NO TEARS FOR SANDRINE

RACHEL GREEN

ALSO BY RACHEL GREEN

Madame Renard Investigates:

Body on the Rocks

Five Dead Men

No Tears for Sandrine

No Tears for Sandrine

1

There were things you could tell about a person from the state of their desk. Here, for example, was the desk of Florian Legrand. Easily two square metres in area yet its entire surface was covered in clutter, so much so that a small bird could have taken up residence in the nests of paper and he probably wouldn't have noticed. Files and folders; boxes and books. Not one, nor two, but *three* separate monitors were hooked up to his computer, each one displaying a screenful of densely worded text. Clearly, the job of a *magistrat*'s clerk was far more demanding than Margot had appreciated. Her eyes moved to the man himself: high forehead, curly black hair; squinting at the screen he was working on even through the thick lenses of his horn-rimmed spectacles – the owner of a brilliant but untidy mind one might reasonably conclude.

"You know," Margot said, standing at the cubby hole that housed the coffee station while waiting for the machine to fill her cup. "I could help tidy some of that for you, if you like."

"No, no. There's no need," Florian smiled good-naturedly. "I like it the way it is. Everything is right here, just at my fingertips."

He wiggled his fingers like he was about to start playing a grand piano. Margot was tempted to accidentally knock some of it to the floor and tidy it for him anyway.

Her eyes drifted across the office to her own desk, nestled beneath the only window. It was half the size of Florian's, and the contrast was stark. All that occupied its surface was her laptop, an A4 writing pad, a mug with a collection of her favourite pens and pencils. On one side lay a small tidy pile of the files she was currently working on; in the corner was a glass vase containing the sprig of *bougainvillea* that she'd cut from her neighbour's trellis this morning. The workspace of someone happy and organised, you might deduce, though this was where her analysis fell down since Margot had never liked working in an office and hated being tied to a desk.

She was also in no place to criticise since this was, after all, Florian's domain. Their boss, Judge Célia Deveraux, had decided that, after several months of working from home, Margot really ought to have a more permanent fixture at the *Palais de Justice* and so Florian, generous soul that he was, had offered to accommodate her. He'd come in specially at the weekend to help rearrange it, sourcing an unused desk from an office on the floor below and helping bring it up in the service elevator. He'd shuffled the filing cabinet out of the corner so that Margot could have the spot by the window, knowing how much she liked the sea (with her head angled correctly she could just about glimpse a modest blue rectangle of Mediterranean). And this morning he'd gone all the way down to the patisserie on the promenade in order to add a slice of *tarte au chocolat* to the collection of cakes and pastries he brought in each day just because she'd mentioned last week how much she liked the ones they made there. Margot's eyes lingered on the fancy white box, taste-buds tingling at the thought of the little sweet slices of joy that lay inside. But it was only nine-thirty, Célia rarely had her break before ten, so she took her coffee back to her desk and got on with some work.

Five minutes later there was a knock on the door. Captain Bouchard entered, removing his kepi and tucking it under one arm. He nodded at Florian before turning his attention to Margot, where his eyes lingered.

"Madame."

She returned his polite nod. "Captain."

"I don't think Madame *le juge* is expecting you," Florian said, briskly searching his diary.

"Actually, it was Madame Renard I was hoping to speak to."

Behind her desk, Margot almost choked on her coffee. She put down her cup and wiped her mouth.

"Me?"

The captain approached, a serious look on his face. "A woman was murdered last night. Here, in Argents."

"How awful. Who was she?"

"Her name was Sandrine Bordes. She was found dead in her home early this morning. She lived on Rue des Arts."

Margot nodded. "I know it." It was a pretty little lane. She and her husband Hugo had viewed a property there when they'd first been looking to buy in the area. Margot remained confused.

"So why did you want to see me?"

"I was wondering ... would you be willing to assist me?"

Margot was tempted to stick a finger in her ear and give it a good wiggle. Had she heard correctly? Captain Bouchard was asking for her help? Since Margot had started working as an advisor for Judge Deveraux she and the captain had been getting along better, but this was a first.

"I'd love to, but how exactly do you think I could help?"

"I understand from the *procureur* that you've been working on the Ginette Clément case."

"That's right."

"Last night's murder showed certain similarities."

The dossier lay at the top of the pile in front of her, in fact. It was one of the cold cases Célia had asked her to look into. Fourteen years ago, eighteen-year-old Ginette Clément had been found dead near the grounds of Argents rugby club. The team had just won an important match and had been having a celebratory dinner for which Ginette and her mother had been doing the catering. Later that night, Ginette had been abducted, taken into some nearby woods, and then smothered with a plastic bag. Despite a year-long investigation, no one had been charged with her murder.

"In what way was it similar?"

"Perhaps I could take you to the scene of the crime and explain."

"Of course," Margot said, intrigued. She put down her half-drunk coffee and grabbed her bag. The *tarte au chocolat* would have to wait.

From Place Jeanne d'Arc they walked briskly along Rue Garenne, heading in the direction of the Gendarmerie. After a hundred metres, they turned left into a cobbled alley and cut through to Rue des Arts, one of the many steep narrow laneways that ran all the way down the hill to the harbour. The house was part of a higgledy-piggledy terrace, three-stories high, a single window flanked by blue shutters on each level. Apart from a small shop selling touristy knickknacks, it was a quiet residential street.

A *policier municipal* stood aside let them in. Margot followed the captain through the front door and into a dark hallway. The crime scene technicians were still at work so they waited, and when there was space to move, entered the salon.

Even with the lights on the room was gloomy. The drawn curtains didn't help, though given that the only window looked directly onto the street Margot could understand why they were keeping them closed. She quickly appraised the layout: a sofa facing the fireplace; an inner door to the kitchen which in turn gave access to a small sunlit courtyard ... a floorplan remarkably similar to her own house.

"The victim was found here."

Captain Bouchard moved to an armchair that was positioned oddly in relation to the rest of the furniture. Marks on the tiled floor suggested it had been moved at least a metre from its original position.

"Who found her?"

"The next-door neighbour. He was leaving for work at five a.m.. He got suspicious when he noticed the gate and the back door were both open."

"Was she killed in the chair?"

The captain nodded. "The killer attacked from behind, pulling a plastic bag tight over her face."

The last of the crime scene technicians briefly looked in. Having finished what they were doing, they gathered their equipment and left. As the house emptied, a chill came over the room. Margot slowly circled the armchair, trying to picture the scene. Just a few hours earlier, the victim and her killer had occupied this same space, breathed the same air. Their smells still lingered; the impressions remained in the cushions. Shards of broken glass littered the floor next to an overturned table.

"It looks like she put up a fight."

"The pathologist's opinion was the killer subdued her with a punch in the face. When the bag was put over her head she must have clawed at it. Traces of plastic were found beneath her fingernails."

"What time was she killed?"

"Between midnight and two a.m.."

"And the killer came in through the back?" Her gaze travelled to the rear door.

"It seems so. There were no signs of forced entry. An alley runs along the rear of these properties, and there's a gate that opens directly into the courtyard. A bell sounds whenever it opens, but there's no lock. According to the neighbour, that was the way her clients normally came and went."

Margot faced him. "Clients?"

"The victim worked as a prostitute. She entertained her clients at home, though it seems she was very discrete. The neighbours said she was never any bother, but seeing a man coming and going in the middle of the night was not unusual."

"So you suspect one of her clients did this?"

"It's a working assumption. It was obviously someone known to her given that she let them into her home at that time of night. Some of the drawers had been searched, but it doesn't look like a robbery. Her jewellery was untouched, and we found a small amount of cash in a tin in one of the kitchen drawers."

"Who did she see last night?"

"She had a client at nine. We found a diary upstairs, though it's not been much use so far. She referred to them by sets of initials. One of the neighbours thought they heard the bell on the gate ring around nine, but nothing after that. The killer could have let himself out through the front, of course."

Margot's eyes travelled slowly around the room. The similarities were her own salon continued, even down to the painted white bookcases on either side of the fireplace, though their taste in books differed: most of these were academic texts, history and politics books, and rather obscure biographies. The furniture smelled of cigarette smoke, and there was a half-full ashtray on the windowsill. Going through the personal effects of a stranger was always intriguing, though at the same time intrusive, seeing things they'd never invited you to see.

"How old was she?"

"Forty-two."

"She lived alone?"

"It would appear so. It's a rental property. According to the lady next door, she moved in around three years ago. My men are checking her background."

Margot wandered through to the kitchen. A two-seater table was pushed against the side wall; the half-gazed door was open onto the courtyard. The yard was a similar size to Margot's, though this was a bare cube of masonry compared to her green haven. Units ran along one side of the kitchen, and a length of marble worktop butted up to an old ceramic sink. The plastic drainer was still loaded with last night's washing-up: one dinner plate, one cup, one wine glass, one knife, one fork, one spoon. No point putting them away when tomorrow you would be using the same ones again. A drill Margot knew only too well.

"We wondered who this might be."

The captain's words pulled Margot from her thoughts. He was pointing to a photograph on the fridge door, held there by a magnet shaped like a penguin: a picture of a baby, just a few months old. Grouped below it were several snaps of what could well have been the same girl, taken a couple of years later, stood next to a man whose head had been cut from the picture.

"A daughter, or a niece?"

"According to the neighbours there was never a child in the house, though there is a child's bedroom upstairs."

Margot paused to think about that for a moment. She opened the fridge door. Nothing out of the ordinary: an open bottle of wine; half a chocolate bar; a drawer full of out-of-date salad vegetables. Three wall cupboards occupied the space above the sink. Crockery was stacked in the left side, tinned and dried food in the centre, and the righthand cupboard was stuffed full of cat food. Noticing a pet carrier under the counter and a dish of water on the floor, Margot looked round.

"Where's her cat?"

Right on cue, a movement on the other side of the window drew their attention. Margot went to the door and looked out into the courtyard. A small black and white cat had just jumped down from the wall, freezing when it saw her, curiosity writ large on its face. Margot squatted and held out her hand.

"Puss-puss."

The cat bobbed its head and wrinkled its whiskers, thinking about coming closer. Margot shuffled forward to try and stroke it, but the cat took fright and in three athletic movements sprang back up to the top of the wall. Safe on its perch, it cast another look back before disappearing down the far side.

"I shouldn't worry about it," Captain Bouchard said. "I imagine one of the neighbours will look after it."

Margot sighed, and raised herself up.

"Can I see upstairs?"

"Of course."

The captain led the way. A narrow winding staircase took them to the room directly above the salon. A low beam forced him to stoop, and he had to duck again to point out the bathroom. The only other room on that floor was the bedroom. Despite the door and window being open the air smelled fusty. A king-size bed took up most of the space, though it looked like only half of it had been slept in. Black duvet, white sheets. Opposite the foot of the bed was a large antique wardrobe with its doors wide open.

"Forensics have been through everything," the captain said. "They've taken away some of the clothes."

Margot looked through the items that remained. Stylish but ordinary clothes. No designer labels, the only noteworthy item being a wedding dress wrapped up in plastic. A small collection of wigs hung from a rack on the inside of one door, and the heart of the wardrobe contained a three-tier integrated drawer set.

"The diaries were found in the bottom drawer," the captain said, coming to her side. "Seven in total. She kept detailed records."

"Of her clients, you mean?"

He nodded. "They're not easy to read. I'll explain when we get back to the Gendarmerie."

Margot looked through the other two drawers. The one in the middle contained a pile of pencil drawings – beautifully detailed fantasy landscapes – while the top one was filled with bric-a-brac. Between the wardrobe and the front wall was a dressing table and mirror. The few bottles of perfume were cheap; the makeup looked like it had been bought from a market.

"The other bedroom is upstairs, I take it?"

The captain nodded.

The second flight of stairs dog-legged up into the roof space. It was a small room but so perfectly formed that Margot had to pause to take it all in. It was like stepping into the pages of a glossy magazine. Everything looked new, from the bedclothes to the flooring to the pictures on the walls. Strings of fairy lights decorated the roof beams; images of galaxies and nebulae covered the only flat area of wall-space. Tucked into the space under the eaves was a study area complete with a child's desk, arm-chair, and cute little bookcase. Amongst the items in the neatly-layered drawers were a brand-new set of drawing pencils, a packet of crayons, a tin of pastels. Margot ran a finger over one of the surfaces. Not a speck of dust came away on her skin.

"Were the neighbours certain they'd never seen a child come to the house?"

"That was what they said. The couple next door both work from home. And they can see the alley from the room they use as a study."

"Was she pregnant?"

"We'll have to wait for the doctor's report, but not obviously so."

The wardrobe was full of clothes: tee-shirts, jeans, underwear, shoes; and all of it looked new. Margot pulled out a lovely silk dress: black, with a stunning silver Barocco pattern. The label was Versace Kids, and there were shoes and underwear, in sizes suitable for a young child. The dress would have cost hundreds, far more than she'd spent on her own clothes. And although the clothes were undoubtedly brand-new, they didn't smell like they'd just been taken out of the wrapper; rather that they'd been washed, ironed and then carefully put away.

But what had she been doing – spending her money on an imaginary child?

2

Returning to Rue Garenne, they continued on foot to the Gendarmerie. As they approached the front door, Margot was reminded of the first time she'd come to this place the day after they'd found little Aswan's body on the rocks. Nothing much had changed inside: the light in the lobby was just as dim; the walls the same depressing shade of brown. The flyer for last year's summer festival was still pinned to the notice-board, even more curling and yellowed than before. Margot waited by the front desk while the captain opened the door to the inner office, but once he had, there was a pause.

"Madame."

"Yes?"

"This way."

He gestured for her to come through.

Margot blinked in surprise – she was being invited into his inner sanctum? Who was this imposter and what had he done with the real Captain Bouchard?

He led her down a long corridor, passing an open-plan office with windows along one side. Around the next corner, he opened the door to his office and, since there were no windows, switched on the light.

"Please, take a seat."

He indicated the chair, but was promptly interrupted by one of his lieutenants. Excusing himself, he stepped back into the corridor. Margot sat down. The last time she'd been brought into this office she'd been too steamed up to pay his desk any attention, but now that she was alone her eyes eagerly roved its surface. What could she ascertain about the personality of Captain Bouchard from the state of his desk? It was, unsurprisingly, incredibly tidy. In- and out-trays were stationed to each side of his blotter, each stacked with a small neat pile of folders. Lined up along the top of the blotter were two pencils, a pen, a ruler, an eraser, and a magnifying glass, arranged so precisely that Margot suspected he'd positioned them with a ruler and a set-square. The remainder of the office was similarly spick and span, few personal touches, a clean military smell. Margot inwardly groaned. This was a level of tidiness that just wasn't healthy. While he was still out of the room, she reached across and set one of his pencils askew.

A few moments later the captain returned, a small collection of folders tucked under his arm.

"The diaries have been sent to the lab for ..."

He spotted it immediately. Pausing halfway to sitting down, his eyes flicked to Margot's; Margot looked back at him like an innocent kitten. She braced herself for a firm rebuke, a dismissal of her services before they'd even begun, a strongly-worded letter of complaint to Judge Deveraux at the *Palais de Justice*, but instead the captain said nothing. He merely set the pencil straight and then lowered himself into his seat. Margot looked at him in befuddlement. Maybe he had a concussion.

"... sent to the lab for analysis," he continued. "But we

photographed the most recent pages. These covered the past few weeks."

He opened one of his files and handed Margot some A4 prints. At first it looked like the pages were covered in hieroglyphics, but on closer inspection she realised the hieroglyphs were actually tiny clusters of words, written in blocks of all shapes and sizes. Practically every square millimetre of paper had been covered, written in different coloured ink: some black, some blue, some green.

"Try this." The captain handed her his magnifying glass.

Viewed up close, the handwriting was extremely neat, the words having been printed rather than written joined-up. The ten or so pages he'd given her must have contained many thousands of words.

"Anything in here about that bedroom?" Margot asked, still marvelling at the intricacy of it all.

"It's not all been read yet. I'm having it transcribed."

Margot had to concentrate hard to get it to make sense. Many of the words were so close together that in places whole sentences looked like continuous streams of letters. In other places, entries had been written in curvilinear text, weaving in and around other strings of words. Here and there, bold sets of initials stood out: PKQ, JKL, UUK.

"So these initials referred to her clients?"

"That was my assumption."

Margot remained puzzled. "Who on earth has the initials 'UUK'?"

"Perhaps she used nicknames."

"Unless," Margot speculated, "it's some kind of code." She tapped a fingernail on the desk. Perhaps she wanted to protect her clients' identities in case the diary ever found its way into the wrong hands. Who knew what secrets might be hidden away in that jungle of text.

The sets of initials were repeated at regular intervals, suggesting a small but loyal coterie of clients. Never more than one per night. None at the weekends. A total of one, two, three different people over the course of the four weeks covered by these few pages. Margot soon became engrossed. Once understood, Sandrine's comments were quite pithy and revealing, particularly when it came to her clients' peccadillos. One of them liked to sit with his head on her lap while she stroked his hair. Another – JNW – sounded more interesting. He liked to get naked as soon as he came into the house and then spend half the session *strutting around, horny as a stag in rutting season*. He liked to do it in front of mirrors, and the last time he'd visited they'd done it in front of the salon window with the curtains drawn:

We could hear people walking by in the street. It seemed to turn him on even more. I was tempted to tear the curtain from the rail so that people could see what kind of a man he really was.

"Have you seen what's she's written about this JNW?"

Margot looked up to find the captain's cheeks had reddened. He'd been sitting patiently, watching her read. Taking that as a yes, she leafed through to the most recent page.

"So, last night her nine o'clock client was GLM," she said.

He brought his camera as usual. We acted like nothing had happened ... were the last words Sandrine had written.

"They'd obviously had some sort of falling out, then. Did you get anything from her phone?"

"Two phones were found at the house. We couldn't unlock them so they're over at the lab, along with her laptop."

Margot flicked back to an earlier entry that related to GLM. He seemed a bit of an oddball. He was averse to physical contact:

Last night he bought me some underwear. He wanted me to put it on and then film me while I was doing the housework. His usual kind of stuff.

In their previous meeting, one week earlier, there was no mention of any disagreement:

Just sat and talked for an hour with GLM. We had the usual debate – who was the greatest influence on New Wave. He seems to think only Truffaut and Godard are worthy of consideration. He has much to learn.

Wow! This guy paid her to talk about esoteric French cinema?

"Have you had any thoughts on the Ginette Clément case?" the captain asked, interrupting her thoughts.

Margot put down the photos.

"Not yet. I was only given the dossier last week. It did strike me as odd that they didn't come up with any real suspects."

The captain nodded. "I was working in the administrative section at that time. But I remember the furore surrounding it. Her face was all over the newspapers."

Ginette had, by all accounts, been a popular figure – a bright, good-looking girl with a promising future. Only two months earlier she'd gained a *mention bien* in her Bac ES and was set to go off to university. There were few obvious parallels with Sandrine's murder, however. First, there was the age difference: Sandrine was forty-two, Ginette eighteen. Second, the killing of Ginette had been a frenzied, sexually-motivated attack, possibly carried out by a stranger, whereas Sandrine's murder appeared to be the work of a cold and calculating killer, most probably known to her. In fact, apart from the method of killing Margot could see nothing to link these two deaths, fourteen years apart.

"It's not a particularly imaginative method of murder," she said. "Suffocating someone with a plastic bag."

"True, but in the fifteen years I've worked here we've had twenty-one cases of murder and of those, these are the only two where the victim was killed in this manner."

"You've checked?"

"I've checked."

"All right. Let's assume for now there is a link. As soon as we work out who these various initials refer to I'll crosscheck their names with the Ginette Clément case. Anyone with any connection to both cases should go to the top of our list of suspects."

"Agreed."

Margot hesitated. "That's assuming you still want my help, of course?"

The captain stiffened, but his reply was unequivocal:

"Most definitely."

Margot smiled. "Good. In that case can I see the body now?"

The captain rose to his feet. "I'll get Lieutenant Martel to drive us."

Lieutenant Martel was a man of speed. With the energy of a sporty thirty-something he seemed to need to do everything at warp factor nine. From the Gendarmerie's back door, he ran across the car park, got into a car, cranked it into reverse, and then sped back to them, skidding to a halt just inches from where Margot and Captain Bouchard stood waiting. Via the rear-view mirror, he shot her a cheeky grin as they climbed in.

They arrived at the hospital fifteen minutes flat. Inside, they got into a lift and went down one floor. After five minutes in the waiting room, an assistant came to get them and then took them down a dingy corridor to the room where the corpses were stored. Margot had never been inside a mortuary before, but the wall of metal drawers that greeted them was familiar from a hundred-and-one cop shops.

The pathologist joined them a few minutes later, kitted out in blue scrubs. A young-looking man with a goatee and tattoos, he seemed far too upbeat to have any kind of job dealing with the dead.

"Captain." The two men shook hands. "A straightforward case this one, I think."

After pulling out the relevant drawer, the assistant stepped aside. The pathologist moved to the head of the tray and folded back the white sheet.

"She died from asphyxiation. There were some bruises on her neck, see here." He pointed to the front and both sides. "I'd say they were knuckle imprints. The tissue damage is consistent with being suffocated from behind with a plastic bag pulled tight over her face, just as you suspected, Captain."

"Was it definitely murder?" Margot asked.

The pathologist frowned. "How do you mean?"

"Could it have been some kind of sex game gone wrong?"

"Breath play, you mean?"

Margot nodded.

He seemed surprised. "That's a bit left field." He considered it for a while but then shook his head. "I don't think so. The bruising extends all the way around the neck. Whoever did this sealed the bag tight, probably twisted it at the back, like this." He mimed the action with his fists, knuckles turning white. "She would have been in distress straight away, and unconsciousness within two minutes."

"How long would she have taken to die?"

"Two, three minutes, tops. Once the brain gets starved of oxygen that's it—" He snapped his fingers. "Game over."

It was sobering to think that all it took to end a person's life was something as simple as a plastic bag. But then, you could kill someone with a biro, or a single well-aimed punch. In many ways the human body was a remarkably fragile thing.

But Sandrine had clearly been a good-looking woman. Even in the harsh light of the mortuary her face held a certain appeal:

petite features; beautifully long eyelashes; a mane of silky black hair. A once exotic-looking human being now reduced to a lump of cold white meat. Twenty-four hours earlier this body had housed a living, breathing person with a mind full of hopes and ambitions. Where had she disappeared to? Transcended to a higher realm? Living on in an afterlife? It would be nice to think so, but Margot was sceptical. You had to consider Occam's razor – all things being equal, the simplest explanation was usually the most likely. And the simplest explanation here was biomechanical: blood had stopped flowing to her brain, cells had died, consciousness was lost. The person who'd had all those hopes and ambitions had simply been switched off.

"Any other injuries?" the captain asked

"As I said earlier, she'd been punched in the face," the pathologist replied. "Hard enough to fracture two of the bones in her cheek. There's also some bruising on the backs of her legs like she'd been forced to sit in a chair." He rolled the sheet to reveal her right leg. "Other than that, she was in very good shape. No signs of disease in any of the internal organs. Heart, liver and lungs were all in excellent condition, for a woman of her age."

"Had she had sex in the past twenty-four hours?" Margot asked.

The pathologist shook his head. "There were no traces of semen internally. Or externally, for that matter. However, she was pregnant."

Margot looked at him in surprise. "How far along?"

"Very early term, only four or five weeks. It's possible she didn't know."

"Had she previously given birth?"

"She had, although I can't say when. Probably several years ago."

With Sandrine's right arm now exposed, Margot noticed

some scaring on the inside of the wrist. Three radial lines, around 50mm in length.

"What did you make of these?"

"Three deep cuts, made with a very shape blade. I couldn't rule out an accident, but most probably the result of a suicide attempt."

"Not self-harm?"

"Unlikely. They would have been deep cuts, enough to sever an artery. It would have been messy."

"Any chance of saying when they were made?"

He pursed his lips. "It would need a specialist to give an accurate assessment, but off the top of my head I'd say they were three to four years old."

Margot stepped back, the cold in the room suddenly reaching her bones. Sometimes it was the person that got switched off; other times the person chose to extinguish the light for themselves.

3

After lunch, Margot returned to the *Palais*. She paused at the half-open door to Célia's office, having heard voices inside. She waited a few moments, knocked, and when she was told to come in, entered to find Célia in consultation with Judge Cousineau, the senior *procureur*.

"Sorry," Margot said. "Shall I come back?"

"No need." Célia waved her in. "I won't be long."

They shared a warm smile.

The office was large enough that Margot could move around the edges without drawing attention to herself. She drifted towards the windows, studying the oil portraits along the way. Each was a former judge, and they were all a little more human to her now that Célia had explained their history and their role in preserving the building that housed them. The *Palais de Justice* in Argents was one of the oldest outside Paris, but also one of the smallest, and the fact that it had not yet been absorbed by the larger facility in Perpignan was in large part due to the actions of these dusty old men. At various points in history, each had argued that this unique courthouse, which dated back to the 1850s, was worthy of preservation. And amongst the group of dusty old men was one woman: taking pride of place on the wall above Célia's chair was a portrait of her grandmother, Agnès Deveraux. This woman deserved an entire history book to herself. After living through two world wars, surviving Nazi persecution and overcoming a crippling illness in her teens, she'd gone on to trailblaze a path for women in the French judiciary, finally ending her career as President of the First Civil Division of the *Cour de cassation*, France's supreme court. It was clear from the way Célia spoke about her that *Mamé* Agnès had been a very special influence on her.

Margot continued her progress towards the windows, giving Cousineau a wide berth. She didn't particularly like the man. It was highly unlikely his portrait would ever earn a place on these walls. A Paris man through and through; superior and chauvinistic; he'd been the senior *procureur* in Argents for over ten years despite claiming to dislike the town and all of its lazy seaside people. Tall, rounded-shouldered, the face of a bat, it was jokingly rumoured he spent his nights hanging upside down from the rafters in the courthouse roof. The few times he and Margot had spoken their personalities had clashed. The last time they'd sparred, he'd delighted in mocking the fact her father had been a High Court judge in London, pouring scorn on the English justice system and how it was a preserve of the rich. Margot didn't necessarily disagree with him, but she loathed his superior attitude.

Nothing much was going on through the windows so she tuned in to their conversation. They were discussing the case of a young drug dealer who was currently being held in *garde à vue*, disagreeing on the seriousness of the charges he should face. Cousineau wanted to upgrade the primary offence to a *crime* (the most serious of criminal offences) rather than a *délit* (middle ranking category of offence) and thus open an *instruction* which would mean that Célia would take charge of the case. This in itself was unusual enough to warrant attention. Normally, an *instruction* was only opened in the most serious of cases, the vast majority being handled by the police under the supervision of the *procureur*. Even then the temptation was to downgrade the offence, railroad it through the system, get it off their books. Such was the workload.

"I don't even know why you're giving me this case," Célia was protesting. "As far as I can see his only crime was being caught in possession of fifty grams of cannabis. In many provinces he wouldn't even have been arrested."

"Oh, come on, Célia. He was seen selling drugs outside the school gates. Two witnesses will attest to that."

"Neither of which is reliable."

"And then there's the assault charge, and breaking and entering. If we let him off with just a slap on the wrist he'll be up to his old tricks again in no time. And you know how keen the mayor is to get these dealers off our streets."

Célia regarded him obstinately. "You do know I currently have over one hundred cases on my books."

"So what difference will one more make?"

Cousineau attempted a smile but his face wasn't built for it. Célia wearily gave in.

"All right. Send him to see me this afternoon."

"Thank you."

He nodded to Margot on his way out, but halted at the door. "You will be coming in next week, won't you?"

Célia nodded. "Don't worry. You're not getting rid of me that easily."

Another pinched smile before he finally departed.

They waited for the door to close. Margot turned to find Célia rolling her eyes.

"We mustn't get on the wrong side of the mayor now must we?" she said in a childish voice.

Margot returned her smile. She knew Célia well enough by now to know when she was being ironic.

"Anyway, Margot. What can I do for you?"

"Captain Bouchard has asked me to assist on the Sandrine Bordes case."

"Oh, yes. I heard. How's he getting on?"

Margot filled her in on what they knew so far. "The victim's a bit of a mystery woman at the moment. No one's come forward, or enquired about her."

"No friends or relatives?"

Margot shook her head. "She lived alone, and it looks like she had a troubled past." She explained about the scars on her wrists. "And we've just been told she was a few weeks' pregnant."

Célia tutted. "Oh dear. What a double tragedy."

"Indeed."

"Any suspects?"

"It was most probably one of her clients, though it's going to be a challenge identifying them. We think she used some kind of code."

"I see."

"So I might be spending some time at the Gendarmerie, if that's okay with you?"

"Of course." A twinkle appeared in the judge's eyes. "Does this mean you and the captain are getting along better now?"

Margot smiled wryly. "It's early days."

"Well, keep me informed."

"I will."

Célia picked up her pen, ready to go back to work, but Margot hesitated.

"Are you certain it's a good idea coming in next week? I'm sure we can manage without you for a few days."

Her uterine cancer had metastasized and come back in her lungs, and they were going to try and eradicate it with a course of radiotherapy. Célia had been putting on a brave face, trying to make out it was routine, but Margot doubted it was so straightforward.

"Don't worry, I'll be fine. Stéphane's coming down from Strasbourg in a few days. He insists on coming with me to the hospital."

"Ever the dutiful son. That's good of him."

"On which note ... perhaps we could get together again. I really enjoyed it last time."

Margot nodded. "Me, too."

Stéphane worked for the European Court of Human Rights, and although outwardly was something of a grey suit, he had an amusingly playful side to his character. After a picnic on the beach, they'd walked a stretch of the coastal path, talking about the break-up of his marriage and the impending divorce. They'd exchanged a few texts since.

"I'll let you know the arrangements," Célia said.

"All right. And if there's anything I can do to help just let me know."

"Thank you, Margot. That's most kind."

It had been a long day and Margot was famished by the time she got home. Her phone pinged as she was unlocking her back door. She pulled the key from the lock, dumped the contents of her arms onto the kitchen table, and then retrieved her phone from her back pocket. A text from Raymond:

If you're in the mood for seafood we have something special on the menu tonight. Shall I reserve you a table?

He'd moved from Le Paname to a restaurant down on the seafront, though for some reason had been cagey about its whereabouts. Margot quickly typed back:

Yes please. I'll be there at eight. Text me the location.

A pin-drop immediately came back. Margot studied the map, but it was nowhere she recognised.

She went upstairs for a shower, and afterwards stood in front of her open wardrobe, deciding what to wear. In the mood for white, she chose white crocheted trousers over white cotton shorts, a white notch-neck blouse, white slip-on pumps. A chunky necklace made from white wooden beads completed the look.

It was dark when she went back out. Pausing on the harbourside to consult her phone, Margot zoomed in on the location Raymond had sent. La Lune Bleue appeared to be right on the edge of the water, somewhere in the remains of the old fortifications. In days gone by, the castle and its walls had defended the town from attacks by sea, and although it was now a mecca for tourists, she'd never heard of any restaurants being down there. She crossed the narrow wooden footbridge to get to the esplanade, and from there descended via a path that curved steeply down the face of the giant defensive wall. According to her phone, she'd actually veered off dry land and was walking on water, but the tinkle of fine glassware drew her on. Through a low stone arch, she followed the glow of soft lights to arrive at a small concourse at the base of the huge fortification. Above her loomed thousands of tonnes of ancient stone masonry.

Margot gazed around in delight. The restaurant appeared to be built into one of the tower buttresses, while the terrace extended to the very edge of the sea, only chunky wooden planters and a post and chain fence to protect them. Dining at its most precarious: one large wave and the whole thing risked being submerged. Inside was only big enough for three or four tables, but a dozen more were spread out on the terrace and it was there that she spotted Raymond, levelling a table on the flagstones by slipping a folded-up coaster under one of its legs.

"Margot – you found us!"

"It wasn't easy." They kissed on both cheeks. "According to my phone we're actually in the sea right now."

"It's a glitch in the GPS," Raymond explained. "Officially we don't exist. The tourists can't find us so we keep the place to the locals. The owner likes it that way."

"Good for him. It's wonderful down here."

Raymond showed her to a table right at the end, sheltered by a small canopy, the sea to both the side and the rear. He switched on the artificial candle. "I thought you might like here."

"Perfect."

"Let me get you a menu."

While he was gone, Margot lit a cigarette and gazed out to sea. It was too dark to see any detail out there, but she could hear the waves, and feel an occasional spritz of seawater carried on the air. Her anxiety soon melted away. The world could be a pretty nice place when it wanted to be.

"The *poisson du jour* is dorade," Raymond said, returning with the menu. "Caught fresh this morning."

"How's it cooked?"

"Grilled with olive oil and a little sea salt, and served with capers and samphire."

"Mmmm, sounds delicious."

Margot's eyes greedily devoured the menu. The Tuna Tartare with wasabi nuts and cream also sounded nice. And then there were oysters, either raw or poached, and mussels in white wine. Margot was rarely indecisive when it came to the desires of her stomach, but she took her time.

"So how come you left Le Paname?"

"It seemed the right time to move on. My brother's girlfriend works behind the bar here. And Chef said he would teach me how to cook one or two of the dishes."

Margot regarded him in surprise. "You're learning to cook?"

Raymond grinned bashfully. "I've been thinking of doing a course, at the *Lycée Hôtelier*. It doesn't start until November, but the applications have to be in next week."

"Have you applied?"

"Not yet. You don't think I'm wasting my time, do you?"

"Of course not!" she tutted. "You have to try, if it's what you want to do."

An excited grin escaped from his face. "I think it is. Thanks, Margot."

"Fill in that form."

"I will."

She ordered the dorade, and a bottle of Spanish Albariño to go with it. When it came, the fish was cooked to perfection – meaty white flakes that literally melted on her tongue. There was only one chocolatey item on the dessert menu, but it was one of her favourites: chocolate cherry tarte. Every mouthful was bliss, and she couldn't resist licking the spoon clean. Sated, she moved her chair away from the table and lit another cigarette while Raymond cleared the plates.

"Did you hear about that murder the other day?"

Margot nodded. "I'm working on the case."

"She used to come into Le Paname."

"Who – Sandrine?"

There were no other diners outside so he left the plates for a moment and bummed a cigarette.

"I didn't know that was her name. I saw her photo in the paper and recognised her."

After lighting his cigarette, Margot shook out the match.

"How often did she come in?"

"Once a week. Maybe twice. She always sat inside, writing in a notebook."

Rue des Arts was just around the corner from Place Saint-

Marc where Le Paname was located. Margot used to go to Le Paname pretty much every day. It was disquieting to think their paths may have crossed at some point.

"What was she like?"

"She never said much. Just sat with her book, scribbling away. She always ordered a double espresso." He lowered his voice, though there was no one to overhear. "They said on the news she was a prostitute."

"That's right."

"She didn't look like one."

Margot gave him a disapproving look. "And what's a prostitute supposed to look like, Raymond? Black stockings and boobs hanging out of her bra?"

He blushed, and averted his eyes. "Sorry. She just seemed nice, that was all I meant."

Margot reached out and squeezed his hand. "We don't know very much about her yet. Who's to say why she ended up living that kind of life?"

He went back to clearing the table. "She was quite generous, I remember that. She always left a good tip."

"Did you ever see her with a child?"

Raymond shook his head. "I did see her with a man once. A few weeks ago."

"Can you remember what he looked like?"

"Tall, white ... they seemed to be getting on well. But generally she was alone. I couldn't understand why someone so good-looking always had such a sad look about her. You'd think she would have had lots of friends."

Ah, the innocence of youth. Perhaps you needed a few decades under your belt before you could understand that one.

He finished clearing the table and went away, but Margot lingered. It was only ten o'clock. Seven empty rooms – that was all that awaited her at home. She stared down at the last of the Albariño, swirling in her glass. Making it last.

Margot paid the bill. She crossed the footbridge to get back to the harbour, and since the marina was quiet went for a stroll along the jetty. Water sloshed against the timber supports, and lights were on in a few of the boats, all cosy inside. She continued all the way down to the old stone turret at the mouth of the harbour. You used to be able to go inside – steps spiralled up to a platform at the top. When she and Hugo used to come down in the summer they would often go up and take in the view, but a few years ago some daredevil teenagers had started using it as a diving platform and the authorities had decided to close it. The entrance was now sealed with a thick metal sheet.

But you could still access the gangway that ran around the base. Margot followed it around to the seaward side, only a thin metal handrail separating her from the water a few metres below. She cupped her hands to her mouth while she lit a cigarette, and after taking a puff held the little white coffin nail up in the air, the tip glowing orange against the smooth dark sea. *Fumer tue*: Smoking kills, said the label. She'd given herself a new limit: no more than ten a day, but how many was she up to now? ... Eight and nine at the restaurant; this one number ten. She smoked it slowly, savouring every lungful.

Dark clouds moved silently overhead. Weakening on her way home, Margot opened the seal on a fresh packet. Who was counting?

4

The church bells were striking nine as Margot approached the Gendarmerie. Spotting her through the small glass panel, Lieutenant Martel quickly threw back the bolts, pulled open the front door, and greeted her with a friendly *Bonjour*.

"If only every day could start as joyous as this," he said, a glint in his eye and a becoming smile upon his face. "Seeing you come to our doorstep, Madame Renard, brings joy to my heart."

A poet and a man of speed? Whatever was fuelling this man Margot wanted it bottled. She returned his smile.

"Is the captain in?"

"The captain is always the first one in. Every morning, eight-forty-five on the dot. Come on through."

"Thank you."

He let her in through the connecting door and then took her down the long corridor that turned several corners. The door to the captain's office was open, but no one was inside. Briefly stumped, Lieutenant Martel took her back to the detectives' office, but the captain wasn't in there, either.

"Ah."

Now it looked like he'd had an unwelcome epiphany.

"Problem?" Margot queried.

"It's Saturday today, isn't it?"

"It is. All day."

"Then he's probably in the barracks. But if he is, he won't want to be disturbed."

"Okay. Shall I come back?"

The lieutenant dithered with indecision. Ever keen to be the helpful gendarme, however, he reconsidered.

"No, no. As it's you, Madame Renard, I'm sure he won't mind. Follow me."

Now he marched her off down a completely different corridor.

From the outside, the Gendarmerie looked every bit the quaint old provincial police station, but inside was a very different story. After walking for at least thirty paces they arrived at a four-way intersection. The lieutenant continued straight on, down yet another long corridor, this one lined with matt olive doors, all of them identical apart from the curious system of numbering – 3152-C; 3153-D:1 – with nothing to indicate what lay beyond. Everything about the place spoke of military efficiency. Margot decided she really must look into its history one day.

A pair of double doors brought them to a glazed arcade, evidently at the rear of the site. This part of the building resembled an Oxford quad, though the buildings here were considerably more recent in construction and enclosed a parade ground rather than a neat green lawn. Tufts of wiry grass poking up through the concrete suggested it hadn't been used in some time.

"This way."

Lieutenant Martell opened a fire escape door. He set off across the parade ground at a brisk pace, instinct perhaps telling him to walk at double-quick time, and they soon reached a gate in the chain-link fence. The barracks formed two sides of the quad and were functional, two-storey blocks with low-pitched roofs. All of the units were boarded up apart from one on the first floor where a light was shining and the sound of a vacuum cleaner could be heard.

They climbed a metal staircase to the first-floor walkway. The sound of the vacuum grew louder as they approached the door at the end, the only one not boarded up, but halfway there the lieutenant paused to ask her to wait. Continuing alone, he halted at the open door, straightened himself, and knocked loudly on the frame.

The sound of the vacuum cleaner slowly died. Curious to see what was going on in there, Margot drifted closer. Inside, she could hear Captain Bouchard having a few choice words with the lieutenant, clearly not happy about being disturbed. Feeling guilty, Margot moved to the door and looked in.

"Don't blame the lieutenant. He was only—"

She froze, unprepared for the sight that greeted her. Captain Bouchard stood in the centre of the salon with a pink feather duster in one hand and the arm of a vacuum cleaner in the other. Green rubber gloves and an army-issue apron completed the rather bizarre sight.

Margot couldn't help staring. Having a hard time concealing her amusement, she had to suck in her cheeks.

"I didn't realise you were the cleaner, as well."

The captain's eyes smouldered like two hot lumps of coal.

"Madame." He thrust the feather duster into the lieutenant's hand. "Is there something I can do for you?"

"Sorry. I didn't mean to intrude. I thought I'd drop by for an update."

He tugged off his apron. "If you'd care to wait in my office I'll be along shortly."

Margot gave her retinas a few extra moments to enjoy the precious image. The apartment looked just as neat and tidy as his desk, exactly what she would have expected of his living quarters. Before she had time to properly take it in, however, Lieutenant Martell gave her a nudge. Without another word Margot was escorted back across the parade ground.

Safely installed in the captain's office, the lieutenant fetched her a coffee, but he was promptly called away leaving Margot on her own. There wasn't much of a personal nature in there, no family photos, nothing to indicate any hobbies. She had no idea if he was married. His entire life probably consisted of the Gendarmerie, nothing better to do than clean his billet on a Saturday morning, polish his boots on a Sunday.

He joined her five minutes later, now fully attired in his immaculate uniform. Their eyes met as he moved to his chair, but neither of them spoke. He scanned his desktop before sitting down, perhaps fearing a second attempt at sabotage, but seeing that everything was in order he settled into his seat. A gendarme brought in an archive box which he set down on a small table.

"We've uncovered a little more detail in the victim's background," the captain began, reaching into the box. He selected a file, spent a few moments flicking through, and then unclipped a page. "Name, Sandrine Bordes; born forty-two years ago in Nice. Her father was a Professor of linguistics at the University of Aix-Marseille. Originally from Lebanon, he moved to France in 1977. Two years later he married a local woman; Sandrine was their only child. It seems he was an eminent figure in his field, specialising in computational linguistics. Apparently, his work was highly influential in the areas of speech synthesis and artificial intelligence. He wrote dozens of papers, published in journals all over the world, and co-authored several books. In the latter stages of his career he went on a very successful lecture tour of the United States. Sadly, he died of a stroke at the age of sixty-two. And then, one year later, his wife also passed away."

"How old was Sandrine at that time?"

"She would have been thirteen when her mother died. She went to live with an aunt in Nice. At eighteen, she followed in her father's footsteps and went to study at Aix-Marseille, though her subject was mathematics. She gained a bachelor's and a master's degree, top grades in both. The head of her faculty said she was one of the most gifted students they'd ever taught, although he also described her as a misfit. She made few friends, didn't get involved in any of the social clubs. She went on to start a doctorate, but apparently there was an incident with her tutor and she left shortly afterwards."

"What kind of incident?"

"The person we spoke to was reluctant to go into detail. It seemed Sandrine had accused her tutor of taking credit for some of her work. Sandrine couldn't come up with anything to substantiate her claim so no action was taken. But she felt so strongly that she quit. They never heard from her again."

"What a waste."

"Indeed."

The captain took another sheet out of the file and handed it over.

"This is a photograph of her, taken at one of her graduation ceremonies."

In life, she certainly had been a beauty: those big black lashes; eyes the colour of brown sugar; the exoticness now explained by her Middle Eastern heritage. Still, there was something of a tortured look about her, a smile that wasn't quite there. She could see what Raymond had meant. The captain went on:

"After she quit university there's a ten-year gap in her

records. The next time she shows up in any official documents was eight years ago when she got married."

"No tax or employment records?"

"None that we've been able to trace."

"Who did she marry?"

He switched to a different file. "Georges Colbert. They were married in Perpignan eight years ago, then divorced two years later. Sandrine reverted to her mother's family name, Bordes. They had one child; a girl named Lya. And here's another odd thing: the father was awarded custody."

Margot blinked. "Why was that?"

"We don't have access to the court papers, only the verdicts."

"So the child would be ... how old now?"

The captain scanned the sheet. "She would be seven years old. She was born two months after they were married."

Was that who the perfect bedroom had been for? But then, why had it never been used?

"Is the ex-husband still around?"

"He's remarried now. He works for an aerospace company based in Montpelier, though their home address is in Elne. I'll be going to see him later." He looked at her from the tops of his eyes. "You're welcome to come along, if you like."

"Yes please," Margot said, smiling inside. It seemed she'd been forgiven.

The captain flicked through to another page.

"The forensic report on the two mobile phones has also come back. No fingerprints were found on either of them. The conclusion was they'd been wiped."

"Anything interesting on the laptop?"

"The tech team are still working on it. But going back to the phones ... one had the usual mundane contacts: utility companies, phone, bank, et cetera; the other had twenty-seven numbers listed in the contacts, none of which had been assigned names. We're guessing she used the second phone for business. I've had one of my men calling the numbers but no luck so far."

"What time did she make her last call?"

"The last activity on the business phone was at five minutes before nine. When we dialled the number, a man answered but then hung up. We're waiting for the phone company to tell us who the numbers are registered to, if anyone. I'm guessing most will be pay-as-you-go phones."

Captain Bouchard put the file back in the box and then took out another folder. "Next, her bank statements. There's not a great deal to see. I'm guessing her business was mainly cash-in-hand. She paid in irregular amounts over the course of each month. Rarely had a balance of more than five hundred, and was often overdrawn. On the 27th of each month she paid a thousand euros into an account in the name of Patrice Fabron. He's listed as the owner of the house Sandrine was living in. But nine months ago the payments stopped."

"You mean she hasn't been paying any rent?"

"Apparently not. Her account was two thousand overdrawn at the time. Since then she's been paying in a little each month. Also, for the past four and a half years she's paid a set amount into the bank account of her ex-husband. First it was four hundred a month, then four-fifty. For the past year it's been five hundred a month. Never a payment missed, even when she was overdrawn."

"So she paid her ex-husband rather than her rent?"

"It would appear so."

"Child maintenance, perhaps?"

"We shall have to ask him."

"How much does the ex-husband earn?"

"He would be on a pretty high salary, I imagine. The company he works for is very successful, and he has an executive position. The only other thing worth mentioning is a bundle of till receipts stuffed into an old shoe box. One of my men is going through them."

"Have you had the diaries transcribed yet?"

"We're still waiting. I'll get a copy to you as soon as I can." The captain gathered up the paperwork and returned it to the archive box. "In the meantime, if there's nothing else, I suggest we go and see what the ex-husband has to say."

5

Georges Colbert lived in the suburbs of Elne, in a cul-de-sac of five newly-built villas. As they drew up outside, Margot was reminded of what she disliked most about suburbs. These five were perfectly agreeable in their own right, but they looked like they'd been designed in a vacuum, or conceived by an android, with scarcely any thought given to their relationship with the properties that surrounded them. More an arrangement of geometric shapes than a place to call home, fronted by fake green lawns and bonded gravel driveways. Holiday homes for the Stepford Wives.

They opened the pedestrian gate and approached the front door, passing a shiny blue Tesla tethered to a charging point. Beside it, a black BMW was positioned oddly, looking like it had been parked in a rush. A man answered right away, no doubt having been alerted by the video doorbell.

"Yes?"

"Georges Colbert?"

He gave the captain a shifty up-and-down look. Presumably realising why they'd come, he stepped out of the house, easing the door to behind him.

"Do you mind if we talk around the back? My wife is still in bed."

He was a man of average height and build. His short black hair was wet and clung to the sides of his head, looking like he'd not long come out of the shower. He wasn't wearing any shoes.

They followed him along a rectilinear path that skirted the building in three broad strokes. He walked gingerly, choosing his footsteps carefully, perhaps regretting his decision to walk barefoot. A small garden lay to the side of the house, but other than a token date palm in the far corner there was little in the way of planting. At the rear, a wooden fence hemmed them in, with most of the space taken up by a swimming pool, but the pool was horribly overlooked, and so small as to be practically useless for swimming. An inflatable pink flamingo drifted listlessly on its surface.

Colbert took them to a patio where an awning covered a set of chairs and an outdoor sofa. He didn't invite them to sit. He seemed distracted; kept looking through the patio doors like he was afraid someone was watching.

"I take it you're here about Sandrine?"

The captain nodded.

"I'm sorry for your loss," Margot said.

Her comment seemed to surprise him. It was a few moments before he acknowledged her sentiment with a small nod. "Thank you. It was quite a shock."

"How's your daughter taking the news?"

He looked away, swallowing. "Actually, I haven't told her yet."

"It's probably best to do it sooner rather than later," Margot said. "If you need any support I'm sure we can put you in touch with someone." She glanced at the captain, who nodded.

"Thank you, but that won't be necessary. Look." Another furtive glance through the glass. "I'm keen to help, but if we could make this quick ..."

"We need someone to formally identify the body," the captain said. "Would you mind coming along to the mortuary with us?"

"No. Not at all."

"And her personal possessions will have to be dealt with. Did Sandrine have any living relatives?"

Colbert shook his head. "Her parents died when she was young. There was a cousin somewhere but I think he passed away a few years back. And I'm afraid I can't offer to help."

Margot pictured the perfect little bedroom being dismantled by workmen. Carted away to the tip. What a waste.

"How did you get on with your ex-wife?" she asked.

He shrugged. "The same as any divorced couple, I suppose."

"Did you see her very often?"

"Hardly at all. We've been divorced for six years, and I rarely go to Argents. My work takes me further afield."

"But what about your daughter? How did the access arrangements work?"

A muscle tightened in his cheek. This time he ignored the patio door and looked unflinchingly back at her.

"Sandrine didn't see our daughter. I was awarded sole custody."

"But she must have had visitation rights."

"She did, but the conditions didn't suit her. The judge ordered the visits take place on neutral ground and with a social worker present. Sandrine wouldn't accept that. The one time we did arrange something she ended up losing her temper and storming off. I didn't want my daughter exposed to that."

"So when was the last time she saw Lya?"

Colbert shrugged. "A few months after the divorce. Five or six years ago."

Margot regarded him in surprise. "And she's had no contact since?"

He grew more irritated. "You don't know the history, do you?"

"Enlighten me."

He exhaled heavily, and cast a longer look at the patio doors. Apparently satisfied no one was in there, he continued:

"When Lya was three months old Sandrine took her to the park and abandoned her. Just left her there, right next to a ditch."

"Was she hurt?" Margot asked, perturbed.

"Fortunately not. A passer-by saw what had gone on and called the police. But then, two days later, she did it again! This time took her into town and left her outside a shop." He broke off, running a hand over his head. "Tell me, what kind of a person could do that to her own flesh and blood?"

Margot wasn't going to jump to judgement. "Did she give a reason?"

"She said the baby had been annoying her, wouldn't stop crying. The person who'd seen her in the park said she'd looked like a zombie."

"Had she been depressed?"

"The doctors called it postpartum psychosis, but she'd never been right in the head. If I'd had my way she would have been carted off to the nearest lunatic asylum right there and then."

"It's an illness, Monsieur Colbert. She wouldn't have known what she doing."

Colbert gave her a hard look, brimming with indignation. "Yes, that's all very easy to say but you try living with someone like that. She was a nightmare."

"Yet you married her."

"We all make mistakes. I spent the next eighteen months trying to get away from her. The day the divorce came through was one of the happiest days of my life."

Margot realised she was staring at him rather intently and so backed down. It had clearly been a difficult relationship. It wasn't her place to judge. The captain took up the questioning:

"Do you mind if I ask where you were on Thursday night?"

Colbert cleared his throat, his eyes shifty again. "I was here, at home."

"All night?"

"Yes. My wife can testify to that. She was here, too."

"When was the last time you spoke to Sandrine?"

"Six or seven months ago. Maybe a year."

"Can you remember what you talked about?"

He puffed out his cheeks. "I honestly don't know. Something to do with her maintenance payments, probably. That was usually the only reason I agreed to talk to her."

"You mean she continued to pay you maintenance even though she had no access to her child?" Margot said. She hadn't meant it to sound like a criticism but Colbert shot her another irritated look.

"My daughter still needs providing for. Had the situation been reversed I'm sure you wouldn't expect the father to get away without paying. Besides, she wanted to."

Just then, a noise came from the house. They all turned to see the patio door begin to slide open. When the gap was wide enough, a young child appeared.

"Papa."

Colbert went straight to her. "Go back inside. Papa's busy." He tried to usher her in, but the little girl stubbornly refused, hanging tightly onto the door handle with both hands.

"But I can't find my ballet pumps!"

"Have you looked in the tall cupboard?"

"*Yes,* and they're not there!"

Margot moved into her line of sight. There was no mistaking this was the girl from the photo on Sandrine's fridge: those same black lashes; the soulful brown eyes. Six years may have passed but she was still her mother's daughter.

"Are you Lya?" Margot asked, crouching to her level.

Suddenly fascinated, the little girl nodded.

"I was always losing my ballet pumps when I was your age."

Lya smiled shyly back. Despite the troubled start in life, she seemed a happy child.

Margot leaned in. With a hand to the side of her mouth, she whispered: "I think adults secretly get up in the middle of the night and hide them from us, don't you?"

The child snickered, nodding her head several times like they'd just shared one of life's great secrets.

"Come on, Lya," her father interrupted. "Go back inside and look again. And wake your mother. She'll have to take you to your class today."

Appeased, the little girl let go of the door. She said goodbye and skipped off, waving as she departed.

Colbert closed the patio door, though for a moment remained with his back to them. It seemed he was unsure what he was going to say next, though when he turned, his head was held high.

"Do you know what – I'm not sure I will tell her. Sandrine has no place in Lya's life anymore. She's better off not knowing."

Margot looked back at him, disheartened. "She'll find out one way or another."

"Maybe she will, maybe she won't. The truth is Lya has a new mother now, and a little baby sister. I don't want anything spoiling that."

Was that the plan – cut her out of their lives, throw away her things, deny her very existence? Colbert went on:

"If there's nothing else, can we go to the mortuary now and get this over with?"

———

Being Saturday, a different assistant was on duty. He left them in the viewing area while he went next door to the cold storage room. After pulling out the cadaver tray he carefully folded back the sheet. Watching through the glazed panel, Margot was astonished to see Colbert barely react. Surely this woman had meant something to him once. There had to be some happy memories hidden away inside him: that first romantic dinner; the first time they'd made love; the day he'd proposed. Love must have come into the equation at some point. Margot stared at the side of his head, expecting at least a flicker of emotion, but when he did react, the look of distress he came up with was clearly fake.

After nodding his head, he quickly looked for the way out.

Margot waited until they were perhaps halfway down the corridor before she spoke.

"There is just one more thing."

With obvious reluctance, Colbert drew to a halt.

"Yes?"

"We noticed some scars on the inside of Sandrine's left wrist. Do you happen to know how she got them?"

He returned a blank look, and then shook his head.

"The pathologist said she'd probably tried to commit suicide," Margot went on. "Maybe four years ago. Did you have any contact with her at that time?"

Colbert thought about it. It may have jogged a memory, but again he shook his head.

"I'm sorry. I can't help you with that."

———

The Gendarmerie closed at four on Saturdays so when the captain went off duty Margot decided to call it a day. On her way out through the front she found Lieutenant Martel closing the shutters on the windows, shutting up shop for the day. After sliding the final bolt home, he yawned wearily and stretched his arms. With all that charging around it was no wonder he'd worn himself out.

"Don't worry," Margot said. "It's Sunday tomorrow. You can have a lie in."

He dropped heavily into his chair. "If only. I have to be up at nine for training, and then we have a match in the afternoon."

"Football?" Margot queried.

"Rugby. The first game of the season, and we're playing Montmélian." He said it with an ominous tone as if it should mean something to her.

"And are they quite good?"

"Good?" Martel seemed surprised. "They thrashed us 38-6 last time we played. Another two points and they'd have gone up to *Fédérale 1*."

If only Margot could share his enthusiasm. It remained a mystery to her: a large group of men running back and forth around a big green field. They were all very earnest about it, but surely there was something more productive they could have been doing with their time.

"Well, good luck with that."

"Thank you. We'll need it."

"I was wondering ... do you have the key to Sandrine's house?"

"Yes. It should be around here somewhere." He patted the desk with his hands.

"I thought I would check on her cat."

"Good idea." He found a small envelope in a tray and passed

it over. "If you could just sign it out, please. That'll keep the captain happy."

In Rue des Arts, the front door was still sealed with police tape. Margot carefully released it, prompting a look of suspicion from a man passing by.

Inside, an eerie quietness had taken over the house. Margot felt a chill as she stood in the salon, thinking of the dreadful scene the walls had witnessed. The chair was still there; the scuff marks still on the floor. The police had taken everything they considered might be of use, but they'd left behind a considerable amount of detritus. Once someone's home; now a collection of junk waiting to be disposed of.

The door to upstairs was closed. With no sign of the cat, Margot carried on through to the kitchen. The water level in the saucer had dropped so he must have been in at some point. She opened the door to the courtyard and stepped out. Walls surrounded her, separating the space from both the neighbour's yard and the alley. She opened the gate, and looked both ways. Still no sign of the little black and white pussycat.

He had to be hungry. He wouldn't have been fed for over a day, unless someone had taken him in. Margot wondered if he'd come back during the night of the murder and seen Sandrine dead in her chair. Traumatised, he'd fled in fright? Though weren't cats notoriously indifferent when it came to the lives of their owners? happy to eat them raw in the absence of any other food.

Margot sighed anxiously. It would be night soon. She couldn't just leave it to fend for itself. The least she could do for Sandrine was look after her cat. Going back to the kitchen, she opened the cupboard with the cat food. It didn't appear to be arranged in any particular order so she took the packet that was nearest. She opened it with a pair of scissors and squeezed a patty onto the saucer, sniffing as she did so. Tuna fillet and mussels, apparently, though it didn't smell particularly appealing.

Back in the courtyard, Margot held the saucer up in the air, letting the aroma circulate. She had no idea if she were doing the right thing. She'd never owned a cat, or had any kind of pet for that matter. She had visions of every feline in the neighbourhood picking up the scent and descending upon her *en masse*. Here was her epitaph:

Margot Renard: trampled to death whilst stupidly attempting to feed the stray cats of Argents.

"Puss, puss," she called out.

As if by magic, a little black and white fur-ball appeared at the top of the wall. Margot smiled. It looked like the same one as yesterday. Careful not to spook it, she set the saucer down on the ground. Would he come close enough for her to stroke? She did rather like the idea of petting him. After a few moments, the cat's interest picked up and he stalked along the narrow strip at the top of the wall, pausing when he got to the end. He stretched his neck, looking like he might jump down. Margot stepped back to give him some space. It was obvious he could smell the food, but after giving it another curious look, the cat changed his mind and parked his derriere, remaining firmly on top of the wall.

"Perhaps you'd prefer to dine alone," Margot said. "Is that it?"

She left the saucer and withdrew into the kitchen, then watched covertly through the window to see if he would change his mind. And he did, turning on a sixpence and jumping down into the neighbour's yard instead.

6

If only the cat would so easily escape from her thoughts. For half the night Margot tossed and turned, imagining the poor little mite out in the dark, alone and unloved. She rose before dawn, even though it was Sunday, put on her swimsuit, and went down to the cove.

Rain was forecast for later in the day but right now the sun was wallowing in its own magnificence. The huge golden globe hung low on the horizon, painting the sky with scarlet and orange. Margot took off her shoes and stepped down onto the shingle, reminded of why this place was her little piece of heaven.

She swam a long way out, way past the line of safety buoys. Bathed in the dawn light, Argents was a dreamy sight, not hard to see why the tourist board had started referring to it as 'The Pearl of the Côte Vermeille'. But the sea was cooler now. Winter would be here soon, and it would be the first Margot had spent in Argents. According to the weather charts, the water dropped to a chilly twelve degrees in February. How would she manage without her daily swim?

After thirty minutes, she turned in the water and swam back.

The sky was already beginning to cloud over as she climbed up onto the rocks. She snapped off her bathing cap and shook out her hair, and gazed around while she towelled herself down. Memories came back to her. This was where it had all begun, that day she'd found Aswan's football shirt concealed in the rocks over there. Margot smiled poignantly as she recalled how she'd marched up to the Gendarmerie, determined to seek justice. Being a few minutes too early, Captain Bouchard had refused to let her in.

She went home, showered, and drank a cup of hot coffee. And still the cat would not get out of her head. She sat on her sofa, arms folded, thumbnail gripped between her teeth, though why she was continuing to worry was a mystery. Cats could fend for themselves, couldn't they? Scrounge from strangers, catch a mouse or two. He surely wouldn't starve. She cast a worried look at the window. It was only ten a.m. yet the sky was already growing dark. It would be raining soon. And cats hated water, didn't they? There was a cat flap in Sandrine's back door – it wasn't like he had nowhere to go – but then, would he want to go back into the house after seeing what had happened to his owner?

Margot hissed with irritation.

She put on her coat, grabbed the keys to Sandrine's house, and went out.

Margot hurried up Rue Voltaire, the sky growing darker by the minute. She turned left at the war memorial and then followed the shortcut through to Rue des Arts.

The lane was empty. Inside, the house was even gloomier than before. How long did it take for a crime scene to go back to being a home? Five years from now, she imagined new owners moving in, oblivious to its history. Margot went through to the kitchen and looked at the floor, relieved to see the food she'd put down had gone. He can't have been that traumatised, then, though there was no sign of him now.

She washed the saucer in the sink and then opened the wall cupboard. What would he like this time: tuna fillet and crab, perhaps? Or maybe chicken cuts in gravy. Margot forked out the chicken, relieved to find this one smelled better. She went through the same procedure as yesterday: stood at the open back door, wafting it around, letting the aroma circulate. She waited a few minutes, but the cat failed to materialise.

Perhaps he'd sensed the impending rain and had holed himself up somewhere. Or perhaps someone had taken him in, the neighbours maybe. Leaving the saucer on the floor, Margot went back through the house and out onto the street. Someone was in – she could hear them talking through the front door – but when she knocked, no one answered. Fed up of being harassed by reporters, no doubt.

Margot wandered back through the house, unsure what to do next. Where did he sleep? There was no sign of a bed. Cats were territorial, weren't they? Perhaps with all those police and technicians clomping around the place, invading his patch, he'd decided to move elsewhere. Just as she reached the kitchen door, however, Margot froze. The little black and white fur-ball was contentedly chomping away at the chicken and gravy.

"I see," she smiled happily. "You'll only eat when I'm not here, is that it?"

The cat looked up, wondering what all the fuss was about. The chicken was clearly far too appealing to consider running away, however, and he carried on eating, happily ignoring her.

A thought popped into Margot's head. One of those thoughts which seem like a good idea at the time but which later she knew she would regret. Her eyes moved to the pet carrier under the counter. It would only be for a few days. She couldn't leave the poor thing here on his own with no one to look after him. And if things didn't work out she could always take him to the cat sanctuary. She wouldn't be able to rest if she did nothing.

But how did one go about catching a cat? It couldn't be that difficult, could it? While the cat was still munching, Margot eased by and slid the carrier out of its space. She pulled out the retaining clip to open the little door, and remembering there was an open packet of treats in the cupboard, sprinkled a few in one corner. As she turned around, the feline wonder paused to give her a curious look, though didn't seem to have realised what she was up to. And when Margot crouched and attempted to stroke him, he didn't shy away.

"Right then, Buster. You're coming home with me."

Cat-like in her own movements, Margot pounced.

Cats, even cute little black and white ones, have very sharp claws, evidently. Margot was left in doubt of this fact as she stood at the kitchen sink, washing the blood from her forearms. It hadn't been pretty; there had been much screeching and caterwauling (and not just from the feline) but at least the little terror was now safely stowed in the carrier, presently not making a peep.

"So, this is the thanks I get, is it?" Margot said tersely. "I'm trying to rescue you, you ungrateful ball of fur!"

The cat moodily stared back at her, the look on his face suggesting this was far from over.

Was there an offence called cat-napping? She would have to look it up when she got home. Article 311-17 of the *Code pénal*: Taking a cat from its home environs without its consent, punishable by three years imprisonment (or the rest of one's life in a mental institution). Margot dried her hands on a towel, draped the towel over the carrier, and then stashed the packet of cheese treats in her pocket.

Thankfully, the street was still empty. She locked the front door behind her and then walked quickly down the hill, taking the back route through to the harbour. She let herself in through the gate to the covered passage, locked it again behind her, and then carried him through to her courtyard.

At least the similar layouts of their houses might help reassure him (and it was a him; Margot had managed to see the evidence during the fight to get him into the carrier). She set him down on the kitchen floor and crouched to peer through the bars. The cat remained huddled in one corner, looking most put out. Margot sighed.

"There's nothing to be afraid of, you silly thing. I'm just going to look after you for a few days, that's all."

Oh dear. Here she was, turning into her worst nightmare – the batty old widow who lived by the sea and talked to her cats.

She pulled out the retaining clip and carefully opened the door. Contrary to her expectations, the cat didn't immediately make a dash for freedom. Thinking some encouragement might be required, she took the treats from her pocket and sprinkled some into her hand. This certainly got his interest, though he refused to take the bait. Although, was that surprising given that the big ugly human who'd just cat-napped you was standing right in front of your cage? Margot put the treats on the floor instead and then took a few steps back.

"Come on, puss-puss. How can you resist? Cheesy treats, yummy!"

She wondered what his name was. He wasn't wearing a collar. She could go back and ask the neighbours, but then, did cats recognise their given names? Weren't they far too haughty for that? She could call him whatever she wanted. Buster?

Tiddles? Mr Mistoffelees? If she ever did have a pet of her own she'd always imagined naming it something fanciful, like Octavia, or Fabiola or ...

And it was while she was thus distracted that the cat, whatever his name might be, made his move. In the blink of an eye he shot out of the carrier, skidded over the treats, and escaped through the door she'd stupidly left open.

Margot dropped her head in dismay. How could she have been so foolish?

Scrambling after him, she got to the courtyard just in time to see his tail disappear behind one of her planters. Margot quickly knelt down and angled her head to the gap. Somehow, the little perisher had managed to squeeze himself into the tiniest of spaces behind her big stone trough. His little face looked back at her, triumphant.

Go on, then – try catching me now, stupid woman!

Margot panicked. She tucked a hand under one edge and tried to pull the trough forward, but the thing weighed a tonne. What was she going to do? Try a big lever? Tie a rope to it and pull? She could ask her neighbour, Madame Barbier, to help. Her husband was as strong as an ox, but then she could just imagine the three of them breaking their backs to shift the thing only to watch the crafty little beggar shoot off and hide somewhere else. There were so many nooks and crannies in her raised beds the feline wonder would be spoilt for choice when it came to hiding places.

Margot exhaled in defeat. There was no point trying to force him out. She would just have to leave him. He would come out when he was ready. She stood up and dusted off her hands.

"All right, little man. Your food's inside if you want it. I'll leave the door open. But today is Sunday and I'm going inside to read my book. Good-day."

It may have been touted as the Pearl of the Côte Vermeille, blessed with over three hundred days of sunshine per year, but even in Argents-sur-Mer it rained. Fifteen minutes after Margot went in, big fat globules of water started falling out of the sky. She put down her book and went to the window. It had gone so dark out there she had to switch on the light.

Unable to concentrate, she sauntered back to the kitchen. Arms folded, she gazed out from the threshold of her back door. Right before her eyes a virtual emptying of the heavens was under way, pouring off the roof slopes, overwhelming the gutters. A veritable cascade was tumbling from the section of gutter directly over her head, landing just inches from her feet and splashing back at her. Margot cast a forlorn look across at the planter.

"Come on, pussy cat. You're going to get wet."

Weren't cats supposed to hate water? According to the weather forecast the rain was in for the day. Surely the thing would see sense, realise he had more to fear from getting wet than anything he might encounter in her kitchen. Unless he'd escaped while she hadn't been looking ...

Margot grabbed a jacket from the rack. Hooking it over her head, she tiptoed into the yard, raindrops pelting her hood like a hundred tiny hammers. The puddles had grown so large there wasn't a single dry place to stand, and when she knelt down her knees got soaked. She bent her neck to peer into the gap. A pair of amber eyes looked back at her.

"You can't stay out in weather like this, you silly thing. Why don't you come in?"

The cat, however, appeared to think otherwise.

Margot reassessed her options. She could call the *pompiers* and get them to shift the planter, though how ridiculous would she look: stealing someone's cat and then allowing it to get stuck. They would bar her from owning a pet for life. Maybe she could scare him out, prod him with a stick or something, but that was hardly a way to build trust. She had another idea – more carrot, less stick – and lowered her face to the gap once more.

"How about I get you some more treats, hmmm? Or a different type of food."

She looked at her watch. 11:36. Would pet-shops be open on a Sunday? She could only but try.

He seemed safe enough for now. The trough was tight against the wall, and the overhanging plants were giving him some shelter. Which was more than could be said for her jacket: the rain was now seeping through the seams and onto her skin.

"Stay there. I'll be back as soon as I can."

Margot got to her feet and ran back inside.

Luckily, there was a pet shop in Argents. And more to the point, it was open, at least for the next fifteen minutes. Margot hurriedly put on her shoes, dug out her properly waterproof coat, and set off.

Racing up Rue Voltaire, she slipped on a wet drain cover and twisted her knee. She cursed blue murder. She made it to the pet shop with two minutes to spare, and in her eagerness to get out of the rain thrust open the door so sharply it made the shopkeeper jump in surprise.

"Sorry."

"Terrible out there, isn't it?"

"Raining cats and dogs, you might say."

Margot shook the water from her sleeves.

The shop was a haven of peace and tranquillity. Packed to the gills with every conceivable item one's beloved pet might need: raw and frozen food; baskets of cows' ears, lambs' tails, puffed chicken feet. They even had chunky pizzles which she assumed were a treat for dogs. She moved through the grooming and medication area, passed shelves full of toys and treats, until finally she discovered the cat section. The food came in a whole variety of flavours: liver mousse pate; duck meat, gizzard and liver; natural dried sprats ... These things ate better than she did. Reasoning she might as well stock up whilst she was there, Margot bought two tins of duck meat, gizzard and liver, three tins of tuna and crab, and a box of chicken cuts in gravy. At the till, she added a packet of cheesy treats. The readout came to €47!

Ten minutes later she was back on her knees in the big giant puddle, packet of cheese treats in hand. The bag tore awkwardly when she opened it, scattering half the contents into the water. Margot glared in disbelief. What on earth had made her think this was a good idea? She shook a few dry ones into her palm.

"Here you go, pussycat. Look what I brought you."

She tossed them into the gap, hoping to encourage him, but instead the cat backed even further into the crevice, regarding her in pure astonishment.

Now she's throwing things at me!?

Margot glared back. "Now don't look at me like that! You liked them earlier."

If he did he'd clearly forgotten.

Margot hissed in frustration. This really was not the way she'd envisaged spending her Sunday.

"Fine! If that's the way you want it, stay out here. See if I care."

With that, she stuffed the soggy treats back into the packet and retreated into the house.

This is what her life had been reduced to – outsmarted by a creature with a brain the size of a walnut.

Determined not to give him another moment's thought, Margot made lunch: a baguette torn in two, a large chunk of Roquefort, three raw figs. On another small plate she arranged some olives and a few pieces of charcuterie. Fully deserving of a treat, she opened the five-year-old bottle of Sauternes that she'd been saving for a special occasion and poured herself a large one.

She plonked herself down on the sofa, tray on her lap, and turned on the TV. She wasn't going to worry about him anymore. He'd had his chance. If he wanted to stay out there and get wet that was his choice. There was nothing for her to feel guilty about. She'd done everything she reasonably could. If he got soaked and died a slow and painful death he only had himself to blame.

Margot popped a piece of the Roquefort into her mouth, wrapped it in her tongue, allowed her teeth to bite into it. She chewed, and then chewed some more. Cheese was surely one of nature's great gifts to man, yet swallowing it brought no pleasure whatsoever. Her plate of food looked totally delicious, yet suddenly, inexplicably, Margot had no appetite.

Damn that cat and whatever warped emotion had made her rescue it.

She snapped off the TV. After returning her tray to the kitchen she stood at the open door. Out in the courtyard, the rain was still falling like stair rods, the overflowing gutters rapidly turning her pretty courtyard into a lake. She'd been foolish to take him in. She didn't know the first thing about owning a pet. She should have left him where he was, he would have made a far better job fending for himself. The only upside was that she was safe from her future as the batty old cat lady.

Margot came away from the door and wandered through the

house. She remembered what it had looked like six months ago, in the aftermath of the fire, when the pain she'd felt had been like a punch in her heart. She would never forget that horrible smell of smoke. The whole house had since been redecorated, but sometimes, particularly on wet days, she was sure she could still smell it, seeping out of the walls, creeping up through the floorboards.

She went upstairs and stooped to look through her dormer window. The sky over the Mediterranean was a broiling mass of raincloud; even the boats in the marina looked washed out. How many hours had she spent here, searching for the meaning of life on the other side of a windowpane? She tried to imagine pushing a baby down to the park and abandoning her. Surely Sandrine had regretted it afterwards, when her mind had settled and the realisation of what she'd done filtered through. Margot refused to believe that any mother would intentionally harm her own child.

She went to the cupboard in the eaves and took out her tin of valuables. Ever since the fire she'd kept Hugo's medal in there, posthumously awarded for bravery, along with her other treasured possessions. Next to the medal was her locket. She opened it, and touched the curl of blond hair with her fingertips, all she had left of her own baby, snipped from his head when he'd been just a few days old. Margot had carried it on a chain around her neck for nearly a decade before Hugo had persuaded her it was time to move on.

Another burst of rain lashed the windowpane. Margot tutted. He wouldn't stay out there all day, would he? Unless he'd been injured – she had had to grab him pretty tightly to get him into the carrier. And he must have virtually flattened himself to squeeze behind the trough. Perhaps he'd crushed a rib in the process. The poor little mite was dying a long slow death and it would all be her fault.

Four o'clock. Still no sign of the rain letting up. Margot went downstairs and resumed her lookout from the threshold. The entire courtyard was now submerged, and water was making its way into the passage. What would she do when it got dark? Leave the door open all night in the hope he would come in? With a murderer on the loose that probably wasn't such a good idea. She could make some kind of temporary cat flap; cut a hole in the door; or leave a window open ... now she was trashing her house for the sake of the darned thing.

She picked up her tray from lunchtime and went back to the salon, her appetite slowly returning. After she'd eaten, she closed her eyes and managed to doze off.

She woke some time later with the impression of having heard something. Was that the sound of crockery slipping against hard tiles? Not sure if she'd imagined it, Margot carefully removed the tray from her lap and set it to one side. She approached the kitchen door with trepidation, trying not to get her hopes up. But then, there he was, the little black and white pussy cat, face down in the saucer of food, merrily chomping away.

He was so keen to get the food inside him he didn't even flinch when Margot sat beside him. Poor little thing. All she'd been concerned with was how it had affected her, yet what an ordeal it must have been for him. Margot reached out and tenderly stroked the fur on his back. All was forgiven.

"See. It's not so bad in here, is it?"

He chased the final morsel around the greasy plate with his tongue before snagging it with a tooth. Then his amber eyes looked gratefully up at her.

"Does that mean you want some more now? I suppose that's all right, given you haven't eaten all day." She got up and went to the cupboard. “How about some duck meat this time? Would that suit his Lordship?”

And it was as she was squeezing it out onto the plate that she turned just in time to see the cat bolt out the door she’d once again stupidly left open. Margot was stunned. Feed it and love it, and then watch it scarper at the first available opportunity.

She closed the door and went up to bed, physically and emotionally exhausted.

7

Florian had this annoying conversational tic. If, for example, one should ask him: "Did you see the documentary about the banking scandal last night?" his inevitable response would be: "Banking scandal?" If, perchance, one should encounter him on the promenade on a bright and sunny afternoon and enquire of him: "Where's the best place to buy ice cream?" he would surely reply with: "Ice cream?" Margot loved him dearly and knew it was only a reflex – having been asked an unexpected question that giant untidy brain of his needed an extra few moments to come up with an answer. But it did rather annoy her at times.

And so, when Margot arrived at the office next morning and said to him: "Do you know of a good local carpenter?" the first word that came out of his mouth was ...?

"Carpenter?"

Margot rolled her eyes. "*Yes*. A person who makes things with wood," she said, rather more tersely than intended. After the Sunday she'd had, her one remaining nerve had been reduced to a shred.

"Not off the top of my head," Florian responded. "But I can find out for you. Any particular job you want doing?"

Margot's irritation drained away.

"I need a cat flap installing. Don't ask. It's been a long weekend. And I have the scars to prove it." She kissed her fingertips and planted them on his forehead. "If you could let me know, please. And I'm sorry I snapped."

Half an hour later she decamped to the Gendarmerie. She found Captain Bouchard in the detectives' office, talking to some of his men, but the moment he spotted her he came away.

"No cleaning today?" Margot smiled as he intercepted her at the door. "If you're interested, I've got a rather nice pinny you could borrow."

He was not amused. "That won't be necessary."

Margot continued to regard him, hoping he might say more, but the captain remained tight-lipped. He walked her around the corner to his office.

"The phones we took from the scene have been analysed," he said as they settled in at his desk. A file was already open. "All but three of her contacts are unregistered phones."

"Who are the other three registered to?"

"The number she called just before nine belonged to Gy Berger. He's a local man; thirty-one years of age; works at the railway station. She also received a call from him at eight-fifteen. That call lasted three and a half minutes. Then he called her again at ten-thirty, this time a thirty-second call. Finally, there was a four-second call at ten-forty-five, followed by two attempted calls which were immediately cut off."

Margot frowned. "That sounds a little obsessive."

"She also sent him a text earlier in the day asking if he would be calling round at his usual time. He replied simply to say that he was. The exchange was quite cold in comparison with earlier messages. There had clearly been a falling out of some kind."

Margot recalled the final entry Sandrine had made in her diary: *We acted like nothing had happened.* The captain went on:

"And if Gy Berger was her nine o'clock appointment, he was the last person we know who saw her alive."

"Have you contacted him?"

"Not yet. We're still trying to locate him. But we found this image on file."

He handed her a headshot. A pasty white face, curly blond hair, a man with a lost look in his eyes. Margot handed it back.

"What about the other two numbers?"

"The second number belongs to her landlord, Patrice Fabron. He owns a string of properties in the area. In the past few weeks she received just one call from him, last Friday afternoon. Prior to that he texted her once a month, usually on a Thursday night, giving a time to meet the following day. This Thursday, however, the night she was murdered, there was nothing."

"So she wasn't paying him rent but she was seeing him on a monthly basis?"

"'Seeing' being the operative word." The captain met her eye, no doubt having the same thought.

"And there's potentially a third person of interest," he went on. "This time on her personal phone. Four weeks ago, over twenty calls were made and received to a Doctor Lucien Roche. Many of them at night, some of them lasting over an hour. All the calls were made over a period of eight days, and then three weeks ago they suddenly stopped."

"Who is he?"

"All we have so far is his name and an address in Aix. The phone is still active, but when we call it there's no answer."

After a pause, he reached into a box and took out a couple of spiralbound A4 books, one of which he handed over.

"This is a transcript of her most recent diary. You can keep this copy."

Margot flicked through. They'd done a good job on it. The

pages on the left carried photographic enlargements of each page of the diary while on the right someone had painstakingly typed up the various blocks of text. Margot turned to the page for the night of the murder. The initials she'd used to refer to her nine o'clock were GLM.

"Does Gy Berger have a middle name?"

Captain Bouchard checked his notes. "Nicholas."

"So, GLM was code for GNB," Margot mused out loud. It was hardly likely to be a random association. Given that Sandrine was a maths genius there would surely be some kind of formula to it. Margot was itching to have a go at cracking it. If they could decipher the code they could find out who these other sets of initials referred to. She was particularly keen on finding the identity of JNW, the *horny stag*. Spotting his initials on another page, she read:

JNW, not much fun last night. While he was doing it he grabbed my hair and called me a dirty little whore. He seemed to get off on it. Afterwards he sort of apologised. Said it just came out in the heat of the moment. But isn't it in the heat of the moment that we see a man's true colours? I bet he never says that to his wife.

He sounded like an unsavoury piece of work.

"We've also been going through the shoe box of till receipts," Captain Bouchard went on, bringing Margot out of her thoughts. "She rarely made any extravagant purchases. She seemed to spend an awful lot of money on her pet cat." (*Tell me about it*, Margot thought). "But when it came to the child's bedroom it was a different story. She spent one and half thousand euros on furniture from BUT. Another six hundred from Monsieur Meuble. She paid nine hundred euros to have the floorboards sanded and waxed. All together it came to well over five thousand, and at that point she was seriously overdrawn at the bank."

"When did she do all of this?"

"July, August."

Margot frowned, baffled.

"Could she have been planning to adopt?"

The captain shook his head. "We checked. She wasn't registered with any of the local adoption agencies, and they had no record of her contacting them."

Maybe she was fantasising, imagining she still had a child. The mind was adept at playing tricks, a fact Margot knew only too well.

Lieutenant Martell appeared at the door. They both gave him a querying look.

"Yes, lieutenant?"

"Guess what – Gy Berger didn't go into work this morning. And according to his boss at the station, that's highly unusual."

"Any idea where he is?"

"I was about to try calling his home. He lives with his mother."

The captain got to his feet. "No need." He looked at Margot. "Let's go and surprise him."

According to the records, Gy Berger and his mother lived in one of the social housing projects north of the town. The road leading to it was closed for roadworks, so they had to park down the street and walk, giving a wide berth to the clattering jackhammers. A series of numbered signs directed them up a cascade of concrete steps, and when they finally located the one they were after they found themselves standing on a plateau four storeys higher than where they'd set out. The house was part of a squat terrace, facing the sea.

A woman in her sixties came to the door, flinching at the sight of the captain's uniform.

"What do you want?"

"We're looking for Gy Berger," the captain said, having to raise his voice over the rattle of the jackhammers, the noise of the roadworks having followed them.

"He's not here."

"Are you Gy's mother?" Margot asked.

"I told you – he's not here. Now leave us alone."

She attempted to close the door, but Margot stayed it with her hand.

"Please, Madame Berger. We only want to ask him a few questions."

The captain, meanwhile, had stepped back to look up at the front of the building. Lowering his eyes, he looked triumphant.

"So who's that up at the window?"

Margot looked, too, and found the face of a young man looking down on them. The mother scowled.

"His dinner'll be ready soon!"

"Then we'll try not to keep him."

The captain moved swiftly past. His long legs carried him halfway up the stairs before Madame Berger could even respond.

"Gy! It's the police."

Margot followed hot on his heels. At the top of the stairs, the captain selected one of the three closed doors and entered immediately. The spooked young man stood with his back to a desk full of computer equipment, childishly attempting to hide what was on one of the screens.

"Gy Berger?"

"Y—yes."

"Stop whatever it is you are doing and move away from the computer."

He moved, though only by a few inches. Suddenly, everyone was still. Margot quickly scanned the room: cameras on tripods, lights on rigs, a microphone on a boom ... all of it linked to two huge monitors behind him on the desk. A bedroom come studio, it seemed. When the captain ushered him aside, the image he'd been trying to hide was simply the feed from one of the cameras pointed at a table upon which was arranged a collection of miniature figures.

A confused silence came over them. The mother had appeared on the landing and was anxious to come in, but the captain closed the door, shutting her out. Margot studied the table, careful not to touch anything.

"What are you making?"

"A film."

"What kind of film?" the captain asked impatiently.

"Claymation?" Margot suggested. It was a stage in miniature: several plasticine figures arranged on a surreal landscape. Above it, a cyberpunk spaceship hung from a wire, while a hideous green monster lurked in a cave. She turned to find Berger nodding.

"Why were you trying to hide it?"

"It's for a competition. I've written the script, and planned it all out."

Margot frowned. "You were worried we might copy your idea?"

He seemed a little unsure but nodded. "The winner gets a thousand euros."

He was holding himself awkwardly, looking very ill-at-ease. Every time he met Margot's eye he quickly looked away. She smiled to try and get him to relax, but it had no effect.

The captain was less sympathetic. When he'd finished appraising the room he faced the young man squarely.

"Do you know why we're here?"

"If it's about Sandrine I know she's dead."

"And how do you know that?"

"I heard it on the radio."

Captain Bouchard eyed him suspiciously. "When did you last see her?"

"On Thursday night."

"You went to her house?"

"Yes."

"What time did you leave?"

"Ten-o-four."

"Ten-o-four?" the captain repeated with curiosity. "That's very precise."

"I work with trains. I like timetables."

"So where did you go, at ten-o-four precisely?"

"I came home."

He glanced nervously between the two of them, his gaze always falling just short of their faces. The captain gave him a long hard stare which only served to make the young man even more uncomfortable. He twitched repeatedly, his body not quite sure what it wanted to do with itself.

"How were things between the two of you?" Margot asked.

He raised and lowered his shoulders, more of a twitch than a shrug.

"Had you quarrelled?"

He shook his head.

"Why aren't you working today?" the captain asked.

"I didn't feel well."

"Have you called a doctor?"

Again, he shook his head. It was difficult to tell whether he was lying or not. His body language might be interpreted as guilt, but equally it could have been the pressure of the questioning. The captain took out his notebook.

"Were you aware Sandrine kept a diary?"

Another shake of the head.

"One of the very last things she wrote, and this was just after you'd left on Thursday night, was this: 'We acted like nothing had happened'. What did she mean by that?"

"You shouldn't have been reading her diary. It's private."

"Nothing is private in a murder investigation, Monsieur. What did you argue about?"

"We didn't argue."

"Then why did she write that?"

"It's better if you tell us the truth, Gy," Margot said. "How long had you been seeing Sandrine?"

"Three years and five months."

"You must have got to know her well in that time."

He tightly knotted his arms, his manner becoming more and more child-like.

"Sandrine was my friend. She liked me."

"I'm sure she did, but even friends fall out. Had she done something to upset you?"

They gave him time, but Berger remained silent. Growing impatient, the captain flipped the page in his notebook.

"According to Sandrine's phone records, you called her several times on the night she was killed. First at eight-fifteen, then at ten-thirty, again at ten-forty-five, and twice more just before eleven. Why did you keep calling her?"

"I wanted to tell her something."

"Tell her what?"

"It's private."

"You'd seen her at nine o'clock; you'd spent an hour at her house. Why didn't you tell her then?"

The young man grew increasingly agitated. His forehead was glazed, he kept clenching his fists.

"You don't understand."

"Then explain it to me."

"She wasn't what you think. She was better than that."

"How was she better?"

His frustration continued to build, but the captain didn't let up.

"We know what you liked to do when you were alone with her. The videos you liked to make. It's all there in her diary, described in every detail."

Berger blushed fiercely. "You shouldn't have been reading that!"

"Can you show us the videos?"

"No!"

"Are they on here?"

The captain moved towards the computer, but Berger panicked. He barged into the captain's shoulder and quickly reached round to the back of the computer. It happened so quickly Margot wasn't sure what he'd done but she guessed he'd snatched out a memory stick. Eyes wide in panic, he faced them like a cornered animal.

Despite the provocation, the captain remained calm. "Let's not do anything hasty, Monsieur. If that's a memory stick you've just taken out then I'd like to see it."

"You can't! It's mine."

"Either you give it to me or I'll be forced to arrest you."

"I didn't do anything wrong."

"In which case you've got nothing to hide."

Margot ventured a step closer. "Do as the captain says, Gy."

He spun to face her. "But I loved Sandrine. I would never have harmed her."

She flinched. "You *loved* her?"

"She meant the world to me. I wanted her to take her away. I was going to—"

A knock sounded on the door.

"Gy?"

Now it was Berger who flinched. As if pulled from a trance, it took him a few moments to compose himself.

"I'll be right out, *Maman*."

He briefly seemed stumped, as if regretting having come out with it. He lowered his eyes and slowly backed down. Captain Bouchard held out his hand.

"The memory stick, Monsieur."

The young man delayed a little longer, but then unfolded his arms and opened his fist.

They waited for a forensics officer to arrive. When he came, the captain instructed him to search the room and take every piece of computer equipment he could find. His phone rang as they were descending the cascade of stairs. Detouring into a side street to escape the noise of the roadworks, the captain stood and listened for the best part of two minutes. Finally, he said, "Send me the address," and hung up.

Margot gave him an inquisitive look. "Anything interesting?"

"Martel's dug up some background on the landlord, Patrice Fabron. He has a previous conviction for assault – he punched one of his tenants in the face and left her hospitalised."

"When was this?"

"Two years ago. She was living on a barge he owned in the canal du Midi. He claimed it was self-defence and got off with a hundred hours of community service."

Margot despaired. "And they call that justice?"

"More pertinently, perhaps, the argument was over money. In his statement, he alleged the tenant hadn't paid him her rent."

8

In addition to owning a string of houses and apartments in the area, Patrice Fabron was also the proprietor of a motorhome dealership on the outskirts of Narbonne. After spotting it from the main road, they came off at the next junction, looped around a supermarket, and drove back through a jumble of fast-food outlets, *jardineries* and DIY stores. The captain swung in through a wide pair of steel gates and pulled up beside a huge white camping car.

The doors to the glass-fronted sales centre opened automatically. Inside, a woman in her sixties crossed the floor to greet them, the slogan on her pale blue tee-shirt becoming clearer as she neared: *Camp more, work less.*

"Bonjour, Captain; Madame. How can I help?"

"We're looking for Patrice Fabron."

Her friendly smile turned to something more rueful.

"What's he been up to now? Nothing too serious, I hope."

"Are you Madame Fabron?"

"For my sins."

Margot wondered how long they'd been married, how much of her husband's history she knew.

Her jollity having fallen upon deaf ears, she sucked up her smile.

"My husband's out in the yard. Shall I call him for you?"

"No need. We'll find him."

The sales yard was crammed with motorhomes, boxy white behemoths, some of them with staggeringly high price tags. They were so large and packed so tightly that the spaces in between had become a warren of narrow walkways. Honing in on the sound of voices, they found Fabron (identifiable by the same blue tee-shirt as worn by his wife) extolling the features of a brand-new Laika to a couple of grey nomads. Though he spotted them immediately, he barely batted an eyelid and carried on with his spiel. While they were waiting, Margot looked in through the camper van's open door: cream leather upholstery, walnut veneered cupboards, high-end kitchen appliances. An Italian gin palace on wheels.

Growing impatient, Captain Bouchard noisily cleared his throat. Fabron took the hint. He invited the grey nomads to explore the rest of the van on their own and then came away.

"Just give me two minutes to speak to my friend the Captain here."

He signalled for them to follow. Around the back of the gin palace, a chain-link fence separated them from a rather sorry-looking canal. He drew them over to a wooden hut where the bottles of liquid gas were stored and then leaned in conspiratorially.

"I'm guessing you're not in the market for a camping car," he chuckled.

Margot flashed him an up-and-down look. He was the epitome of the oily used-car salesman, all white teeth and tacky jewellery. Shorter than average height, overweight (the tucked-in tee-shirt was doing him no favours), though despite his flabby physique his hands were strong, his fingers cord-like. Potent weapons when balled as fists. As if reading her mind, he tucked them away in his pockets.

"I take it you're here about Sandrine. I heard the news yesterday. What a tragedy. A nice sweet thing like that. I hope you find the bastard who did it."

"I'm sure we will," Margot said.

He looked her in the eye, not quite getting her meaning.

"Well, whatever I can do to help. Ask away."

Another customer was strolling between the motorhomes so the captain waited until they'd moved out of earshot.

"Have long had she been your tenant?"

"Three years. Never had any trouble from her. She always kept the place clean and tidy. I only wish they were all like her."

"And the rent?"

"What about it?"

"Were her payments always on time?"

"Always. Every month, without fail."

The captain raised an eyebrow. "According to her bank statements she stopped paying the rent nine months ago."

Fabron hesitated, doing his best to return a blank look.

"Did she? To be honest, I leave all the financials to my wife. Most of the money ends up in her pocket, anyway."

"Do you know what Sandrine did for a living?"

He frowned. "Wasn't she a physiotherapist of some kind?"

"No, Monsieur, she was not a physiotherapist. She worked as a prostitute."

"Is that a fact?"

"It is."

He heaved a fake sigh. "Well, whatever she chose to get up to behind closed doors was no business of mine."

The captain squared his shoulders, losing patience. "Don't play games with us. Do you seriously expect me to believe you were unaware she hadn't paid any rent for nine months?"

"Like I said, my wife deals—"

"Then perhaps we should go inside and speak to your wife," Margot cut in. "See what else she knows about you."

His oily grin lost some of its sheen. He spent a few moments giving Margot a look of disgust before turning his attention back to the captain.

"All right. So maybe she did have problems paying her rent. But we came to an arrangement."

"Which was?"

"Do you want me to spell it out for you?"

"You demanded sex from her in lieu of rent," Margot said, more than happy to spell it out for him.

Fabron looked peeved. "I didn't demand anything from her. It was her idea. She called me just after Christmas and said she was short of money. I told her I wasn't happy about it so she offered payment in kind. And, correct me if I'm wrong, that's not illegal."

"I'm not sure the tax office would see it that way," the captain replied.

This time the salesman had no comeback.

"It's not the first time one of your tenants has been late with her rent, is it, Monsieur Fabron?" Margot said.

"What do you mean by that?"

"Your barge on the canal du Midi."

He bridled. "What are you talking about? That was self-defence. She came at me with a boat hook!"

"So you punched her in the face," Margot said. "Did that make you feel like a big strong man?"

He pulled his hands from his pockets and came at her, eyes shining with hatred. "What is this?"

"A simple enough question."

He glared, his face just inches from hers. "You weren't there. You don't know what happened."

"Does your wife?"

"Yes! And I've served my time."

Margot scoffed. A slap on the wrist and a hundred hours of picking up litter. She continued to stare back into his eyeballs, refusing to be intimidated, until the captain put a hand between them, prompting Fabron to back off. When things had calmed down, the captain resumed:

"You normally contacted Sandrine on a Thursday. Why not this Thursday?"

"I was busy."

"Doing what?"

"Look. If you're trying to insinuate I had anything to do with Sandrine's death you're wrong. Totally wrong. I actually did like her. Granted, she was a bit weird, and she was hopeless with money, but she was harmless. And, since you've asked, the night she was killed I was at a card game. With some friends. It finished at midnight, and afterwards I went straight home and got into bed with my wife. More's the pity."

"We'll need the names of those friends."

"No problem. Give me your card and I'll send you the list."

After a pause, the captain handed it over.

"Fine. Is that it?"

"Just one other question," Margot said. "When was the last time you actually saw Sandrine?"

"It would have been the end of last month."

"On the Friday?"

"Yes."

"What time?"

He looked irritated. "What does it matter?"

If they knew the exact time and date Margot could look up his codename in the diary and use it to help work out the cipher.

"Just answer the question," the captain said.

Fabron exhaled. "I don't actually remember since I do,

funnily enough, have other things to think about. But it was probably around seven. That's when my wife does her Pilates class."

Poor woman. Having to put up with this excuse of a human being for a husband.

The captain glanced at her to see if she were done. Margot nodded. He touched the peak of his kepi and they turned to leave.

"Hold on."

They waited.

"Have you finished with the house yet?"

"I'll have to check with forensics but I think so. Why?"

Fabron turned his head and spat through the chain-link fence, into the canal. "I need to get some men in there. Clear the place out before I re-let it."

After locking the gate behind her, Margot crept along the covered passage. The carpenter Florian had found had promised to call round later to install the cat flap, but this morning she'd risked leaving the back door open and the saucer of food on the kitchen floor. Not only that, she'd cleared a space in the corner and put down a blanket in case he wanted something soft to curl up on (and had been fighting the urge to go back to the pet shop and buy him one of the proper cat beds she'd seen). There was no sign of him in the courtyard. Margot pushed open the back door and was unsurprised to see that the food had been eaten. When she stooped to inspect the blanket, she found a dozen hairs snagged in the fibres.

"Hmmm. Eats my food and then buggers off elsewhere," she muttered to herself, getting the feeling she was being taken for a sucker.

Margot opened the cupboard and selected his lordship's evening meal: chicken and liver in gravy tonight? Or maybe salmon terrine? Perhaps Sir would like it served on a silver platter, warmed in the microwave, with a few choice biscuits on the side? Afterwards, Sir could lounge on his blanket while his slave gave him a mani-pedi. *You've got your paws well under the table there, mate,* his feline buddies most probably said to him when they'd been out for a night on the tiles.

Sucker.

Turning, Margot jumped, spooked by the sight of his royal furriness installed on her threshold. The look on his face suggested he knew exactly what she'd been thinking. After sampling the air with a twitch of his nose, he got off his rear and deigned to come in.

Well, are you going to stand there looking at me like a lunatic or put that food down here where I can eat it?

Margot emptied the rest of the packet. Instead of putting the saucer straight down, however, she held it out of reach. It was time they came to an understanding.

"Now listen, Buster. You can have this on two conditions. One, you let me stroke you while you're eating it. And two, when you've finished you'll come and join me in my salon. Deal?"

The cat chirruped with delight.

Oh yes, yes, of course. Give me the food. Give it to me now, and I'll do anything you want. Anything at all.

Margot put down the saucer, grinning from ear to ear. Suddenly everything was right in the world. The cat got on with his meal while Margot crouched beside him, running her palm all the way down his back to his tail. Suddenly the attractions of owning a pet became clear. And the statistics were there to prove it: pet owners lived longer than non-pet owners, had lower blood pressure, were generally less stressed. It made sense on every level. The cat ran his tongue around the saucer, keen to lap up every last drop of sauce. Finding a morsel stuck between his teeth, he chewed and swallowed, content now that his belly was full. A successful love-in all round, it seemed.

"Right then." Margot got up and went to the door of the salon. "Remember part two of our deal?"

The cat looked up, appearing not to have the faintest clue what she was talking about. Interest evaporated, he sat on his spot and wetted a paw. He ran it over his right eye, and then over his left.

"Come on," Margot encouraged. "If you're a very good boy I'll let you sit next to me on the sofa."

If cats could sneer this one would have. After subjecting her to a long disdainful stare, he rose to his paws and merrily walked out the door.

Margot's head fell onto her chest. Perhaps she had the word tattooed on her forehead:

SUCKER!

9

Behind on her caseload, Margot spent the next morning at the *Palais*, bogged down in paperwork. For four hours solid she sat with a pile of dossiers in front of her, checking that each one had been compiled in accordance with the *Code de Procédure Pénale*. The dossier was the key component of the French justice system, forming the central feature of both the investigation and the subsequent trial. Unlike the adversarial approach favoured by other countries (where justice largely depended upon which side came up with the better argument), the French system relied upon the written record, and this meant that every piece of evidence, every transcript of every interview, each snippet of background information all had to go into the dossier, and then each piece of paper had to be checked and double-checked to ensure that correct procedure had been followed. Statements were required to be signed in triplicate; a proper record of the *garde à vue* had to be provided, showing the times of each interview, details of rest breaks and any medical visits. It was all very thorough; the only downside being there was precious little time available for the judge herself to direct the investigation. More often than not, supervision these days consisted of a retrospective review of the evidence gathered by the police, a bureaucratic more than a judicial role. And going through it all was so tedious it made Margot's brain go numb.

"Florian," she said, surfacing for air one time. "Do you happen to have a revolver in that desk of yours?"

"A *revolver*?"

Margot threw a book at him. Though only in her head.

"Yes. Another hour of this and I might just shoot myself."

In her break, Margot exchanged the dossiers for one of Sandrine's diaries. All seven had now been transcribed and, if anything, the earlier ones were even more indecipherable than the most recent. Much of what she'd written was stream of consciousness stuff, the subject matter dark and brooding, interspersed with weird and wonderful doodles. Sandrine had clearly had a lot going on in her head. Every page had been used apart from four years ago where ten white pages stood out. At first Margot had wondered if the transcribers had missed something, but then she checked the date: April, four years ago – the time they'd assumed Sandrine had attempted to commit suicide.

The entries leading up to the blank pages contained hints of what she'd been planning. She clearly felt guilty, and had been tormented by thoughts that she'd let both Lya and herself down. It seemed to have been a one-off, however, and after the ten white pages there was no mention of it.

The codenames had first appeared three years ago. Her clients seemed to be people already known to her. Other than PKQ (whom she'd now been able to deduce was her landlord, Patrice Fabron) she never mentioned anyone other than a regular set of six. And for most of them the sex was secondary; what they really wanted was someone to talk to, to touch, to confirm that they were actually still living. As for Gy Berger, he didn't even like to touch her – all he wanted was to film her. The entries during this latter period became rather more playful and humorous; far less dark than some of her earlier jottings. For whatever reason it seemed her mind had cooled. And in the past few months Margot found comments on how she was planning to give up the sex work and make a fresh start. Still, it was depressing to think that someone of such high intellect had ever been reduced to living that kind of life.

At lunchtime, she walked down to the harbour and followed the curving path that led to La Lune Bleue. It wasn't busy. The table at the end of the terrace was free, and finding no sign of Raymond, Margot took a seat. Eyes closed, she sat with her face to the sea, letting the breeze blow away the cobwebs.

She took out the most recent of Sandrine's diaries and set it down on the table. Next to it she placed a blank sheet of paper, weighted with the candle holder and a bottle of olive oil. After searching her bag for a pencil, she wrote:

GLM was the codename for GNB (Gy Nicholas Berger)

PKQ was the codename for PMF (Patrice Maximillien Fabron)

Having two names should now give her something to work with. Margot gripped the end of the pencil between her teeth. There had to be some kind of formula to describe how the code worked. G remained as G so that was a shift of 0 places along the alphabet; N to L was a shift of 24; and B to M was 11 places so it wasn't just a simple linear shift. She scribbled out what she'd written.

Raymond appeared, approaching the table with a mortified look on his face.

"Sorry, Margot. I didn't see you come in."

"That's perfectly all right."

"Let me get you some wine. We've got a very nice bottle of Chablis open at the bar."

"Am I that predictable?"

He grinned as he backed off to get it. When he returned a few moments later, Margot moved aside her things to let him set up.

"Do you know anything about ciphers, Raymond?"

"Ciphers?"

Margot ground her teeth. Was this thing catching?

"You know – codes."

He pulled a face. "Not really. I wasn't very good at maths at school."

That was true. Margot had home-tutored him in English for a while, and although he'd tried hard, academia was not his calling. Pausing, Raymond looked into space, appearing to have had second thoughts.

"Though I do remember something about Caesar codes. My friend and I used to send cryptic messages to each other when we were kids."

"So what's a Caesar code?"

"It's where you substitute one letter for another further down the alphabet. So, A becomes ... D; B becomes ... E; C becomes—" he had to think about it "—F. And so on."

"Mmm." Margot chewed the end of her pencil. "I already thought of that. The problem is, this code was designed by a maths grad. I'm guessing it's going to be a little more complex."

"Oh." He gave her a downcast look. "Is this a case you're working on?"

"It is. And I have a feeling it's going to drive me nuts."

Raymond finished setting the table. "Sorry, Margot. I wish I could be more help."

"Never mind. I'm sure I'll figure it out."

On her way home after work Margot called in at the pet store. The owner was just about to shut up shop, but seeing Margot's face appear at the door she changed her mind. Hardly surprising given the fact she'd already spent a small fortune in there.

"Back already?"

"I think I'm going to need considerably bigger treats."

They both laughed.

Margot moved between the racks. Perhaps a toy might help lure him in. He seemed quite a young cat; he probably liked to play. A feathery bird thing tethered to the end of a stick took her fancy.

"I'm not sure why I'm buying him this," Margot said when she got to the till. "He's the one who's got me on a string."

"Cats are experts at it. Have you had him long?"

"Only a couple of days. He's a rescue. His owner died recently."

"I'm sorry to hear that."

"I was wondering if he'd been traumatised. He spent the first day hiding behind a trough in my garden."

"That's not unusual," the shopkeeper said, bagging up her purchase. "When a cat finds itself in a strange new environment they'll usually look for somewhere to hide."

"Any tips on how I might encourage him to come into my house? He'll eat the food I put down in the kitchen but come no further."

"You mean you've let him out?"

"Well, he sort of escaped."

The shopkeeper pulled an unhappy face. "It's usually best to keep them indoors for the first two weeks. Cats are very territorial – he may try and find his way back to his original home. If he does come back, you could try one of these." She reached behind her and took a small box from a shelf. "It's a diffuser.

Plug it into a socket and leave it switched on for an hour or so. It's meant to create a relaxed environment."

Margot glanced at the writing on the box. "Lure him in with pheromones, you mean?"

"Something like that."

"Thank you."

Margot walked home, weighed down with another hefty bag of shopping.

The carpenter had been to install the cat flap. There was no sign of the fur-ball inside or out, but it seemed he hadn't entirely abandoned her: the food she'd left in the kitchen that morning was gone. She must have been doing something right. Lacking the headspace to pander to him right now, however, Margot plugged in the diffuser, fed herself, and then watched ten minutes of news on TV. Leaving the dirty dishes on the tray, she settled in at her bureau, armed herself with a pencil and a pad of paper, and then set to work on the diary code.

She reviewed the notes she'd made at lunchtime:

GNB was encrypted to GLM

PMF was encrypted to PKQ

Looking at it again, something immediately struck her as odd. The first letter in each example remained the same yet the other two letters were scrambled. Hmm. This clearly was no simple Caesar code. There was bound to be a computer program somewhere where all you had to do was type in the two pieces of ciphertext and the program would spit out the solution in a millisecond. She could also just leave it to the tech guys to figure out, but Margot's stubborn streak was coming through. Sandrine's unique mind had come up with this code and she felt that cracking it would give her another telling insight.

She tore off a clean sheet and wrote down the numbers 1 to 26. Below them she wrote the letters of the alphabet. Then she noted the positions of each letter in her two examples: 7-14-2; 16-

13-6. Below that she wrote the ciphertext equivalent: 7-12-13; 16-11-17. Now, what could be the relationship between those two sets of numbers? Margot stared at the digits until her eyesight began to go blurry. She tapped her pencil on the bureau, willing her brain to work. She'd been quite good at maths at school, but when you get to fifty school becomes a distant memory. She struggled on for another ten minutes, but failing to come up with any sparkling ideas put down her pencil. Some research on the internet was needed.

She poured herself a small cognac and took her phone to the sofa. There were many famous codebreakers throughout history, of course; chief amongst them the team at Bletchley Park. Alan Turing was the one who routinely got the credit, but Margot was surprised to discover that at the height of the second world war over nine thousand people had worked at the site, and 80% of them had been women. Few of the names were familiar to her: Margaret Rock, Mavis Lever, Rozanne Colchester, Joan Clarke, Mavis Batey, Winifred White, Cicily Mayhew ... Margot felt compelled to speak their names out loud, feeling they should be heard. It came as no surprise to read that all of them were paid less and ranked lower than their male counterparts.

It was a similar story in the United States where, during the course of the war, ten thousand women were drafted into the Army and Navy, all of them educated, preferably unmarried. Some groups tested America's own codes, others worked on breaking the systems used by the enemy. Margot was intrigued to read that, although women were considered to be better code-breakers than men, it wasn't a compliment; the logic being that much of the work was tedious and boring – better for women to slog away at their desks and leave the men to come up with the insightful breakthroughs. Though integral to many of the successes, the contributions of this invisible army were ignored for decades, sworn to secrecy during the years of the war and afterwards glossed over by the writers of history books.

Yet many of them were outstanding codebreakers in their own right. Genevieve Grotjan, for example: an American mathematician whose insights into the workings of the Japanese cipher machine had proved pivotal. Her speciality had been something called a 'one-time pad encryption' which, apparently, was a form of encryption that used a random secret key and hence could not be cracked. If that was the model Sandrine had used Margot's prospects did not look good.

Buoyed by such inspirational stories, she went back to her bureau.

She wrote out the list of letters and numbers on a clean sheet and studied the digits again. How could each letter be shifted by a different amount? It had to be governed by some sort of rule. Something more complex than a simple linear shift, like multiplication or division, for example. Or perhaps it could be expressed as a quadratic equation. Margot chewed the end of her pencil while she tried to remember how it worked. It was bound to be something like: $x^2+b=y$ where x is the position of the plaintext letter in the alphabet, b is a constant, and y is the ciphertext equivalent. But then, raising any number to the power of 2 could quickly send her off the scale: 26^2 for example – her pencil would be going round and round like a mad thing.

And there were an infinite number of possible equations, of course. Her brain began to fog. How on earth was she going to guess which one Sandrine had used without a clue of some kind? This was the point at which some smart Aleck from tech would come along and say there was a far easier way of doing it: *Why are you wasting your time doing that? All you need to do is this, and then this, and then this. See?* Margot would be forced to take her imaginary revolver and shoot him dead on the spot. *In my defence, it had been a trying day ...*

She dropped her pencil, folded her arms, and moodily gave up. The world was so unfair. Why couldn't she be smarter?

Her phone rang. Pouncing on the distraction, Margot hurried to the sofa and snatched her phone from the cushion.

"Yes."

"I haven't called at a bad time, have I?"

Margot froze. "Stéphane?"

Her mind took a moment to untangle itself. She dropped onto the arm of the sofa while she recalibrated.

"Sorry. My mind's an alphabet soup at the moment."

He laughed. "You've not been eating that alphabet spaghetti again, have you?"

The last time they'd met, she'd told him that one of her favourite meals as a teenager had been Heinz Alphabetti on toast. *Pasta. Out of a tin? In the shape of letters?* He'd been mortified. Though Margot had subsequently been heartened to discover that the French, in fact, had a version of their own, albeit a rather more tasteful variety that came dried and in a packet.

"Are you mocking my ancestry again?"

"Margot, I wouldn't dare."

"Good. What can I do for you?"

"I'm coming down at the weekend. I was thinking we might meet up."

Meet up, she was tempted to say, taking a leaf out of Florian's book.

Instead, she slid down the arm of the sofa and sank her back into the cushions, staring up at the ceiling. She tutted in disgust. Just look at the size of those cobwebs up there. She really ought to get around to cleaning it. Dig out her feather duster. Or maybe ask Captain Bouchard to drop by and do it for her.

"Your mother's way ahead of you," Margot said. "She's already asked me round to dinner."

"How very presumptuous of her. I take it you accepted?"

"Hmmm ... well, that rather depends."

"On what?"

"On who's doing the cooking."

"I'm sure *Maman* and I will rustle up something between us. But don't worry, I'll have plenty of tins of spaghetti on standby just in case."

"Stéphane, if I see you with a single tin of spaghetti in your hand you'll be wearing it for the rest of the week. Do I make myself clear?"

He laughed. "Perfectly."

A plaintive *meow* came from the kitchen. Margot rolled her eyes in exasperation. He really chose his moments.

"*All right*!" she snapped, flattening the phone to her shoulder. "I'll be there in a minute."

"Sorry?"

Margot placed the phone back to her ear. "Not you. I was talking to my new lodger."

"Oh, really?"

Was that a hint of jealously in his voice? She rolled onto her side, and then sat up, smothering her grin.

"Yes. He's very demanding. If I don't have his food out at the allotted time he'll tear me to shreds."

"He sounds an absolute beast."

"Oh, he is. Although ..." Margot looked across the room to the socket where she'd plugged in the diffuser. It was still switched on, and had been pumping out pheromones for the past few hours.

"Oh."

"What is it?"

"I have a funny feeling I've got him high on drugs. I'd better go."

Registering the stunned silence at the end of the line, Margot smiled.

"Don't worry. I'll tell you all about him at the weekend."

Buster was waiting for her in the kitchen, not looking the least bit impressed.

Get off that damn phone, woman, and give me some food.

10

It didn't look much like the office of a lawyer – two white plastic windows above a backstreet auto-parts store – but this was the correct address: 42, Rue de la Port, the office of the *avocat* Sandrine had used for her divorce.

Margot held her finger on the plastic door buzzer, letting it ring. A few seconds later the lock unclicked without anyone asking her name. At the top of the stairs, a stocky woman in black tights stood waiting to greet her.

"Madame Renard?"

Margot smiled as she reached the same level. "Charlotte Bassot, I presume?"

They shook hands.

"Pleased to meet you. Come through."

An inner door led to a cramped office. Filing cabinets covered one wall, and the windowsill was piled with so many papers that little natural light made it through. It was a far cry from the sleek offices of the Paris law firm where Margot had once worked.

"You'll have to excuse the mess. I'm a one-woman band these days."

The desk was just as cluttered as the rest of the room though little analysis was required here. The framed family photos, the *Asterix* lunchbox, the child's artwork on the pinboard: Charlotte was clearly an overworked wife and mother.

"Can I get you a coffee?"

"No thanks."

They made themselves comfortable.

"I was terribly saddened to hear of Sandrine's death," Charlotte said. "I'd like to help in any way I can."

"You said on the phone you got to know her quite well."

"Yes, I did. Her divorce became quite contentious and we ended up spending a good deal of time together. I don't usually get personally involved with my clients but I have to say I liked Sandrine. She was a unique woman."

"I gather it was the husband who filed for the divorce."

"It was. He cited violent and unreasonable behaviour, towards both himself and the child. I take it you're aware of what happened when Lya was a baby?"

Margot nodded. "Didn't they take her PPD into account?"

"They did, but abandoning your baby in a park is pretty extreme. The child's welfare must always come first, of course."

"Of course," Margot agreed. "But it's still a shame. I've been reading her diaries. It's obvious Lya was important to her."

"At the time of the divorce, Sandrine still hadn't bonded with the child and was happy to give her up. It was only later that she changed her mind. But then his lawyers argued she was an unfit mother. I didn't believe that to be the case. As far as I was aware the psychosis was a one-off episode, and although she admitted to a history of depression she was taking medication for it. But they put up a strong argument, and unfortunately the judge sided with them."

"You say he claimed violent behaviour towards him ... Was there any truth in that?"

"She admitted to hitting him once, slapping his face during an argument. But it was nothing compared to the emotional abuse he'd subjected her to. Then again, Sandrine didn't make life easy for herself. Once she'd decided she wanted Lya back, she kept visiting their house, demanding to see Lya. He then applied for a restraining order, which was granted."

"Did she say why she'd changed her mind?"

"She said she felt guilty. She thought she'd let her daughter down and wanted to make amends. So she came back to me around a year after the divorce and said she wanted to appeal."

"And she lost the appeal as well?" Margot asked in surprise.

Charlotte nodded resignedly. "They argued she represented a clear and continuing danger to the child. And unfortunately, Sandrine wasn't in a strong position. She had little money, no proper job. She wasn't really looking after herself, never mind being fit enough to care for a small child. Compare her situation with that of her ex-husband who'd subsequently remarried, had a nice new house, a well-paid job ... he could offer a strong stable family whereas Sandrine had pretty much nothing. His *avocat* argued that bringing Sandrine back into the equation would only unsettle Lya. The only concession the court made was to extend her visitation rights, but that wasn't what she wanted."

Margot nodded. "Her ex told us about the restrictions."

"I can't imagine that having to have a social worker present when you visited your child was a particularly gratifying experience. Sandrine didn't want her daughter thinking of her as some kind of freak."

So why the bedroom? Margot wondered. If she had no chance of getting Lya back, had she just been living a fantasy; deluding herself into thinking it was going to happen?

"I can't pretend to understand her feelings," Margot said. "They were obviously complex."

Charlotte nodded in agreement. "We had several long chats about it. As a young woman, she said she'd never wanted to have children. She lacked maternal instincts, and ultimately felt pressured into it."

"By the husband?"

"By the husband, by society in general. It's easy to get trapped by the narrative you're not a complete woman unless you've given birth. Having a baby seemed the only way out. In the months leading up to the birth she said all she could feel was dread. She wanted to turn back time and undo the mistake she'd made. Then afterwards, she was plagued by a crippling sense of anxiety. She hated being left alone with the child, and was terrified she wouldn't be able to look after her properly."

"I suppose her unconscious mind was giving her a message: abandon the baby in the park and problem over."

"Perhaps. I think it was more a case of wanting to put Lya out of harm's way. She thought that if someone else found her they'd probably do a better job of looking after her. She wouldn't have been thinking logically during the psychosis, of course. She told me that, at the time, the baby had kept her awake for days. Later on, when people told her what she'd done, she was shocked."

Margot heaved a sad sigh. "It's a sorry story whichever way you look at it."

"It certainly is. I think one of the problems was she didn't communicate well. People misunderstood her. But the truth was she was a caring, intelligent woman, and for whatever reason life had let her down."

Margot could only imagine what it must have been like for her: looking at her baby and knowing she wasn't feeling the same things about it that other mothers felt. The fear of failing to live up to expectations must have been crippling. And before that, seeing her embryo as some kind of monster growing inside her, intent on taking away the life she knew.

"How long has it been since she lost the appeal?"

"Four years."

"Was it in April, by any chance?"

Charlotte checked her notes. "Yes, that's right. Four years ago, in April. How did you know?"

The ten blank pages; the scars on her wrist.

"Just a hunch," Margot said. "Have you seen her since?"

"Sadly, no. We didn't part on the best of terms. She left owning me money, though I've never pursued her for it. Quite frankly, I thought she deserved better. No woman should have been treated the way she was. It just wasn't fair."

Captain Bouchard was busy on another case so Lieutenant Martell took Margot into the detectives' office and installed her at the desk next to his. He fetched her a coffee, asked if she wanted anything to eat, and then dashed back to the other side of the room to get the two files she'd requested.

"The background checks on Gy Berger," he said, dropping the first file onto the desk. "And everything we have so far on Patrice Fabron." He dropped the second file beside it. "There's not much on Fabron yet. We're waiting for some people to get back to us."

"Okay. Thanks."

"You're most welcome. Anything else I can do for you, Madame Renard? Anything at all."

Margot regarded him from the tops of her eyes. Did this man's exuberance never take a day off?

"Any news on that mystery doctor?"

"Ah, the mysterious Doctor Roche. Kind of." He perched on the corner of the desk. "I tracked him down to a hospital in Aix, but the person I spoke to wasn't much help. According to her, their Doctor Roche was on assignment with *Médicins Sans Frontièrs*, working in some remote village in Somalia. I'm not entirely sure we were talking about the same person."

"Well, keep trying."

"I will. Anything else?"

"If I think of something I'll be sure to ask."

With some reluctance, the lieutenant went back to his computer.

Margot opened Gy Berger's file. She was keen to see whether either of them had any connection to the Ginette Clément case though she'd barely got started when her attention was drawn to the screen of Lieutenant Martell's computer. He'd gone back to watching one of Gy Berger's videos – the one where Sandrine was walking around the house in her underwear. Eleven memory sticks had been taken from his room, each containing at least twenty videos (an estimated hundred and fifty hours of footage, someone had calculated), but none of those Margot had seen so far contained anything that need concern them. Most were arty and esoteric, often tight close-ups of Sandrine's face as she answered questions put to her by Gy, off-screen. In others she was simply sitting on a chair, musing about life in general, a video equivalent of her diary. She was a natural in front of the camera. She didn't smile very often, but when she did her eyes shone with vitality. Berger had edited them into short films, each around forty minutes in length, and intercut the talking heads with footage of birds in flight, trees blowing in the wind, time-lapse sequences of clouds speeding across a moody sky, usually filmed in monochrome. They made *Bicycle Thieves* look like a trashy Hollywood blockbuster.

And in amongst the esoterica was some softcore erotica; thinly-disguised personal fetishes: Sandrine having a shower; exercising naked; that kind of thing. And it was the one where she was doing the housework in her underwear which the lieutenant just happened to be studying at that particular moment. Margot tutted pointedly.

"Do you have to watch that one?"

The lieutenant looked over his shoulder, eyes full of innocent surprise. "The captain's orders. He asked for a full report."

"Sheer dumb luck you found one where she's half naked, I suppose?"

Stuck for a response, Martel gaped. But then he turned back to his computer and immediately closed down the video.

"Sorry," he said. "Though that actually was the next one on the list. Honest."

Margot looked him in the eyes, believing him. "They're just a young man's private fantasies. Would you want someone looking at your innermost desires?"

The lieutenant firmly shook his head. "Un-un. No way. My fantasies stay firmly inside my head."

That was a can of worms Margot had no desire to see opened.

Arms folded, Martell remained sheepish for a while, but then, unable to stay still, he grabbed a tennis ball from a bowl and started throwing it up into the air and catching it.

"Do you think he did it?" he asked.

Margot watched the ball shoot up over their heads, narrowly miss one of the light fittings, and then drop into his cupped hands.

"You mean Gy Berger?"

"He was the last one who saw her alive, wasn't he?"

"As far as we know."

After stretching to catch the ball one more time, the lieutenant paused, and turned his seat, regarding her thoughtfully.

"I watched this documentary about Marilyn Monroe last night. They reckoned one of the last people to see her alive was Bobby Kennedy. Apparently, her diary was full of secrets that the Kennedys didn't want anyone finding. So, that got me thinking: what if Sandrine had someone's secrets hidden in her diary?"

Margot looked at him with newfound respect.

"Actually, lieutenant, I've been thinking the very same thing." She retrieved her copy of the diary from her bag and located one of the passages she'd marked. "I keep coming back to this JNW. Here's one of the things she wrote about him: 'I wonder if he'd be so smug if the whole town knew what I know. That would wipe the smile off his arrogant face.'"

"Any idea who he is?"

"Not yet. Someone smug and arrogant, obviously. But I need to work out the code to find his true initials."

The lieutenant thought about it for a few moments, but then, unable to offer any further insights, went back to throwing his ball. After making another two catches he was put off by his phone ringing and missed the next one. The ball landed on the edge of his desk, bounced onto Margot's, knocked over an empty cup, and then trickled over her papers before dropping into her lap. Martell grinned.

"Sorry."

Margot gave him a weary look. Lieutenant Martell had a heart of gold but it would be nice if someone occasionally took out his batteries. He answered his phone, but it was no one interesting. Margot hid the ball in a drawer while he wasn't looking.

"How did you get on in your match?"

"Our match? Oh, we lost. 20 – 14." Forgetting all about the ball, the lieutenant lounged in his chair. "Though it was quite funny at the end," he chuckled to himself. "Their flyhalf had a bust-up with the referee, so when the game was over they waited for him to go to the portaloo, and then six of their forwards turned the cabin onto its side. You should have seen his face when he climbed out. It was hilarious."

Despite her best efforts, Margot couldn't help smiling.

"Actually, lieutenant, there is something you can do for me."

Jumping to attention, he sat up, straight as a bolt.

"Name it."

"Could you find out which school Sandrine's daughter attends?"

"No problem. Give me two minutes."

He sprang out of his seat and literally ran to one of the filing cabinets on other side of the room. He was back within ninety seconds, a sheet of paper in his hand. Margot took it from him: Elne Elemental. The school just around the corner from Colbert's house.

"What time does it close?"

Another sprint across the room. This time he shouted back:

"Four-thirty."

Margot looked at her watch. Ten past four. She had time.

The line of vehicles parked outside the school extended all the way down the street. Margot had the taxi drop her at the end and then walked back.

She crossed the road as she neared the gates, avoiding the tight knot of mothers chatting outside. Others sat waiting in cars. The school run – probably a chore for most of them, never stopping to think how some would give the world to trade places. Margot thought of all the things Sandrine had missed out on in the past six years: her baby learning to walk; her first day at school; six years of growing up. Ordinary and everyday things taken for granted.

The bell rang. Half a minute later the children began to emerge, burdened with backpacks and folders. Margot had no idea what Colbert's new wife looked like but she was certain she would recognise Lya. As the tide of happy/sad faces came to the gate, there she was, cute as a pin in a fuchsia top and blue denim skirt. A tall blonde took her by the hand and quickly set off, looking like she was in a hurry. They walked back along the line of cars without stopping to talk. Margot crossed the road and watched them arrive at the black BMW she'd seen parked oddly on Colbert's drive. After giving them a moment to sort themselves out, Margot approached.

"Victoria Colbert?"

The woman turned sharply. "Yes?"

Margot looked past her, through the gap between the two front seats, to where Lya was settling into her booster seat. She smiled.

"Did you find your ballet pumps?"

Lya smiled brightly back. "Yes, thank you."

"Excuse me. Can I help you?"

Margot switched focus. Despite her obvious good looks, there was something quite mousey about Colbert's second wife. She was trying to look affronted but couldn't maintain eye contact for long. He'd clearly gone for someone less challenging second time around. Margot apologised, and then introduced herself.

"I came by your house on Saturday morning. I presume your husband told you?"

Victoria briefly looked flummoxed. In the front passenger seat, her toddler had dropped her drinking bottle and was pulling a face. Victoria stretched across the driver's seat to retrieve it, and by the time she turned back had managed to compose herself.

"Oh yes. I remember now. Is there a problem?"

"I just wanted to ask you about Thursday night."

"What about it?"

"Your husband told us he was at home all night."

Victoria Colbert blinked. "Thursday night?"

Margot nodded.

"Well, yes. That's right. We were both at home, all night."

The toddler immediately threw the bottle back into the footwell, and this time started to cry. Hissing impatience, Victoria quickly retrieved it.

"Look. I don't mean to be rude, but I'm in a bit of a rush. We're booked in at the dentist's in ten minutes."

"That's all right. I can see you're stressed. When you get a chance, would you mind calling into the Gendarmerie and giving a statement?"

"Of course not."

Margot stepped aside to allow her to get in.

Lya waved through the window as they drove off. A happy little family indeed. Though not, perhaps, the rightful one.

11

Captain Bouchard was back in his office when Margot returned from Elne. She brought him up to speed on her talk with Sandrine's former *avocat* and her brief visit to the school.

"Can you imagine what it must have been like for her?" Margot said, dropping into the chair and turning it through ninety degrees. "Wanting your daughter back and then being told you couldn't have her."

"It was a sad state of affairs," the captain replied, "but you can understand the court's point of view. The child was settled in a stable family. From Lya's perspective, Sandrine was a stranger."

Margot nodded reflectively. Perhaps she had been spending too much time seeing things through Sandrine's eyes. Lya and her stepmother clearly got on. Breaking them apart wouldn't have been fair.

"Have you found anything in Berger's past to link him to the Ginette Clément case?" the captain asked.

Margot shook her head. She reached into her bag and took out the two files Martell had given her.

"I've been checking his history, but nothing as yet. He would have been seventeen fourteen years ago, and living in Rivesaltes. At the time of Ginette's murder he was studying at the *lycée* in Perpignan. That's forty kilometres from the school Ginette attended. His father also worked for the railway, and had done for over forty years, as did Gy's grandfather. Gy's an only child, and get this ... his mother was *forty-nine* when she had him. That makes her eighty years old now."

The captain raised an eyebrow. She was certainly spritely for her age.

"I can't see there's anything incriminating on the memory stick he was trying to hide," Margot went on. "I think he just didn't want us seeing his films. They were obviously very personal to him. Has anything been found on his laptop?"

"We're still waiting for the lab. But keep looking into his background. If we dig a little deeper something might turn up."

Margot turned to Fabron's file. "As for her loathsome landlord ... Fourteen years ago he was working for a shipping company in Caen. There's no record of him having any connection with this area until nine years ago when he got married in Narbonne. There's nothing in here to say how he managed to acquire such a large property portfolio."

"Apparently, six months before they got married his wife had a big win on the lottery."

"Whoopy-doo," Margot said flatly. She closed both files and took out her copy of the diary. "What I'd really like to know is: who is JNM?"

"The horny stag?"

They shared a small smile.

She read him the extract she'd discussed with Martell. "I'm guessing he's quite high-profile; she talks about escorting him to various functions and fashionable parties. If he'd found out Sandrine had some dirt on him then that gives him a motive."

"But if she was killed for the secrets in her diary why was it left at the house?"

Margot shrugged. "Maybe he didn't know she'd written any of it down, but it's a lead worth pursuing, isn't it? According to the diary, she saw him two days before she died."

The look on the captain's face suggested he wasn't entirely in agreement but he kept his thoughts to himself. Margot continued:

"And then there's the question of who got her pregnant. It's unlikely to be Gy Berger. The impression I'm getting from the diary is they weren't even having sex."

The captain nodded. "How are you getting on with the code?"

"Slowly. Without knowing which method of encryption she used I'm not sure how we'll crack it."

"That's pretty much what the tech team said."

"Is it?"

The captain nodded again.

Margot felt relieved. At least it wasn't her just being dim, then.

Lieutenant Martell came to the door, a worried look on his face. The captain jutted his chin.

"What is it, Lieutenant?"

"Gy Berger's mother has just turned up at the front desk." He leaned down to rub his shins, grimacing. "She hit me with her walking stick! I was outside, watering the window boxes, and she just took a swipe at me."

"What does she want?"

"She's asking for her son's computer back. And she's pretty steamed up. I think you'll need to speak to her, Captain."

Madame Berger was glaring so intently at the Perspex screen that Margot feared it might just crack. The captain and Lieutenant Martell followed her into the office, but it was the captain the elderly woman's eyes immediately latched on to.

"You!" She rapped the screen with her stick. "You're the one! Coming round to our house like that, saying things to my poor Gy! What have you done with his computer? I want it back, right now!"

This was an eighty-year-old not to be messed with.

The captain stepped up to the desk, though kept his distance from the screen.

"Will you please refrain from attacking Gendarmerie property, Madame."

Undeterred, Madame Berger raised her stick again, ready for another assault. This time, however, Margot stepped in.

"Stay there, Madame Berger. I'm coming through."

The lieutenant and the captain both regarded her as if she'd gone insane.

Margot entered the waiting room via the connecting door and approached with caution, though Madame Berger kept her distance.

"Gy's computer is still being examined by our technical team," Margot said calmly. "But I promise, it will all be returned just as soon as they've finished with it."

Madame Berger turned down her suspicion a notch. Margot indicated they sit, and in the absence of any other chairs braved one of the grubby moulded plastic seats.

"You had half the street talking," Madame Berger lamented. "Turning up at our house like that."

"I'm sorry."

"And Gy was so upset. He wouldn't go to work again this morning, and that's not like him at all."

"Did he ever talk to you about Sandrine?"

"Yes. He talked about her a lot. I knew he was fond of her. And now she's dead, and you're asking him all these questions ..." she trailed off, shaking her head in exasperation.

The captain came to the door, though remained on the threshold. When Margot gave him a questioning look, he nodded, letting her continue.

"You do know what Sandrine did for a living, don't you?"

"I know she was a prostitute, if that's what you mean. There's no shame in that, is there?"

Margot shook her head.

"In any case, they were friends. Gy said she enjoyed spending time with him."

"The problem is, Gy was with her the night she died. He admitted to being at her house just a few hours before she was killed."

"That doesn't mean he killed her."

"I know. Do you remember what time he got in that night?"

"He always comes home at ten-thirty when he's been to see her."

"And you're sure it was ten-thirty that night?"

"Yes," she insisted. "If it had been any later I would have thought something of it."

"Did you speak to him?"

"We said a few words. Then he made himself a drink and went up to his room."

"What kind of mood was he in?"

"It's not always easy to tell with Gy. He often doesn't say much. I said goodnight to him and then went to bed."

"And what time was that?"

"Eleven o'clock."

That last flurry of phones calls between Gy and Sandrine had taken place between ten-thirty and eleven, just minutes after he got home if this account were to be believed. What had he been so desperate to tell her?

"Could he have gone out again after you've gone to bed? Would you have noticed?"

"He often goes out after dark, especially if he's having trouble sleeping."

The captain stepped forward. "Excuse me, Madame – are you saying it's possible your son left the house after he came back from Sandrine's?"

"Yes, but there's nothing unusual about that. I just said, he often goes out."

Margot looked at her more closely. "Where does he go?"

"Here, there, nowhere. He just likes to walk around. He says things look different when no one's around."

"But did you *hear* him go out?"

"No, but then I wouldn't. He's very considerate. He never makes a sound when he knows I'm in bed."

"So when was the next time you saw him?"

"Seven o'clock the next morning, when I took him his coffee."

Captain Bouchard remained in a thoughtful mood as they strolled back to his office. As they turned a corner, Margot gave him a probing look.

"What are you thinking?"

The captain breathed in slowly through his mouth. "If his mother didn't see him between eleven p.m. and seven the next morning she can't corroborate his alibi. And if he regularly goes out walking the streets at night he could easily have gone back to her house."

"So what next?" Margot asked.

"We'll wait to see what we find on his computer."

Reaching the door to the detectives' office, he called out to Martell, seated at his computer:

"Lieutenant – get onto the crime scene lab. See if they've found anything on either Gy Berger's computer or Sandrine's laptop. And tell them to make it their top priority."

"Yes, Captain. And I've just had a call from one of the landlord's friends. He confirmed there was a card game that night. He says Fabron left just after midnight. And Victoria Colbert also left a message. She wants to come in tomorrow to make a statement confirming her husband's alibi."

"Thank you. Call me if anything else comes in."

Whichever way they looked at it, things were not stacking up well for Gy Berger.

They entered the captain's office, where he immediately paused to consult his watch. Ten minutes to five.

"I'm afraid I'm going to have to leave early today," he said. "I need to pick up my son from football practice."

Margot flinched. "I never realised you had a son."

He gave a tiny nod of his head.

"How old?"

The captain tidied the loose papers on his desk. For a few moments he acted like he hadn't heard. Finally, he replied: "Thirteen."

"He lives with you in the barracks?"

He glanced up, a mystified look on his face. "I don't live in the barracks, Madame. We all live off-site these days."

Margot remained confused. So why had he been cleaning that apartment the other day? She gave him an enquiring look, hoping he might say more, but he seemed to have decided he'd shared enough. Happy with the state of his desk, he picked up his keys, wished her a good day, and then quietly left.

Still bemused, Margot wandered back to the detectives'

office. Lieutenant Martell almost bumped into her on his way out.

"Has the captain left?"

"Just this minute. Why?"

"You'd better see this."

They returned to the lieutenant's desk. He let her take his seat at the computer while he leaned over and clicked through. An email appeared on the screen.

"The lab guys have found some deleted messages on the computers. They just sent this."

He clicked on the attachment and then let Margot take control of the mouse. A document came up, showing a series of messages dated the night of the murder:

22:32 Have you thought about what I said?

22:34 Yes Gy. And the answer is still no. I won't change my mind.

22:37 But I can take you away from this. You said you wanted to escape. I told you – I have some money saved. We can go away together.

22:40 I do want to escape but not like this. And not now. I take responsibility for what's happened in my life and I'm finding my own way out of this. Please don't ask again. I told you I have to stop seeing you and I meant it.

22:41 I love you.

22:41 No you don't.

22:43 You are the only one who's ever truly understood me. I would do anything for you. Without you my life isn't worth living.

22:44 Please don't talk like that, Gy. We had an arrangement that suited us both. Nothing more. And now I'm afraid it's over. Please stop sending me these messages.

Margot pictured him sitting in his room that night, alone at his computer. Moments after receiving that final message from Sandrine he'd tried calling her, and then in all probability had left the house again shortly afterwards. Margot looked up at Martell.

"Were these erased from Sandrine's laptop as well?"

He leaned across and clicked back to the email. "Yes. They'd been erased from both his computer and her laptop."

Which could mean only one thing – Berger had gone back to her house sometime after eleven. The final nail in the coffin, it seemed. Margot breathed deeply.

"You'd better get the captain back."

12

The two Gendarmerie cars swung into the car park in quick succession, one pulling up outside the station's main entrance, the other blocking the ramp to the platform. As gendarmes spilled out of both vehicles, Captain Bouchard gave his orders: two men up onto the platform to block off escape routes; the other two with him. He strode up some steps, and burst in through the front doors.

Margot was the last one out of the car. Keeping her distance, she moved across the front of the building until she drew level with the brightly-lit window of the ticket office. Inside, Gy Berger was working the nightshift. Eyes on his screen, checking timetables, oblivious to the fact his orderly little world was about to come crashing down on him. The captain and his men had disappeared from view, but Margot was able to watch the scene unfold from Berger's reaction. First, he froze, stunned by the invasion. Then he backed away in fright, looking as if the devil himself were about to lay hands on him. Fright turned to panic, and as the gendarmes forced their way into the ticket office, Berger scrambled away, silent shouts trapped behind the glass. He upended a desk, threw a bundle of papers into the air. The struggle continued for another ten seconds until he finally broke free and all three men disappeared from view.

Shouts drew Margot to the floodlit platform. She hurried up the ramp just in time to see Berger escaping through a back door. With his exit route blocked, he turned and ran for the bridge, unable to see the fourth gendarme closing in from the opposite side. The young man raced up the steps, light on his feet, only to come to a juddering halt when he realised he'd run into a trap.

Even from a distance, Margot could sense his desperation. He swung his legs over the handrail and tried to perch, heels seeking an edge on the narrowest strip of ironwork. Margot watched in horror as the headlights of a train appeared, fearing the inevitable were about happen and Gy Berger would end his life down on the rails. But something made him hesitate, and that was enough. The assembled gendarmes closed in, grabbing him with half a dozen hands.

Not that he showed his saviours any gratitude. He continued to resist as they hauled him down the stairs, spitting at the captain as they passed by.

———

Even with his wrists cuffed Berger refused go quietly. Seated in the following car, Margot could see the struggle continue through the lead vehicle's windows. The short trip back to the Gendarmerie took twice the normal time.

They drove in through the electric gates and pulled up at the rear door. The two harassed gendarmes hauled him out of his seat and frogmarched him into the corridor, struggling all the way. At the door to the interview room he flared up again and refused to go in, hands, legs and feet clinging desperately to the sides of the door frame. One of the gendarmes got elbowed in the face; losing his temper, he immediately struck back, catching the top of Berger's head with his knuckles. They'd no sooner manhandled him into the room and got him seated when he sprang back up as if he'd just sat on hot coals. The captain responded by slamming the desk hard with the base of his fist.

"Enough!"

Like a switch had been flicked, Berger dropped into the seat. A marionette with his strings cut. The change was so abrupt that the gendarmes were caught unawares and they stood at his sides, chests heaving, unsure whether or not to back off. As the dust settled, the captain gave the nod. The gendarmes unfastened the cuffs, threaded the chain through a gap in the chair, and then immediately refastened them.

The room fell silent. All three men stood down, taking a minute to straighten themselves. The gendarme who'd been hit dabbed his cheek with a hand, checking for blood. Realising Margot had come in with them, the captain had one of his men take her out, closing the door behind them.

He tried to escort her to an exit, but Margot held back.

"Is there somewhere I can observe?"

He pointed to the corner. Margot found a door and let herself into an empty, windowless room: two chairs; a desk with a monitor. When she switched on the monitor a brightly-lit image of the interview room appeared. Captain Bouchard was now seated at the table, calmly arranging his paperwork, while facing him, Gy Berger remained subdued, chin on his chest, barely recognisable as the wild thing they'd just brought in.

"I would like a glass of water, please."

With his head down it was difficult to hear what he'd said. After a pause, the captain signalled to the gendarme at the door who promptly went off to get it.

The silence resumed. The captain turned the pages in his

file slowly and with consideration, intentionally taking his time, no doubt. As the seconds continued to pass, Gy Berger raised his eyes and gave the captain an inquisitive look.

"Why have you brought me here?"

Captain Bouchard ignored him. He continued to sort through his papers, eyes down, and only when a further minute had gone by did he lean forward and give the curious young man his fullest attention.

"You've been brought here to answer some questions."

"I've already answered your questions. I told you, I didn't do anything wrong."

"In that case why did you run away just now?"

Berger lowered his eyes. The gendarme came back with a cup of water and set it down on the desk, but he didn't unlock the handcuffs and Berger showed no interest in drinking it.

"Let's start by examining your movements on the night Sandrine was killed," the captain began. He picked up one of his sheets of paper. "You told us you arrived at her house at three minutes past nine and left at ten-o-four. You walked home, which should have taken you no more than twenty minutes. Your mother confirmed you arrived home at ten-thirty and went straight up to your room. So, what happened next?"

Berger looked up, though not quite far enough to meet the captain's eye. The captain waited. When no reply was forthcoming he went on.

"Did you leave the house again that night? Because, according to your mother, you often go out after dark, wandering the streets on your own."

"Is that what she said?"

"Where did you wander off to that night?"

Berger's upper body went rigid and he began rocking back and forth on his seat.

"I would like my computer back."

"You'll have your computer back when I say you can have it back. Now answer my questions: did you leave the house again that night?"

Berger carried on rocking. Half a minute or more must have passed while they sat in silence, the captain's stare unwavering. Failing to elicit a response, he heaved a sigh and turned to another page.

"All right, let's talk about your computer, since it's clearly important to you. Our experts have examined it, along with the phones and the laptop we took from Sandrine's house. They recovered a series of deleted messages between you and Sandrine, the final one being sent at ten-forty-four on the night of the murder. As we've just established, you were at home in your room at that time. So would you care to explain to me how those messages came to be deleted?"

"Those messages were private. You had no right to look at them."

"Did you delete them?"

The frequency of his rocking increased.

"Is that why you went back there, because of what she'd said in her message? Shall I remind you of the exchange?" The captain read from his sheet: "'I love you.' 'I would do anything for you.' 'Without you my life isn't worth living.'"

"Stop it."

"To which Sandrine replied: 'I'm afraid it's over. Please stop sending me these messages.'" He put down his sheet and returned his eyes to the young man. "Why didn't she want to see you anymore?"

"She didn't mean it."

"Had she grown tired of you? Or got bored with you?"

"Sandrine understood me."

"Did you do something to upset her, was that it?"

"I would never do anything to upset her."

"Yet the message is clear. You were no longer of interest to her and she wanted you to stop contacting her."

Berger shook his head. "I was special to her."

"I imagine she said that to all her clients."

"No – she hated those men."

"And yet you were the only one she no longer wanted to see. How did that make you feel – jealous? Angry? So angry you wanted to punish her?"

Berger suddenly stopped rocking. His chin dropped onto his chest and he began sobbing. It took the captain a moment to realise he was crying so he waited, squirming a little on his seat. It wasn't pleasant to watch. At least a minute passed before Berger was able to gather his emotions. The captain continued:

"I'll ask you again, Monsieur Berger, did you delete those messages?"

"Yes."

The captain made a note in his file.

"So, you went back to her house. What then?"

"She was already dead."

He'd spoken so quietly that the captain didn't appear to have caught what had been said, though the microphone had picked it up.

"Say that again."

Berger sniffed, and wiped his nose on his shoulder. A sense of calm had come over him now and he breathed in deeply through his mouth.

"She was already dead. I went into her salon and found her sitting in her chair, all the life gone out of her."

"How did you get in?"

"The back door was open. I called out. When she didn't reply I went in."

"How did you know she was dead?"

"Her face was pale. She wasn't breathing."

"Did you touch her?"

He blinked several times. "No."

"Are you sure about that?"

A movement of his head that looked like a nod.

"What did you do then?"

Berger attempted to shift his position on the chair but appeared to have forgotten his wrists were bound. He looked down at the handcuffs as if seeing them for the first time.

"I didn't want her to be alone so I sat with her. Then I remembered the messages and went to look for her laptop."

"Why didn't you call the police?"

For perhaps only the second time during the interview Berger's eyes drew level with the captain's.

"I know what you people are like. You wouldn't have believed me. If you'd found me there with her body and then seen the messages you would think that I'd killed her. But I didn't."

"How did you get into her laptop?"

"She'd given me her password once. Her computer was infected and she asked me to fix it. We would do things like that for each other."

"What time was this?"

"Two-thirty-three."

"And after you'd erased the messages ...?"

"I went home."

"You left through the back door?"

"Yes."

"Leaving it open, or closing it?"

"I left it open. I didn't want to disturb anything. I thought it would help the police find the person who'd killed her."

"Was the light in the salon on or off when you entered?"

"It was on."

"Did you switch it off when you left?"

"No."

The captain tapped his pencil on the desk, considering. Berger appeared to have attained some kind of inner peace now and an aura of contentment had settled upon him. As the silence grew, he was the one who finally broke it.

"Can I go home now?"

The captain stared at him for a long time, tapping his pencil repeatedly.

"We've seen your videos. My men have studied them in great detail. We know all about your peculiar fantasies."

Berger went red in the face.

"I'm curious: why didn't you want to touch her? There she was, an attractive, full-bodied woman. Willing to let you do pretty much anything you wanted to her."

"Sandrine wasn't like that."

"Wasn't she? She let other men touch her."

"She understood me, and I understood her. She knew what it was like to not fit in; to feel you were different to other people. She wanted me to be happy."

"She only wanted you to be happy because you paid her. Just like all the other men."

"She only took the money because she needed to pay bills. I wasn't like the others. She said."

"Did you know she was pregnant?"

Berger flinched. "What?"

The captain seemed pleased to have caught him unawares.

"Sandrine was pregnant. And the father was most likely one of her clients."

Berger pinched shut his eyes, retreating into his shell once more. Captain Bouchard went on:

"Come on, Monsieur Berger. It must have made you angry

knowing she saw other men. What did you think when you pictured them, doing things to her that you couldn't?"

"I want to go home now, please."

"Admit it. You told Sandrine you loved her, she said she didn't feel the same way, so you went back to her house, intending to have it out with her. You were upset. You were angry. And we've seen what a temper you've got. You argued, and then you killed her. Isn't that the truth?"

Berger suddenly lashed out, kicking the leg of the table and toppling the cup of water. The captain sprang back to avoid getting splashed, while the gendarme at the door jumped to life, ready to take action. The most intense look they'd yet seen appeared in the younger man's eyes.

"I *said*, I want to go home now."

The captain spent a long time looking back at him. Satisfied the outburst was over, he had the gendarme stand down. He waited another few moments and then gathered his papers.

"I'm afraid, Monsieur Berger, you won't be going home. You'll be spending the night in the cells. And in the morning, when I ask you again, perhaps you'll tell me what really happened on the night Sandrine Bordes was killed."

Margot waited for Berger to be taken down to the cells and then caught up with the captain as he headed for the exit.

"You really think he's lying?"

The captain rubbed his forehead, looking tired. Reaching the back door, he paused.

"It's all very convenient, turning up to find her dead. The facts remain, he admits he was there, he had the opportunity, and now we know he had a motive. He's an obsessive young man who can't handle rejection."

"But what he said about the door being open was true."

"So what? It would have been true either way." He pushed the button to release the lock. "I'll get forensics to check out their house in the morning; see if they can come up with anything. And in the meantime, I'll have another go at him tomorrow. Push hard enough and I'm sure he'll crack."

13

Another long day of paperwork loomed. When Florian came into the office and added three more dossiers to her pile, Margot fired daggers at him with her eyes. She wondered if there were anything she'd less rather be doing.

At ten o'clock, Célia called them in. Florian carried the coffee tray, Margot took charge of the box of cakes.

"I hear the captain's got a suspect in *garde à vue*?" the judge said as they settled into the easy chairs in the corner.

Margot brought her up to speed on what Berger had said in his interview, along with her doubts.

"You think the captain's got the wrong man?"

"It's just that Berger seemed so genuine in his denials. My only worry is, now he's got his eyes on a credible suspect the captain won't want to look elsewhere."

"Are there any other credible suspects?"

Margot nodded while she cut a small chunk off the slice of chocolate tarte. She filled Célia in on JNW and, after taking the diary out of her bag, showed her some of the highlighted passages, in particular one she'd come across only last night:

Went to a conference with JNW. He left me talking to some mega boring people so I went off to find him. And there he was in the gents, this blonde nymphet on her knees in front of him, shirt tails covering her face. He saw me. Turned and grinned, but stood there, letting her carry on.

Célia raised her eyebrows. "Well, he sounds a real charmer."

"Would he treat a mistress like that?"

"And these initials ... are they the code you talked about?"

Margot popped the piece of tarte into her mouth and brushed the crumbs from her fingertips.

"Yes. In my opinion we really need to concentrate on cracking it."

"Can't the tech team help?" Florian asked.

"They are looking into, but I'm hoping to figure it out myself." She washed the tarte down with a mouthful of coffee. "My other concern is Gy Berger. The captain was pretty hard on him last night. He really ought to be treated as a vulnerable person."

Célia gave her a sympathetic look as she handed back the diary. "I can have a discrete word with Cousineau, if you like."

"When's he planning on opening an *information*?"

"He'll wait as long as possible; give the Gendarmerie time to do what they need to do."

In other words, give them time to extract a confession. An *information* had to be opened within fourteen days, and only then did the suspect enjoy the better rights of access to a defence *avocat* and full sight of the dossier. More importantly, perhaps, once an *information* had been opened, the suspect could only be questioned by the JI and normally that would take place in the judge's office rather than the relative anonymity of the police station.

Margot's phone beeped. She read the message and then put the phone away.

"That was Captain Bouchard. He's just had another go at Gy Berger. He's sticking to his story."

Time was ticking. Cracking that code had to be her top priority.

Margot left the office at five on the dot and called in at the pet shop on her way home: 3 packets of duck meat, gizzard and liver; 1 packet of natural dried sprats; 1 bag of cheesy treats. Wouldn't it be nice if His Imperial Fluffiness was waiting for her to come home, curled up on her sofa, purring with delight the moment she set foot through the door. As it was, Margot opened the back door to find the food eaten, water on the floor and the cat gone.

She stood under a steaming hot shower for a full ten minutes and then came downstairs in her bathrobe. After pouring herself a large glass of white wine she went to her bureau and got to work on the code. A quick trawl of the internet brought up something called a Vignère Cipher, also known as a 'polyalphabetic substitution cipher'. In this type of encryption, a keyword determined the number shifts along the alphabet with each letter of the keyword being matched with a letter of the message to be encoded. So if, for example, she wanted to encrypt the message: THE KIPPER FLIES AT MIDNIGHT using the keyword: CODENAME, she would write the word CODENAME underneath the message and repeat it until they were both the same length.

The letters of the alphabet were then labelled from 0 to 25 (A being 0 and Z 25) which meant that, in her example, the first letter of her message – T – would be shifted 2 places (since C corresponded to 2); the second letter – H – would be shifted 14 places (since O was in position 14); and so on. All of which meant that her original message, THE KIPPER FLIES AT MIDNIGHT, would become:

VVH OVPBIT TOMRS MX OWGRVGTX

Margot slurped a mouthful of wine, impressed with herself. So far, so bizarre. The cipher could also be described by the equation:

$$C_i = E_k(M_i) = (M_i + K_i) \bmod 26$$

where $M = M_1 \ldots M_n$ is the message; $C = C_1 \ldots C_n$ is the ciphertext; and $K = K_1 \ldots K_n$ is the keyword.

But when Margot laid eyes on this her mind went into meltdown. Did mathematicians belong to the same species as everyone else?

Fortunately, there was an easier method – something called a Vignère Square. This was a grid composed of the alphabet written out in twenty-six rows, starting with A-Z and then shifting one space along on each subsequent row. Margot started to draw one out with a pencil and ruler but quickly lost patience. Instead, she found one on the internet and printed it off.

So now she had a Vignère Square. She pinched shut her eyes. Her brain was starting to hurt. But she pushed on, determined to figure it out.

Would it be possible to work out the keyword from the two examples she already had?

GNB became GLM

PMF became PKQ

That was the six-million-dollar question. Margot tapped her forehead.

Come on, brain. Work, damn you.

She got up and retrieved her cigarettes from the table, disappointed to find only one row left. Ration gone for the day. She left them undisturbed and hid the packet in the back of a drawer. Forcing herself to return to the bureau, Margot held her head in her hands and thought long and hard. If she'd understood it correctly, the method of finding the keyword would be to simply reverse the steps. Starting with GNB, she ran the letters through the grid and discovered that if the codename was GLM then the keyword would be: AYL. She tried it with PMF, and surprisingly, the keyword AYL also gave her PKQ. But she stared at the results in bafflement. What kind of a keyword was AYL?

Margot dropped her pencil on the desk. It couldn't be right. She must have gone wrong somewhere, or had failed to understand it correctly. Aside from which there was nothing to say that this was the cipher Sandrine had used, and even if it was they were any number of variations. She was clutching at straws. She should just accept she'd reached the limit of her intellectual capabilities, acknowledge that there was stuff out there that she was never going to understand no matter how hard she tried. Or maybe it was an age thing. Her brain was too old; her thoughts too woolly. Twenty years ago she would have cracked it for sure.

Her head was starting to throb so she emptied her wine glass and lay down on the sofa, planting her face in a cushion. With any luck she would wake up in that magical place where everything was warm and cosy and problems simply melted away.

A little voice was speaking to her: *You're not a quitter, Margot. Get up. You just need to work harder.*

Margot hauled herself off the sofa, ate some bread and cheese, downed a second glass of wine, and gave herself a stern talking to. Ten minutes later she was back at her bureau, ready for round 2.

Deciding to leave the codenames for a moment, she went back to Sandrine's diary, hoping to spot a clue as to the type of encryption she'd used. Margot had read pretty much every page of it by now, pored over each snippet of text, every random jotting. She looked again at the front and back pages. One thing the facsimile hadn't reproduced was the front and back covers. From what she remembered of the photographs, the original diary had been a red, leather-bound hardback.

Then something on the very last page caught her eye. Down in the bottom righthand corner was written the word KEY, though only half of the letter Y was showing. Margot switched on the angle-poise lamp and examined it under the bright light. It looked like a corner of the lining paper had curled back and was concealing the rest of the word. Perhaps she'd written the keyword under the lining of the back cover.

Margot looked at the clock. The time had flown by and it had already gone nine, but she called the captain's phone.

No answer.

She rang the out-of-hours number for the Gendarmerie and got straight through to Lieutenant Martell.

"Do you have Sandrine's original diaries there, or are they at the lab?"

"Working late, aren't you, Madame Renard?"

"This wretched cipher."

"Give me one second. I'll check."

She heard him tapping away at his keyboard.

"According to the log it's here. Safely locked away in evidence room 2."

"Could I come over and look at it?"

"You mean now?"

"If you don't mind."

"Of course not. Come to the front door and I'll let you in."

Margot grabbed her bag and made to leave, only realising when she got to the door that she was still wearing her bathrobe.

Suitably re-attired, she set off up Rue Voltaire. The Gendarmerie's front door was already open and Lieutenant Martell was waiting for her in reception. After locking the door behind her, he led the way down another long corridor, one that Margot had not even seen before. They went through a double door, down a flight of concrete stairs, and into what must have been a sub-ground level, lights coming on every few footsteps. Margot began to suspect the place doubled as a nuclear shelter – the bowels of the building appeared large enough to accommodate half the population of Argents.

The lieutenant halted outside one of the ubiquitous matt olive doors. He tapped a code into the keypad and waited for the green light to come on. Margot expected it to slide aside with a *hiss* of escaping air, but instead the building showed its age and the hinges creaked as he pushed. Lieutenant Martell flicked on the lights, revealing dozens of bays of racking.

"We're looking for bay 6, shelf 3, box 4.2," he read from the scrap of paper in his hand.

Margot followed as he weaved through, marvelling at the efficiency of it all.

"Ah. Here it is."

He hauled an archive box off the shelf. A small table was attached to the bay so he put the box down and lifted the lid. The diaries were on the top of a small pile of personal possessions, all individually sealed in evidence bags.

"They've all been signed off by the lab," Lieutenant Martell said. "So you can open them, if you like."

Spotting the red cover of the most recent diary, Margot unpacked it. The lighting in the room was a little on the dim side so she examined it with the torch on her phone. She set it down on the table and opened it at the back cover.

"What exactly are you looking for?" Lieutenant Martell asked, peering over her shoulder.

Margot focussed on the lower righthand corner. Just as she'd surmised, the lining paper was slightly peeled back. Teasing it with a fingernail, she managed to ease it back a little further and found what she was looking for: KEYWORD = and then a symbol of a heart next to an arrow pointing to the left.

Lieutenant Martell frowned. "What does that mean?"

Margot tried to peel the paper back a little further, but it was stuck fast and there was no sign anything else was written there. She sighed, disappointed.

"Blast."

"Were you expecting something else?"

"I was hoping it would be the keyword to Sandrine's code. But what on earth does heart with an arrow mean?" It was just one puzzle after another.

Undeterred, the lieutenant gave it some thought.

"Maybe the keyword is written in invisible ink."

He reached across and looked for himself, but Margot shook her head.

"Don't bother. I give up."

This thing had officially driven her crazy.

Taking pity on her, Lieutenant Martell took her back up to the detectives' office and insisted she stay for coffee. He sat her down at his desk while he went off to the kitchenette. Margot was too restless to be seated, however, so after a few moments she went after him. The Gendarmerie's facilities were rather plusher than their cubby hole at the *Palais*, boasting a full-size fridge, a nice clean worktop, and a range of modern cabinets. He made the coffee in a Moka pot, and after delicately packing the grounds into the filter, put it onto the hotplate to boil.

"How come you're working nights?" Margot asked, watching him from the door.

"My wife's just started a new job. She's a nurse. They put her on the nightshift this week, so I volunteered."

"Doesn't it get lonely?" Margot cast her eyes back at the empty office. It seemed a different place with everyone gone home. "Mooching around all on your own."

"It's not always this quiet. Saturday nights can be hectic, especially in summer. It doesn't really bother me, though. Days or nights. I'm easy."

Margot suspected he took pretty much everything in his stride.

"What about you?" he went on. "Here you are, at ten o'clock at night, and you don't even work here."

When the alternative was sitting at home, pandering to a stolen cat, it wasn't really a difficult choice.

"I suppose, when a case gets under your skin, it's hard to let go," Margot said. "Criminals should be behind bars, not out on the streets."

"Quiet right," Lieutenant Martell agreed.

As the coffee brewed, he removed the pot from the heat. He took two small cups out of a wall cupboard, stirred the pot, filled both cups with thick black liquid and transferred one to a saucer, adding an amaretti biscuit. He smiled, pleased with his efforts, as he carefully handed it over.

"All I can say, Madame, is we're lucky to have someone as diligent as you on the case."

Margot scoffed. "I think it would be more use having someone smarter."

"Nonsense. If anyone's going to crack this code I'm sure it will be you. And the captain speaks very highly of you."

"Does he?" Margot said, faintly astonished.

"Well, he's never actually said those words, but I can tell from the way he acts. He's different around you. I think he's a little bit in awe of you, to be honest."

Margot blew across the surface of her coffee, remembering the day they first met. "We didn't get off to the best of starts. I may have called him a few choice names."

The lieutenant laughed. "We all call him a few choice names every now and then."

They took their coffees back into the office. Martell pulled out his chair and sat down.

"No, the captain's a good man. He took me under his wing when I first came down here."

"How long has it been?"

"Six years. I joined straight out of the army. My family are from the Vosges, so I didn't know anyone here. He went out of his way to make me feel welcome."

"That's nice. I never realised he was a family man. His son plays football, I hear."

"He does. And he's quite good, actually; I've watched him play. They were talking about getting him a try-out with Toulouse."

"And are they a good team?"

A dimple formed in the lieutenant's cheek as he grinned.

"Sometimes, Madame, I think you are pulling my leg. Yes, Toulouse are a very good team."

Margot put down her cup. She probably had heard that somewhere but hadn't the heart to tell him that she wasn't pulling his leg. She wandered over to the window, and with a finger made a slit in the venetian blind. The office overlooked the parade ground, and the dark mass of the barracks beyond. The windows were all dark.

"Why was he cleaning that apartment the other day?"

"The one in the barracks?"

"Yes."

Margot turned to find the humour drained from the lieutenant's face. He rubbed his chin, and looked away, seeming reluctant to answer. His silence only served to make Margot more curious, however, and she went back to his desk.

"It was the only one that looked lived in. All the others are boarded up."

"Well ... that was where he and his wife used to live."

"And he still cleans it, even though they live off-site?"

Martell looked her straight in the eye. "Hasn't he told you?"

"Told me what?"

He held her eye for a few seconds, but then got out of his seat and perched on a corner of the desk. Arms folded, he breathed a sad sigh.

"His wife died a couple of years ago. A road accident. It was all very sudden."

Margot bit her lip. "Oh my god. That's awful."

The lieutenant nodded. "The captain's not one to show emotion, but I think it very nearly destroyed him. And as for the apartment ... well. We don't like to pry, but I think he goes in there because it reminds him of her. They must have had lots of happy times together."

Margot felt crushed. And all this time she'd been making fun of him. She mutely nodded her head, turning away to blink back a tear.

The hands on the wall clock turned painfully slowly. Eleven o'clock came and went, and apart from a phone call to report a barking dog, little seemed to be happening on the night-time streets of Argents-sur-Mer. Lieutenant Martell sat with his boots on the desk, engrossed in a game on his mobile phone, while Margot had gone back to her Vignère Square, her pad and her pencils, having decided to start again from scratch.

Heart backwards – the two symbols continued to play on her mind. It had to mean something, and there must have been a reason Sandrine had tried to conceal it under the lining.

As if reading her thoughts, Lieutenant Martell suddenly raised his head.

"Isn't Sandrine's daughter named Lya?" he said, a thoughtful look on his face.

Margot looked across at him. "Yes. Why?"

"Maybe the heart refers to the one she loved i.e. Lya. Then the arrow means spell it backwards, making AYL."

A spark ran down Margot's spine.

"Lieutenant Martell – you're a genius."

"Am I? That's very kind of you to say."

She quickly sorted through her papers and tore off a clean sheet. Curious, Martell took his boots off the desk, got out of his chair and came over.

"What is it?"

Margot showed him her notes. "AYL was the keyword I came up with earlier, but I didn't think it was right. See this – it's called a Vignère Square. It's used to encrypt messages. You can also use an equation."

She showed him the formula.

The lieutenant blanched.

"But it's easier using the grid. The way we encrypt is like this: we take our plaintext GNB; write the keyword AYL directly beneath it; then code it by going to row G and column A in the square. That gives us the letter G. Do the same with the other two letters and we get GLM. See? GLM is ciphertext for GNB, just as Sandrine used in her diary."

"Madame, it's you who's the genius."

"And then we have Patrice Fabron: PMF. Put him through the same process and we get ... PKQ. Again, exactly what Sandrine used." She glanced at the lieutenant and found him watching keenly with his mouth slightly hung open. "With me so far?"

Martell nodded slowly. "I think so. So, to *de*-cipher a code-name—" he picked up her grid "—you go to column A, look along the alphabet until you reach the correct letter, and then see which row it's in."

Margot flicked him a smile. "Go to the top of the class. And the purpose of all this," she took the grid back off him, "is to find the identity of JNW." She quickly got to work. "The first letter should be J. Which it is. And then the other two letters become ... P and ... L." She flung her pencil across the desk and sat back, arms folded. "That's it, lieutenant. JNW is JPL. Those are the initials of the man we have to find."

Lieutenant Martel looked briefly triumphant, before his optimism faded.

"But how are we going to do that? There must be thousands of JPLs in France."

"I'm sure there are, but we can narrow it down." Margot retrieved the pencil. "It has to be someone high-profile. And probably local."

There was silence while they both wracked their brains.

"I wonder if there's a search engine for people's initials."

"Or we could try the census," Martell suggested. "I know someone who works at the statistics institute."

"Or maybe the records office at the Mairie," Margot added.

The bolt of lightning struck simultaneously. They locked eyes.

"Are you thinking what I'm thinking?"

Martell hesitated, but then blinked. "You don't mean—?"

Margot nodded. "Jean-Paul Lefève. The mayor of Argents."

The lieutenant had to sit down.

Margot put a hand to her mouth, flabbergasted.

"Oh my God, lieutenant. We've done it. We've found our horny stag."

It was twenty past midnight. A buzzer sounded in the office as a car pulled in through the electric gates, headlights strobing through chinks in the Gendarmerie's shutters. Martell was in the front office, dealing with a call, so Margot made her way to the rear entrance alone.

The captain was hardly recognisable in civilian clothes. He met her in the corridor, dressed in a thin black pullover and light grey slacks.

"I got your message. What's all the excitement about?"

"We've cracked the code."

"From Sandrine's diary?"

Margot filled him in as they walked back to the detectives' office.

"She was using something called a Vignère Cipher. She'd written the keyword under the back flap of her diary. JNW's real initials are JPL."

She waited a moment to see if that would register. The captain's face remained blank.

"You think you know who that is?"

Margot took a breath. "Jean-Paul Lefève."

The captain came to a halt. He regarded her closely, though his face gave nothing away.

"You're sure about this?"

Margot nodded. "I'll show you."

She took him across to Martell's desk where her papers were still spread out. She explained in detail the process she'd gone through, thinking it might go over his head, but the captain appeared to grasp it immediately and promptly tore off a clean sheet of paper. He began writing down letters for himself, using the formula to check her findings. After a minute or so he came up with the exact same result, though with little enthusiasm.

"Well," Margot said. "We're right, aren't we?"

He leaned against the desk.

"All it proves is that she had a client with those initials. It doesn't necessarily mean it's our mayor."

"True. But if you can find me another local dignitary with those same three initials I'll eat my swimsuit."

The captain conceded a thin smile.

"Don't forget, we have those unregistered contacts from Sandrine's phone," Margot went on. "If we can establish one of those belongs to Lefève that'll prove he was a client."

"And how do you suppose we do that?"

"I take it you've met him?"

"A couple of times."

"Would you recognise his voice on the other end of a phone?"

The captain squirmed, seeming to pick up on where she was going. "Madame—"

"Let's call those numbers right now. See if Lefève answers."

Captain Bouchard gave it a few moments' thought, but then shook his head.

"You're getting ahead of yourself. In all likelihood, whoever owned those phones will have ditched them the moment they heard of Sandrine's death. And even if they didn't, and you are correct about the mayor, calling him now would achieve nothing other than putting him on his guard."

Margot had to concede the logic in that, but she was still itching to do something.

"We can at least question him, can't we? We have reasonable grounds. And if the secret Sandrine knew about was worth killing for that would give him a motive."

The captain considered. He picked up one of her papers, and then put it back down again.

"Very well. I'll speak to Cousineau first thing in the morning. I don't imagine he'll be entirely happy about it, but I'll do my best."

"Thank you."

"Is that all?"

Margot nodded. "Sorry for disturbing you so late."

"Not at all. I'll see you tomorrow at the *Palais*."

Margot accompanied him into the corridor, but then stopped at the door. She called out as he headed for the exit:

"Oh, and Captain."

He turned. "Yes, Madame?"

Margot pictured him ten years earlier, returning to his home in the barracks, his wife and son patiently waiting. Another happy little family. She smiled fondly.

"It doesn't matter."

14

"Absolutely not! It's totally out of the question. Have you any idea what the press would make of such a thing: questioning the mayor of Argents in relation to a murder enquiry?"

Cousineau had gone so red in the face it looked like his head might just explode. Seated beside her, facing the *procureur* across his desk, Captain Bouchard sent Margot a sideways glance: *See what you've got me into,* his eyes appeared to be saying. He squared his shoulders and took a deep breath.

"I appreciate the delicacy of the matter, Monsieur *le procureur*, but we have very good reason to believe the mayor was one of Sandrine's clients. It's only right and proper that we speak to him, if merely to eliminate him from our enquiries."

"What about this man you have in custody? What's he got to say for himself?"

"Gy Berger admits he went back to the house but he claims Sandrine was already dead when he got there."

"And you believe that?"

The captain returned a neutral look. "We're waiting to see what we get from forensics."

"If you need more time to work on him I can let you have the full ninety-six hours."

"That may help."

Margot sat up, pointedly clearing her throat. "Aren't we forgetting something? Paying for sex is a crime."

In France, receiving money for sexual services was no longer a criminal offence but paying for them was, the aim being to criminalise the customer rather than the sex worker. If found guilty, the mayor would be looking at a fine of €1500 and a criminal record.

"You don't need to remind me of the law, Madame."

"I was simply stating a fact."

"Have you any evidence he paid for her services?"

"Not yet," Margot conceded. "I imagine men in such exalted positions manage to find some way around it, don't you?" Margot fixed him with an accusatory look.

Cousineau didn't like it one little bit. "Forgive me, Madame Renard, but why are you here?"

"I—"

"Madame Renard has been helping with my enquiries," Captain Bouchard quickly put in. "She was the one who deciphered the code."

"Code?"

"Yes," Margot said, just about managing to keep the irritation out of her voice. "Sandrine used a code to conceal her clients' identities. Something called a Vignère Cipher. Have you heard of it?"

"No, Madame. I have not heard of it."

"In that case allow me to explain."

Without waiting for permission, Margot got out of her seat and went around to the *procureur*'s side of the desk. She began arranging her papers over his things, pushing his files aside to make room. Cousineau shrank back as if fearing she were about to pull nits from his hair, but Margot carried on regardless. She explained the workings of the Vignère Square, how they'd found the keyword and used it to work out the identity of JNW. It was clear the technicalities were going straight over the *procureur*'s head, but Margot was not put off. She showed him the formula (he grumbled irritably) and continued with her explanation until his patience finally ran out and he angrily tore off his glasses, his lily-white eyes glaring up at her like two little pieces of frogspawn.

"Just tell me this, Madame Renard: what are the chances of your analysis being incorrect?"

"Sixteen-point-seven-million to one," Margot said with absolute certainty, though in reality had no idea whatsoever what the odds were. "Numbers don't lie." Though people, for good reason, often did.

"It's clear the victim knew this man had a secret," Captain Bouchard put in. "She stated in her diary that she was afraid of what he might do should the truth come out."

"You're surely not suggesting the mayor of Argents was involved in a *murder*?" Cousineau said, faintly amazed.

"You're surely not suggesting the mayor of Argents should be excused from questioning simply because of who he is?" Margot fired back.

Cousineau screwed up his face, regarding her like she was something unpleasant he'd had the misfortune of treading in. He shooed her away with his hand, though it was clear from his manner that he'd conceded the argument. Margot gathered her papers and went back to her seat, smiling inside.

"Are you still considering a link with the Ginette Clément case?" Cousineau went on, a little less combative this time.

"We are," said the captain. "We've been looking into the backgrounds of all the suspects."

"And that should include the mayor," Margot added. "It

would be interesting to know what he was up to fourteen years ago."

Cousineau emphatically shook his head.

"No. You can go ahead and interview him in relation to your current enquiry, but nothing more. The only grounds you have is your suspicion he was a client of this woman's. That is the only basis upon which you have grounds to question him."

Margot narrowed her eyes. This 'woman' would be getting justice, no matter whose toes got trodden upon.

It seemed the mayor's secretary was not playing ball. Margot could sense the captain's frustration build as she observed his side of the telephone conversation from across his desk.

"Yes, Madame ... I appreciate the mayor has a very full schedule, but ...Yes ... Yes, Madame... No, this is not a matter for the prefect. I really ... Yes ... Yes, Madame ..." When he briefly glanced in her direction, Margot could see his eyes had glazed over. Finally, when the opportunity arose, he jumped in with both feet: "*Madame*, I assure you, this is a very important matter and I would very much like to speak to the mayor today, if possible."

Such was his urgency to squeeze in a complete sentence that the last few words tumbled out of his mouth in a raised tone. Several seconds passed during which he appeared to be holding his breath. Then relief shone from his eyes.

"Yes ... Thank you ... Very well ... I will."

He couldn't put the phone down quickly enough.

"She says if we can be there in fifteen minutes the mayor will see us right away."

How very gracious of him.

The Mairie was only a five-minute walk from the

Gendarmerie so they didn't rush. For such a small town, Argents was blessed with a selection of grand old buildings and the Mairie, occupying a generous plot on the southern flank of Place Jeanne d'Arc, was one of its finer examples. Tall white windows, pink rendered walls – Margot associated it most with the Bastille Day celebrations where, each 14th of July, a crowd gathered outside to sing *La Marseillaise*. A few years ago, she and Hugo had joined the parade, starting at the war memorial where a wreath was laid and then following a band, a small troop of gendarmes, and half a dozen *pompiers* on their march through the town. The mayor must surely have been there that day, though someone different had probably been in the role back then.

They passed through a black iron gate into a small green garden. A path took them to a heavy oak door held open by a wedge. Over their heads, an oversized tricolour dangled from a pole jutting out of a first-floor balcony. Despite the bright sunshine, it was gloomy inside: all dark wood and an old marble floor. The woman at the reception desk looked up as they approached, though seemed disappointed to see them.

"Ah, Captain Bouchard."

"Was it you I was speaking to on the phone just now?"

"It was."

"Can we go straight up?" He pointed to the stairs.

The receptionist pulled a face. "Unfortunately not."

The captain's shoulders dropped. "But you said he was free …"

Despite how she must have been jabbering on the phone the receptionist now seemed strangely reluctant to communicate.

"I'm afraid I was mistaken."

"Mistaken? How?"

"I do apologise, Captain, but Monsieur *le Maire* left just a few minutes ago. He had an appointment on the other side of town. I must have missed it in his diary." She gestured at her computer as if it were responsible for the oversight though at the same time didn't appear to believe her own words.

For once it was Margot who took on the role of conciliator. "Will he be gone long?"

"I'd have to check."

"We're happy to wait."

The receptionist didn't seem pleased but she consulted her computer. She seemed to waste an awful lot of time aimlessly clicking around. Either she was deliberately being unhelpful or didn't know what she was doing.

"I'm afraid he's busy now for the rest of the day. Could you come back next week?"

Margot opened her mouth to respond, but the captain had reached his limit.

"Could you please tell Monsieur Lefève that I would like to speak to him in connection with the murder of Sandrine Bordes? And if a meeting at the Mairie is not convenient then we can always arrange one at the Gendarmerie."

Margot felt a warm glow inside. Had she doubted this man before, there was no mistaking where his loyalties lay now.

They'd barely been back at the Gendarmerie two minutes when Lieutenant Martel caught up with them.

"The Mairie just called. Lefève will see you at eleven."

This time the receptionist told them to go straight up and wait in the waiting room. They crossed the marble floor to an L-shaped staircase and found the waiting area in an alcove off a wide, wood-panelled corridor. A bright red carpet covered the floor, and a row of what appeared to be dining chairs were pushed against one wall. The doors to the mayor's office were so fanciful they could have come straight from the Palace of Versailles: wide ornate architraves, a carved wooden pediment. The place was deathly quiet, the only sound coming from the ticking brass clock on the wall at the end. It was ten-fifty-seven but there was no sign of anyone coming out.

"I suppose we'd better wait," the captain said reluctantly, looking at the doors like he would much rather burst through them and give the mayor a piece of his mind.

Margot chose the centre of the seven seats. A few moments later the captain relented and picked a seat at one end. They sat in silence until eleven o'clock arrived, at which point Captain Bouchard got back on his feet and began pacing. After two laps across the mouth of the alcove he went to the only window and looked out, heaving a bored sigh. No doubt he thought they were wasting their time. In his eyes, Gy Berger was their man and Lefève was a distraction at best, but the fact he was willing to keep an open mind did him credit. Margot thought about his wife, and the road accident, and that neat little apartment in the barracks. And she remembered that day she'd first encountered him, when he'd called her 'the police inspector's widow', a phrase which had irritated her immensely at the time. *"I'm sorry for your loss,"* he'd said – the only compassionate words to have come out of his mouth during the entirety of their previous encounter. Only now could she appreciate how difficult those words must have been for him.

Another ten minutes crawled by. Margot stared at the dial of her watch, then returned her eyes to the double doors. Not a single peep had come from inside. She wondered if they were waiting in the wrong place, but the receptionist's directions had been clear and these were the only doors on this section of corridor. Margot began to suspect he was intentionally keeping them waiting. A show of power. Men like him were like that.

Men like him ... Margot repeated to herself. Shouldn't she be keeping an open mind as well? She knew nothing of the mayor other than what she'd read in Sandrine's diary and a few brief mentions in articles she'd found on the internet. According to the captain, he'd only been in the post for three years so it wouldn't have been him she'd seen on that 14th July parade. But the fact Sandrine had disliked him was good enough for Margot.

Twenty-past-eleven. She rose to her feet and quietly approached the door. Still at the window, the captain sensed her movement and unfolded his arms, turning to keep a curious eye upon what she was doing. Margot lowered an ear to the door. Voices, and vague sounds could be heard inside, but the acoustics suggested the room was large and she couldn't make out what was going on.

"Shall I knock?" she whispered.

The captain looked tempted, but then shook his head.

Margot contemplated doing it anyway, but after another few moments gave in and reluctantly returned to her seat.

Finally, at eleven-twenty-five, the door handle turned. They both looked up as a young woman appeared, looking equally surprised to find them there. A petite blonde twentysomething, face flushed, ears burning red.

"Bon*jour*?" Her intonation turned it into a question

The captain was the first to advance on her. "We're here to see Mayor Lefève."

"We've been waiting for half an hour," Margot said, opening up a second line of attack. "Our appointment was for eleven."

"Oh," said the blonde. "Could you wait there a moment?"

She flicked them a smile before retreating into the office, pulling the door shut behind her.

Margot and the captain traded looks of disbelief. This was getting beyond a joke. The delay was short, however, and when the door opened for a second time it was Lefève himself who greeted them, full of bonhomie.

"Captain, good to see you again." He snatched up his hand and shook it vigorously. "Sorry I missed you earlier. Something came up at the very last minute."

I bet it did, Margot thought, fighting to keep the comment to herself.

"And you would be?"

In the flesh, the mayor of Argents was not quite the ogre she'd been building him up to be: tall, broad shouldered, a rounded baby face that belied his forty-two years, unblemished apart from the crooked line of his nose which had clearly been broken at some point. She glanced down at his feet, clad in size eleven loafers, and then at his outstretched hand, tanned and stubby and with nails that were buffed and trimmed. He looked like the kind of man who used a handshake as a weapon so Margot hesitated, and when the pause grew noticeable gave him just the ends of her fingers to latch on to. It was enough to neutralise him.

"Margot Renard. I work as an assistant to Judge Deveraux."

"Ah, Célia – how is she? I'd heard she was unwell."

"She's bearing up. You can't keep a good woman down."

"Well, give her my best. Do come in, both of you."

He withdrew into the office. He showed them to an assembly of leather armchairs arranged around a low circular table and invited them to sit. The furniture was oddly laid out: the desk too close to the wall; the floorboards bare apart from a rug positioned diagonally in one corner. The bookcase next to the fireplace was virtually empty whereas the trophy cabinet beside it was stuffed with silverware. The objects on his desk were all very masculine: photos in heavy silver frames; a thick glass ashtray, a large leather-bound ledger of some kind. There was no sign of the blonde, and nothing to indicate a second exit. Perhaps he'd hidden her under the desk.

Margot returned her attention to the man himself. Lefève:

their illustrious mayor. It was clear from the way he held himself in the armchair that here was a man who relished power. Back straight, forearms flat on the armrests, legs widely parted. His tailored blue shirt was stretched over a barrel chest, and he was a man who knew how to wear a tie. To Margot's mind, however, he was more silverback than stag, and she couldn't help picturing him naked, strutting around Sandrine's house like a tinpot king of the jungle, beating his chest with his fists and then *flapping his manhood around like a helicopter blade*. Another quote from Sandrine's diary came to mind: she'd likened his lovemaking technique to *a walrus inflating an air bed*.

"Forgive me, Madame. Have I said something to amuse you?"

Margot blinked. Realising she'd been smiling, she straightened her face.

"Sorry. I got distracted."

"Distracted? Well, my time is valuable so perhaps you could make an effort to concentrate on the matter at hand."

And *poof* – just like that the veil came down, the bonhomie was gone. Margot knew his type in an instant. She narrowed her eyes, but let him have his victory.

Thinking her suitably chastened he turned back to the captain, but some kind of reflex made Margot fire back:

"What was the nature of your relationship with Sandrine Bordes?"

He looked at her without speaking for a few moments, doing his best not to appear irritated.

"I thought you were here to consult on your enquiry, as a courtesy."

Margot opened her mouth to speak but it was the captain's words that came out:

"I'm afraid we'll have to be a little more formal than that. Your name came up during the course of our enquiries and there are a few questions we'll need to ask."

Lefève still tried to look blank. "What makes you think I had any kind of relationship with her?"

"We've found evidence to suggest you were seeing the victim on a regular basis."

"What evidence? I thought you had a man in custody."

"We do, but we're pursuing several lines of enquiry."

The mayor flicked his attention between them, appearing to weigh his options. After a little consideration, he altered his posture and leaned forward, elbows on his thighs. Classic silverback.

"All right. I'm more than happy to save us all some time and talk freely, but first I'll need an assurance from you. Whatever I say must not go beyond these four walls. I have a reputation to consider, and you know how the press like to twist things."

"With respect, Monsieur *le Maire*, this is a murder enquiry. We expect you to cooperate, regardless of the effect upon your reputation."

Lefève's nostrils flared. Clearly, the silverback was not happy being put in his place by a mere captain of the Gendarmerie.

"However," Captain Bouchard continued, "I can assure you that my officers are not in the habit of talking to newspaper reporters."

Lefève paused again. He gave the matter some more thought, still unsure. For a moment Margot feared they'd lost him, but then he seemed to make up his mind. The tension went out of him and he relaxed into his chair.

"Very well. I did know her. We've seen each other regularly for the past couple of years, maybe a dozen times this year. The last occasion was around three weeks ago. We were on good terms. Never argued." He smiled. "So I hope you're not treating me as a suspect, Captain."

"Where did you usually meet?"

"Sometimes I would go to her house, sometimes she would

come with me to various engagements. With all the functions I have to attend my wife's not always available. Sandrine looked good on my arm. It's a tragedy to think that she's gone."

"Did you pay for her services?" Margot asked.

"Don't be absurd," he scoffed.

She gave him a sterner look. "You are aware she worked as a prostitute?"

"Yes."

"So you're saying she let you have it for free?"

He chuckled. "I think there's been a misunderstanding, Madame – Sandrine was my mistress."

Margot gaped. "Your *mistress*?"

"Yes. And before you ask, my wife did know about her and no, she did not give one jot."

Margot shook her head in disbelief. That was quite possibly the biggest load of guff she'd ever heard. Captain Bouchard continued while she was still getting over her amazement:

"You say it's been three weeks since you last saw her?"

He thought about it, and then nodded. "Yes, that's right."

"Sandrine made a note in her diary suggesting she saw you two days before she died."

Lefève frowned before appearing to remember something. "I think I spoke to her on the phone around that time, but we didn't meet up."

"May I ask what that phone call was about?"

"Nothing much. I wanted her to accompany me to a function next month. There's a big conference going on in Marseilles. But she said she was busy."

That didn't ring true to Margot's ears. He didn't strike her as a man who so easily took no for an answer.

"How did the two of you meet?" Margot asked.

"As far as I recall, a mutual friend introduced us. It was a long time ago."

"What kind of functions did you take her to?"

Lefève shrugged. "All sorts: dinner parties, conventions, conferences ... does it matter?"

"I was just wondering what the two of you talked about."

He seemed perplexed. "The same things anyone talks about. What are you trying to imply?"

"I'm just curious, that's all. With all these events you were taking her to you must have got to know her quite well."

"Maybe I did. But then she didn't really talk much about herself. I knew she was an only child. Her parents had died when she was little. She never mentioned any family. But she had a fine mind and a witty tongue. I liked that about her."

Margot could barely believe what she was hearing. Sandrine loathed him. Either he was tone deaf to her feelings or every word coming out of his mouth was a lie.

"Do you know if she had any enemies?" the captain asked.

"No."

"Disputes with anyone?"

"If she had she didn't tell me."

"Did you ever see Sandrine's diary?" Margot asked.

"No. Why would I?"

"She used it to record all sorts of details ... her clients' peccadillos, secrets they might have told her."

He returned another innocent look. "And?"

Margot looked him in the eye, waiting to see if he would flinch, but his face was giving nothing away. *I've dealt with far more worthy opponents than you*, his expression appeared to be saying. He went on:

"I think I see where you're going with this. You suspect one of her clients killed her for the secrets she had in her diary – is that it?"

He said it so casually it rather took the wind out of Margot's sails. She hadn't been expecting him to call her bluff.

"We're keeping an open mind," the captain replied.

"Do you have possession of the diary?"

"It was found at the house."

"Then that rather pours cold water on your theory, doesn't it? I mean, if the diary contained such incendiary information then why would the killer leave it behind?" His eyes flicked back and forth between them, seeking an answer. And when neither of them had anything to offer, Lefève went on: "Are you sure it wasn't drugs related?"

The captain returned a baffled look. "There's no evidence to suggest drugs were involved."

"An intruder, then? Or one of her clients? Wasn't she attacked at home?"

"She was. The killer suffocated her with a plastic bag."

The mayor ground his teeth angrily. "The kind of man who can do a thing like that needs taking to the guillotine, if you want my opinion. But if you're looking for advice, I'd say you're looking for one of her clients who has a history of domestic abuse. You can guarantee at least one of those low-lives regularly beats his wife. I'd say that's where you need to concentrate your efforts, Captain."

Margot bit her tongue. They were meant to be interviewing him as a suspect, not getting his advice on how to conduct the investigation.

"Would you mind telling us where you were last Thursday night?" Margot asked

"You're talking about the night she was murdered?"

"Yes. Between midnight and two a.m.."

He smiled wryly. "So, you are treating me as a suspect?"

"It's just a formality," the captain replied. "If we're to eliminate you from our enquiries."

Lefève remained amused as if unsure whether or not to take them seriously.

"I would have to check my diary. I did have rather a busy week last week."

The captain nodded. "Of course. Could you contact me when you find out?"

"No problem."

They rose to their feet as one; took turns shaking hands.

"And do keep me up to speed on your investigation. Sandrine was a good person. We really need to catch the bastard who did this."

The captain touched the peak of his kepi and they went on their way. As they neared the door, however, Lefève called them back.

"Actually, it's just come to me."

They both gave him an inquisitive look.

"I can tell you exactly where I was last Thursday night. I went to an exhibition in Sète. The photographer, Sylvie B., was showing her latest collection. She's a friend of the family."

"What time did you leave?" the captain asked.

He puffed out his cheeks. "It was late. Well after midnight. Then after the exhibition I went to a party with some friends. It must have been two or three o'clock by the time we left Sète. My secretary will have all the details." He smiled. "So there – I couldn't possibly be your murderer."

The captain nodded. He reached for the door handle, but this time it was Margot who stopped them.

"Just one final question, if I may?"

Lefève had just taken his phone from his pocket and started to type. He didn't seem pleased to be interrupted. He lowered the phone and produced a smile.

"Yes, Madame?"

"Did you know Ginette Clément?"

A look of steel hardened his eyes. "I beg your pardon?"

"Ginette Clément," Margot repeated. "The young woman who was murdered fourteen years ago."

The intensity of his stare didn't diminish. "I'm well aware of who she was. But I think you've taken up enough of my time as it is. Good-day."

15

Another visit to the pet shop on her way home: 3 packets of duck meat, gizzard and liver; 1 sachet of chicken cuts in gravy; 2 bags of cheesy treats. Margot had been trying a new tactic: instead of putting the food down in the morning and allowing the royal puffball the entire day to enjoy it at his solitary leisure, she waited until she got home, reasoning he would be so hungry he would race to her feet and at least give up a little bit of affection in appreciation of her opening the packet.

The first half of the plan went well. Returning home at six, she found Buster installed on top of the courtyard wall, clearly wondering what on earth was going on. He raised himself onto his paws and watched with interest as she moved to the kitchen door.

Woman, where's my food?

Since he'd been so patient, Margot rewarded him with a packet of lamb and liver in jelly. She forked it onto a saucer, and sprinkled it with turkey treats as an extra bonus. He still hadn't come in, so she took it to the door and found His Imperial Majesty now patrolling the top of the wall, showing no inclination of coming down. Either he didn't like the food she'd chosen or was protesting about this new regime of hers. When Margot called out to him, he promptly sat down and turned the other cheek.

"I see. Having a sulk, are we?"

She wafted the saucer around a little bit more, but he still wouldn't budge. Grinding her teeth, Margot looked at her watch. She was due at Célia's at seven.

"All right. You win."

She left the food in the kitchen and went upstairs for a shower.

Afterwards, she put on a pair of blue denim jeans, a low-cut white shirt and, since it was a cool evening, a cream blazer with a Hermès silk scarf. A pair of dangly silver ear-rings and her chunky platinum watch completed the look. In the kitchen, she was unsurprised to see the cat food gone. She found His Majesty out in the courtyard, sprawled on top of her wrought-iron table, happily washing his bits. He gave her a disdainful sneer as she walked by – *See you later, sucker!* – and Margot shook her head as she departed. If cats ever learned how to open tins the human race would be doomed.

Already running late, she walked briskly up Rue Voltaire. On the far side of town, Célia's apartment block was lit up in spotlights, shadowy palm trees swaying in the breeze. She took the lift to the top floor, and found the door to Célia's penthouse ajar.

"Knock-knock." Margot peered in.

Stéphane appeared in the hall. "*Bon soir*, Margot."

She tilted her cheeks for kissing. "*Bon soir*, Stéphane."

"You're looking well."

"Thank you." She handed him the bottle of champagne she'd bought on the way, but held onto the flowers. Stéphane smiled fondly.

"Ah, Margot, that's very sweet of you, but there's no need to buy me flowers."

Margot smacked them lightly against his chest. "These are for your mother, cheeky. How is she?"

"She's okay. Come on through. We're in the kitchen."

The soundproofing in the building was clearly effective since Célia hadn't heard her arrive; entering the kitchen, they found her seated at the island with a faraway look in her eyes. Noticing Margot approach, however, she instantly brightened.

"Margot, what lovely flowers. Thank you."

"How did it go at the hospital?"

"As well as can be expected, I suppose. It's only five minutes in the machine, but all the waiting around takes it out of you." She took the flowers across to the sink to unwrap them.

"One down, fifteen to go," Stéphane commented. "They said the tiredness would catch up on her in a few days. You need to remember to take little breaks now and again, don't you, *Maman*?" he added like he'd already had to remind her a dozen times.

Célia threw out a weary look. "He's such a fusspot, Margot. Honestly, you would think I'm incapable of taking care of myself despite all these years living on my own."

Catching the look of consternation on Stéphane's face, Margot gave him a sympathetic smile. She was with him on this one. She diplomatically changed the subject.

"Dinner smells good." She cast a glance at the stove. Onion and garlic were sizzling in a pan of foamy butter. "Is there anything I can do to help?"

Célia ushered her away. "Absolutely not. You're our guest. Stéphane – fetch Margot a drink, will you, please?"

"Yes, mother. What would you like, Margot?"

"Ooh ... a glass of that champagne would be nice."

"Make that two," Célia said. "And when you've done that, could you pop down to the basement for me? You'll find a nice white vase in my storage room. It'll be perfect for these."

"Yes, mother. Of course, mother. Whatever you say, mother."

Stéphane playfully rolled his eyes at Margot as he went to do as he was told.

As soon as he'd gone off down to the basement, Célia left the flowers and patted the stool beside her. They sat side by side at the countertop, drinks in hand.

"I hear you've been ruffling someone's feathers."

"Our illustrious mayor, you mean?"

"Cousineau said you'd cracked the diary code."

Margot gave her a brief account of how they'd solved it. "He tried to make out she was his mistress, but it's a complete pack of lies."

"I don't imagine the council would be very impressed."

"Quite. It's unlikely we'll prove anything – he'll have covered his tracks somehow. It would be interesting to find out if he was the one who got Sandrine pregnant. I don't suppose we can request a DNA sample ..."

Célia smiled dryly. "I can't see Cousineau sanctioning that."

"Do you know much about him?"

"Lefève?" Célia put down her drink, glass clinking on the granite. "I've always found him quite personable, to be honest, although I certainly wouldn't trust him. The same as most politicians, I suppose. He's certainly been a popular mayor. He came down from Sète a few years ago and campaigned on a right-wing agenda – anti-immigration, tough on crime. He was the one who brought in the zero-tolerance policy on drug use and pickpocketing, and last year he had a purge on rough sleepers."

Margot shook her head in dismay. "So he doesn't want homeless people spoiling the look of the town but he'll happily pay a prostitute?"

Célia smiled with irony. "You don't need to tell me the hypocrisy in that. What else did he have to say for himself?"

"He had an alibi for the night of the murder. He claimed he

was at an art exhibition in Sète, though we've yet to corroborate that. According to Lefève they got on famously, but you've seen the way Sandrine describes him in her diary. She loathed him. It makes you wonder why she went on seeing him. He must have had some kind of hold over her."

"You think she was afraid of him?"

"He's a powerful man, in more ways than one."

"I have to confess, I have heard rumours."

"What kind of rumours?"

"Wandering hands, inappropriate touching."

"And no one's done anything about it?"

"Well, no one's actually made a complaint as such. At least, not to my knowledge. They're just rumours. And you can't rule out them being malicious. Politics is a murky world."

"What did he do before he became mayor?"

"I believe he used to work in the textile industry. His wife's employed by one of the big advertising agencies, and before that she was a model." The onions started to sizzle a little too fiercely so Célia got up and took the pan off the heat. She came back with the champagne bottle and topped up Margot's glass. "Do you seriously suspect he's involved?"

"I think we should seriously consider it. If we can at least find out what his secret was we'll know whether it was something worth killing for."

"Well, Cousineau's opened an *information* now so I'll be getting the dossier next week. Whatever he's been up to we'll get to the bottom of it, don't worry." She patted Margot's hand reassuringly.

Stéphane came back with the vase, and since Célia needed to get on with the cooking, Margot arranged the flowers and took them out to the table on the terrace. The penthouse was arranged over three floors: the living area in the middle, the bedrooms below, and a solarium/garden on the roof. From the salon, frameless glass doors opened onto an expansive terrace where dark wood decking wrapped around two corners. Planters divided the space into more intimate areas, and in the central section the table had already been laid: covered in a crisp white cloth and lit with candles. Over the handrail, spotlights lit up the towering trunks of the palm trees, and in the distance the soft lights of Argents curved gently around the bay. They were close enough to the sea to hear waves washing the rocks, five storeys below. Pausing to take it all in, Margot could happily have stayed out there all night.

Célia had outdone herself with the meal: four courses, starting with an *amuse-bouch* of pickled baby beetroots and kumquats and finishing with a lemon merengue pie, the lemon filling so sharp it made Margot's gums shrink. The beef tenderloin for the main was cooked just the way she liked it: seared to a smoky sweet perfection on the outside; juicily pink in the centre. Margot was frankly amazed at the effort she'd put in – a manic response to having spent half the morning at the hospital, Stéphane had commented while his mother was away from the table at one point. Célia gave him credit for doing all the prep, but it had still been an admirable effort.

Suitably sated, they moved to the loungers. Warm air was ducting up through grilles in the floor, insulating them from the chill in the evening air.

"I hear you have a new partner," Stéphane said, pulling the cork from a bottle of Pichon Lalande, one of Margot's favourites (checking the label, she'd been delighted to see it was a ten-year-old vintage). "Mother's been telling me all about your adventures with Captain Bouchard."

Margot smiled as he filled her glass. "We've been getting along famously, thank you very much. I misjudged him first time around, although I'm not so sure I approve of his interrogation technique."

Stéphane returned the open bottle to the table and sat back down. "A little too handy with his fists, is he?"

"He doesn't go quite that far."

"Ah, but those were the days, eh? When the police could beat a confession out of a suspect and no one would bat an eyelid. Damn that pesky European Convention on Human Rights for spoiling everyone's fun." He shook a facetious fist in the air.

"Oh, here we go," Célia said, rolling her eyes. "Now you've got him started."

Margot smiled amiably. Stéphane had spent much of his working life incorporating the ECHR into French law, the implementation of which had consistently been resisted by several key factions. The political Right saw it as an unwanted intrusion into French affairs. The *magistrats* objected on the grounds it strengthened the defendant's pre-trial rights. Even the courts were ambivalent to its implementation, arguing that it added unnecessary complication to the judicial process. Stéphane seemed to take the objections personally.

"You're a lawyer, aren't you, Margot?"

"I used to be."

"Then you don't need reminding of the illustrious track record of the French police when it comes to human rights. Until very recently they weren't even obliged to inform a detainee of their right to silence. In the good old days they didn't even have to tell them *why* they'd been detained or, heaven's forbid, grant them access to a defence lawyer. No, they could happily grind a suspect into submission in the anonymity of the police station, and this in our famous inquisitorial system where the investigation is supposedly being supervised by a judge."

"You do realise he'll be going on like this for the rest of the night," Célia said in an aside to Margot. Margot smiled again as she sat back in her seat. He had got a bee in his bonnet, though she couldn't deny it was nice watching someone speak with such passion.

"And then," he went on, "in 1993, when reforms were brought in to give the defendant more rights, one of which was to allow a defence lawyer into the *garde à vue* for the very first time, do you know what happened? The *magistrats* protested! There were mass demonstrations. My mother herself was out on the streets, burning copies of the CPP."

Célia gave him a phlegmatic look. Margot suspected this was a well-worn exchange, acted out so many times it had turned into family theatre.

"I assure you, Margot, I did no such thing. I may have torn out a few pages on the steps of the *Palais de Justice*, but I didn't set light to anything."

"What were you objecting to?" asked Margot.

Célia shuffled on her seat, slowly warming to the discussion. "Well, for one thing, the 1993 reforms were seen as a move to a more adversarial system. Anything which gives the defence a greater role has always been viewed with scepticism. For another, they wanted to take away the power of detention from the JI which, rather pompously, I was very much opposed to at the time." She smiled. "I've mellowed as I've grown older."

Stéphane took a large slurp of wine. "You were a real firebrand at university, though, weren't you, *Maman*?"

"Don't listen to him, Margot."

"Has she told you about the time she organised a 24-hour sit-in? One of the teaching staff was overheard using a racially offensive term. He refused to apologise, so the students blockaded the lecture hall until he agreed to back down."

"Good for you," Margot said.

"I was very headstrong back then."

"Grandfather was less than impressed, though, wasn't he? Didn't he lock you out of the house for a week?"

"My father had some strange ways."

"I'm sure he was proud of you," Margot said. "One thing I've always admired about the French is their willingness to protest."

"Oh, I agree," said Stéphane. "Though it's less easy being sympathetic when it's the tanker drivers who're on strike and you're queuing to buy petrol."

"Spoken like a true slacktivist."

They shared an amused smile. Célia went on:

"It started as morality protests. In the 1780s, gangs of young men would stand outside the houses of people accused of morality crimes, banging pots and pans. Anyone who didn't meet their perceived norms was fair game."

"These days they would just mob them on social media," Margot said, and they all laughed.

Stéphane reached for the wine bottle and topped them all up. "You're right – protesting gives people a voice. The way things are in the world right now we all feel we have less and less power. But the danger is people get funnelled into extremist views, and that then triggers a return to oppression. Look at anti-terror legislation. It comes in, initially for a limited period, but then gets normalised and remains on the statute book. It's the Interior Ministry rather than Ministry of Justice that's the driving force these days."

Margot decided to play devil's advocate. "But is that surprising, given the threat we face from terrorism?"

"If we don't uphold our most fundamental legal principals then what are we protecting?"

"People have a right to feel safe in their own cities."

"Of course they do, but look at what that leads to: video surveillance; facial recognition; racial profiling. Then it's detention without trial; waterboarding; Guantanamo Bay. They say security is our most important freedom, yet the measures they put in place ride roughshod over civil liberties. Did you hear about that case a few years ago where a man was held on terrorism charges? He spent five years in prison before his case came to trial, and only then did the truth come out. All the evidence against him had been fabricated. You can't detain someone just because you think they *might* commit a crime."

"If it stops them from blowing up an aeroplane does anyone really care about human rights?"

"Would you say that if you were the one they imprisoned? Or a member of your family? Put there because of some erroneous piece of intelligence? We like to think our intelligence agencies have our best interests at heart, but believe me, that's not always the case."

Margot lightly shrugged her shoulders. She didn't disagree with him, but in her view the world was never black or white, just many shades of grey.

Realising Célia hadn't spoken for a while, Margot turned to find her slumped in her seat, eyes closed. It seemed the day had finally caught up on her. Stéphane followed her line of sight.

"Mother," he softly called out.

With a sharp intake of breath Célia came back to life. "Sorry. Did I doze off?"

Margot laid a hand on her forearm. "Don't worry. He was boring the pants off me, too."

Stéphane got up and went to her chair. "Why don't you go to bed? I'll clean up."

Célia yawned widely. "Do you mind, Margot? It feels rather rude."

"Don't be silly. You must be exhausted."

The three of them stood.

"It's all these drugs they put you on. I'll be fine after a good night's sleep."

Stéphane gave her a hand up and accompanied her inside. Margot remained on the terrace, watching them go. It was the first time Célia had looked in any way frail, and that wasn't the way things were meant to be.

When Stéphane came back the mood remained subdued. Margot helped him collect the dirty crockery and carry it into the kitchen. He hardly said two words as he rinsed the plates and handed them to Margot to stack in the dishwasher.

"How long are you down here for?" she asked.

"A couple more days. I'll be back next week for her next appointment."

It was good of him to spare the time. From what Célia had said, he was very much in demand in Strasbourg, apparently fighting off head-hunters all the time. Financially, he could probably do far better in the commercial sector, but Margot suspected that wasn't what motivated him.

Dishwasher loaded, she wiped her hands on a towel. Fearing she was intruding now, she looked at her watch.

"Anyway. I should go."

"Sorry we've not been great company."

"On the contrary. The food was wonderful, and the conversation engaging."

"Even though I bored the pants off you?"

"You can make up for it next time."

His face brightened. "Challenge accepted."

"Text me."

"I will. How about I walk you home?"

Margot hesitated, pleasantly surprised. She couldn't remember the last time someone had offered to walk her home. Strange how a simple question could suddenly make you feel twenty years younger.

"Why not?" she smiled. "I'll get my coat."

They took a back-street up to Place Jeanne d'Arc and from there walked down through the town. At the war memorial, Margot steered him into an alley which served as a shortcut to the seafront. The promenade bars and restaurants were humming with life.

"So, tell me about this new lodger of yours."

"Why, are you jealous?"

Strolling along with his hands in his pockets, Stéphane shrugged noncommittally. Margot paused to light a cigarette.

"I'm trying to win the affections of a cat."

"Oh." He seemed relieved. "And how's that going?"

She shook out her match, and tucked it into her portable silver ashtray. "Not good."

"Notoriously fickle creatures."

"Aren't they just?"

"Not that I've ever owned one. But I know of them by reputation."

They grinned. Loud music was spilling out the doors of one of the bars so they went down some steps to a lower section of the promenade where it was quieter.

"You're worried about her, aren't you?" Margot said.

Stéphane drew in a long sad breath. "I just keep remembering what it was like last time. Everything she went through. All that treatment, so many hospital appointments, and it still came back."

"Your mother's a fighter. If anyone can get through it she can."

"Have you had any experience of cancer?"

"Not first-hand, no. I suppose I've been lucky."

"Then forgive me, Margot, but you don't know what it's like. You hear all these wonderful survival stories, read about new wonder-drugs and breakthroughs in treatment. But not everyone survives. I remember visiting her in hospital last time.

The woman in the next cubicle had just passed away. We could hear her family crying behind the curtains."

Margot detected the emotion in his voice. She drew on her cigarette, and gave him a moment.

"I'm sorry. I don't really know much about what she went through last time. Célia never talks about it."

"She had to have a full hysterectomy and her lymph nodes removed. She has a rare gene that expresses itself as an aggressive form. The prognosis wasn't good. I think the doctors were surprised she responded so well, but that doesn't mean the same will happen this time. She thinks she can take it all in her stride, but sometimes I wish she would just face facts. She's in for a tough time."

They walked on for a little while in silence. Reaching the edge of the beach, Margot had an idea to try and lighten the mood. The pavement continued around the back of the beach, but a boardwalk gave access onto the sand. Suddenly buoyed up with life, Margot took off her shoes and ran down the boardwalk. Looking back from the sand, she saw that Stéphane hadn't followed.

"Come on," she called out. "Let's go for a paddle."

"Come on where?" he called back dubiously, eyes searching the darkness. Margot waved, but he couldn't see her.

"You never walked on a beach at night before?"

"There aren't that many beaches in Strasbourg."

"Well, you're not in Strasbourg now, Toto. Live a little."

"Are you sure this is a good idea?"

"Yes! There's no one down here. Come and find me."

Laughing, she ran off towards the sea.

Margot ran down the beach until her feet met wet sand and then opened her lungs to the air. She gazed out over the great body of water with her eyes wide. Lines of white crests were catching the light, and as a wave came in, cool frothy water ran up over her bare feet, drowning her ankles. At times like this she felt at one with the ocean. Twelve degrees or not, she couldn't survive without her daily dip in the sea.

"Margot."

Stéphane's disembodied voice came from somewhere close by.

"Are we playing hide and seek now?"

Margot turned. She could see his grey shape moving gingerly across the beach. He was heading towards her, but not quite in the right direction. Fizzing with mischief, Margot picked up a handful of sand and then stalked him in a wide arc. She snuck up on him from behind, but he sensed her presence at the very last moment and turned, at which point Margot threw the sand at him. The sand was wetter than she'd expected, however, and a chunk broke off and hit him in the face. Horrified, Margot gasped.

"Sorry! I meant to throw it over your head."

Stéphane looked none too impressed. Margot helped brush the bits off his front while he spat lumps out of his mouth.

"That was very childish of you."

"I know. It's a failing of mine."

She could only see shadows on his face, but beyond his peeved expression he seemed to be smiling.

"Shouldn't you have grown out of that kind of behaviour?"

"Think young to stay young. That's my motto."

The sand was all gone, but for a few moments they carried on facing each other. Some half-formed thoughts passed between them before Margot looked away. Realising she'd dropped her cigarette in the sand, she stooped to pick it up, and then crumpled the remains into her ashtray. As they turned to walk on, she lit number ten – the dropped one didn't count.

"This was a good idea, though," Stéphane said, raising his

head to breath in the salty sea air. "And you are right – I never have walked on a beach at night before."

"Not even as a teenager?"

"Ours wasn't the type of family to go on beach holidays. I was surprised when *Maman* decided to move down here. She seemed happy in Lyon."

"So what were holidays like for you growing up? Let me guess: re-enactments of the Grand Tour? Hunting trips to the Scottish Highlands? Glamping in the Serengeti?"

He flinched in surprise. "Hardly. My father was a very modest man. The only places we ever seemed to go on holiday were either Paris or Bruges. He was particularly fond of Belgium, I recall, although I think that was because Simenon was one of his favourite authors."

"That's not what I was expecting, you being a noble and all."

"A noble?" he queried.

"I've heard all about your aristocratic ancestry."

"My what?"

"The illustrious Deverauxs. The grand old Napoleonic Duke ... Célia's told me all about it."

Stéphane laughed heartily. "I can assure you, Margot, it didn't feel very noble growing up."

"Your mother said you lived in a twenty-room château."

"We did, but at least half of those rooms were uninhabitable. And the small section we did inhabit was freezing cold. In winter we used to go to bed in our coats."

Margot drew on her cigarette, orange tip sizzling in the darkness. "That can't have been fun."

"It wasn't, although *Maman* did try to make it fun for us. I remember one year, it was so cold there was frost on the insides of the windowpanes. It snowed for days and days, so heavily the power went out. Mother built us this huge nest of blankets in front of the fire and we slept in there. My brother and I were so disappointed when the power came back on and we had to return to our bedrooms."

"What did your father do for a living?"

"My father? He worked for the government, although I've never found out quite what he did. I know he worked at the Élysée Palace for many years. We were told never to ask. It was all very hush-hush."

"Célia never mentions him."

"She wouldn't. It wasn't a happy marriage. Doomed from the start you might say."

"How so?"

"Her father collapsed on their wedding day and died of a brain aneurism a few days later."

"What a horrible thing to happen."

"*Maman* was devastated. But apparently my father wasn't very sympathetic. I think he was more annoyed they'd had to cancel their honeymoon. It caused a rift, and they never really got over it. They divorced six years later."

"Do you see him at all?"

"Not often. He emigrated to the States a few years back. He married a real-estate broker from New York. They have a wonderful house in the Hamptons. I get a Christmas card every year but that's about it."

A large wave came in and water rushed up to their feet. Stéphane stumbled into her in his eagerness to get out of the way, but the water receded just before it reached them, dissolving into the sand like a hissing serpent. He let go of her arm, apologising.

"What happened to the château?"

"The château – that got sold off. *Maman* bought an apartment in Lyon, in the sixth arrondissement. A fine old building, it was. You would have loved it: high ceilings, huge windows overlooking the Parc de la Tête d'Or. I preferred it to the château, to be honest."

"How old were you?"

He gave it some thought. "I would have been six when we moved. I stayed until I went to university."

"Did Célia ever re-marry?"

Margot sensed him shake his head.

"There was someone she was fond of – a colleague at work – but my mother's from a generation where such things stayed in the closet."

"The closet?"

Stéphane looked into her eyes. "Didn't you know?"

Margot felt her cheeks redden. "It's not something you really discuss with your boss." Though it did make sense of a few things.

They'd reached the end of the beach and had nowhere left to go. Stéphane looked around, hands on hips.

"I'm guessing we have to walk all the way back to the boardwalk."

"Don't be silly." Margot eyed up the concrete wall at the rear of the beach. "We can climb over there."

The wall was barely six feet high. Cigarette in her mouth, Margot hoicked herself up with her hands, then threw a leg over. Safely at the top, she crouched to give Stéphane a hand.

"Walking on a beach at night and now climbing walls," Stéphane said as he dusted himself down. "I'm not sure *Maman* will let me come out to play with you anymore."

Margot smiled. He didn't know the half of it.

"Anyway," she said, stubbing out her cigarette. "I'm going to have to love you and leave you, I'm afraid. My other man is waiting for me at home."

"Your furry companion?"

"He prefers the title: His Royal Highness, Puffball of Argents."

"You must introduce me sometime."

"I'd love to but he'll barely tolerate me, let alone a stranger."

"He sounds like hard work."

"He is. But don't worry, I'll tame him."

Their eyes met in the glow of the streetlight. Margot was surprised when something like electricity sparked between them. But she kissed him lightly on the cheek, and then backed away.

"Goodnight, Stéphane."

"Goodnight, Margot. We must do this again sometime."

"We must. And next time I'll try not to throw sand in your face."

"That's a date."

16

Ten a.m. Sunday – a text from Captain Bouchard:

Forgive me for contacting you at such an unsociable hour but there has been a development. If you're free perhaps you could call at the Gendarmerie.

Leaving her coffee unfinished, Margot went straight round. Lieutenant Martell let her in, and as he was busy with another matter he left her to walk the empty corridors alone. Captain Bouchard was stationed in his office, deep in thought, an assortment of items in plastic evidence bags spread across his desk.

"What's all this?"

Margot moved around the desk, casting her eyes over the collection: various items of clothing, some shoes, a couple of bags. The captain got to his feet.

"Some of the items we found at Gy Berger's house and at the train station. This—" he picked out a bagged-up khaki messenger bag "—was found in his personal locker. And this—" he picked up another bag containing a screwed-up white shirt "—was found inside."

Margot had closer look, but the bloodstains down the front were clear from first sight.

"Is it definitely his?"

"It's the same size as others we found in his house."

"And the blood ...?"

He nodded. "It belongs to Sandrine."

Margot tried to imagine an innocent explanation for how it might have ended up there, but inspiration was lacking.

"More tellingly, perhaps," the captain went on. "We also found this in his locker."

He picked up another evidence bag, this one containing what looked like a clear plastic bag. Margot sensed the hairs rise on the back of her neck.

"It matches the plastic found under Sandrine's fingernails," the captain said. "We have our murder weapon."

Margot pulled out a chair and heavily sat down. The evidence seemed irrefutable.

Lieutenant Martel came in. "He's still refusing to eat. I just went down there and he'd thrown his tray at the wall."

"Who are you talking about?" asked Margot.

"Gy Berger," Martel replied. "He's not eaten anything since we brought him in. He'll sip water, but that's it. What are we meant to do?"

"Has he been seen by a doctor?" Margot asked, turning to face the captain.

Captain Bouchard looked a little bit sheepish.

"We'll put that in hand," he said. "But first I want him back in the interview room. Let's see how he tries to explain away this little lot."

Once again, the captain refused to let her sit in, relegating her to the observation room instead.

Berger was a diminished figure. Pale and washed-out, his

body stayed limp and languid as a gendarme brought him into the interview room and guided him to the chair. His hands were cuffed, but this time they didn't bother securing him. There was no fight left in him.

Captain Bouchard was already seated. He waited until he had the young man's attention and then reached down into a box. He took out the messenger bag and placed it on the table between them.

"Do you recognise this?"

Berger nodded.

Next, the captain produced the evidence bag containing the bloodied shirt and placed it beside the messenger bag.

"What about this?"

Berger nodded again.

"They both belong to you?"

He nodded for a third time.

"And were you wearing this shirt the night you went to Sandrine's?"

Predictably, he nodded again.

The captain laced his fingers. "In that case, would you care to explain how it came to be stained with the victim's blood?"

Berger shuffled on his seat. He spent a few moments clearing his throat, and took several seconds to find his voice.

"I wanted to comfort her. I knelt beside her chair and put her head on my chest. There was some blood on her cheek."

"Why did you want to comfort her? You had no interest in touching her when she was alive."

"Everything had changed."

"How had they changed? Apart from the fact that she was dead."

"You wouldn't understand."

"You preferred her when she was dead, is that it?"

Berger lowered his eyes, slowly shaking his head. The

sadness coming off him was almost palpable. "I don't want to talk to you anymore."

The captain continued to regard him. When a whole minute's worth of silence had passed, he cleared some space on the desk, pulled another item out of his box, and placed the sealed-up plastic bag between them. Berger took no interest at first, but as the silence grew he was unable to resist. He didn't seem surprised by what he saw.

"Do you know what this is?"

Once again he had to build himself up to speaking. He appeared to be swallowing a lot. On the third attempt he managed to get his words out:

"Is that from my locker?"

"Would you care to explain how it got there?"

"I put it there."

"When?"

"The day after."

"And how did it come to be in your possession?"

"It was on her head when I arrived. So I took it off."

"That's not what you told us before."

"That's because I knew what you would think."

"So why did you hide it? Why didn't you just leave it where it was?"

"Because I'd touched it with my bare hands. I thought you'd be able to test it and find out I'd picked it up."

The captain inhaled deeply, frustration beginning to show.

"Unfortunately, Monsieur Berger, I find it hard to believe a single word you're saying. All the evidence points to you killing her yourself. We've found nothing to indicate anyone else was in the house that night. Only you. And when we consider that you had a clear-cut motive: Sandrine was precious to you; you wanted her all to yourself; but she didn't want you ... And somewhere in the twisted logic of your mind you decided that if you couldn't have her then no one would. You killed her, didn't you?"

"I did not kill her," Berger said patiently.

"Admit it, and your conscience will be clear."

"My conscience is already clear."

If anything, his quiet composure only served to rile the captain even more.

"Dammit, man! Save us all some time and confess!"

Berger briefly snapped out of his trance. He looked at the captain as if it were the first time they'd met, but the spark of life faded as quickly as it had appeared.

"Can I go home now?"

Captain Bouchard exhaled lengthily. One by one he took the bags off the table and returned them to the box.

"No, Monsieur Berger, you cannot go home. And if the judge accepts my recommendation and charges you with murder, you won't be going home for a very long time."

Margot caught up with Captain Bouchard in the corridor. Together they watched Gy Berger being taken down to the cells, shuffling along at a snail's pace, barely able to raise his feet off the ground. When he'd finally gone out of sight, they turned around and headed back to the captain's office.

"Was anyone else's DNA found on the plastic bag?" Margot asked.

"A partial fingerprint matching Berger's right thumb was all they could find."

"If he'd gone there with the intention of killing her wouldn't he have worn gloves?"

"He's a volatile man. We've seen how quickly he can flare up.

My guess is he lost his temper and killed her in the heat of the moment, then panicked and tried to cover his tracks."

But does a guilty man go on hunger strike? Margot was tempted to say.

"So what now?"

"I'll speak to the judge first thing in the morning. In my view there's enough evidence to put him on a charge of murder. And I'll be recommending he be held in custody during the period of *instruction*."

The sound of a commotion came from the direction of the front office. They doubled their pace along the corridor and found Lieutenant Martell gesturing angrily at someone through the side window.

"The Gendarmerie is closed on Sundays," he called out. "You'll have to come back in the morning." Sensing their presence, he turned and came away from the glass, looking frustrated. "It's Gy Berger's mother again. She keeps banging on the window, demanding to see him."

Right on cue, the woman's stick appeared above the sill and gave the glass a sharp tap. The captain showed no interest in intervening so Margot stepped forward.

"Shall I speak to her?"

"Be my guest."

Lieutenant Martell accompanied her into the lobby, but after unlocking the front door and letting her out he closed it behind her. Madame Berger promptly came over from the window.

"Is he in there? Can I see him?"

"I'm afraid not. He's just been taken down to the cells."

Madame Berger hissed. "So when's he coming home?"

The midday sun was hot on her head so Margot moved into some shade, drawing Madame Berger with her. She pulled a sympathetic face. "Not for a while, I'm afraid. The captain's going to recommend he be detained in custody."

"But he hasn't done anything wrong!"

"I'm sorry," Margot said. "But given the seriousness of the crime, and the fact Gy resisted arrest, they'll want to make sure he remains at the disposal of the court."

She hissed again, looking like she was slowly deflating. She drifted back out into the sun and started to wander off, but then changed her mind.

"Where will they take him?"

"The local prison, I would imagine. You will be able to visit him. And there is something else you should know – he's refusing to eat."

"He probably doesn't like your food."

"I think it's a little bit more than that. He'll be allowed to refuse nourishment until his life is in danger, but at that point a doctor will have to step in. If all else fails they'll have to force-feed him."

Madame Berger shook her head, muttering.

"Perhaps when you visit him," Margot went on, "you could try and persuade him to change his mind."

"But he's innocent, I tell you. The real killer is still out there. Why aren't you out looking for them?"

Margot returned a neutral look, stopping short of agreeing with her. Despite all the evidence, she was convinced the captain was wrong. She laid a reassuring hand on Madame Berger's arm.

"I'll do my best. I promise."

Margot called her a taxi and waited for it to arrive. She paid the driver in advance, and after watching it depart went back into the Gendarmerie. Lieutenant Martell had changed into civilian clothes and looked like he was ready to lock up.

"Is the captain still here?"

"He was heading back to his office the last time I saw him."

"I'll be two minutes," Margot said, and rushed off down the corridor.

He wasn't in his office. On a hunch, she went around the corner to the glazed arcade. On the far side of the parade ground a light was on in the first-floor apartment. Margot put a hand to the latch on the fire escape door and almost went out, but promptly changed her mind.

She hurried back to the front office, hoping to catch Martell before he left. At the intersection of corridors, she spotted him heading towards the back door.

"Lieutenant."

He halted, and waited for her to reach him.

"Yes, Madame?"

"I was wondering ... has anyone checked out the mayor's alibi yet?"

"I found out the name of the gallery he said he went to. It's called Galerie Soleil, on the Canal Royal. I was going to give them a call tomorrow."

"Do you mind if I do it instead? I was thinking of going over there."

He shrugged. "Not at all. It'll save me a job."

17

Galerie Soleil was on Quai Général Durand, in a tall thin building squeezed into a terrace of small shops. Margot spotted it too late, and since there was nowhere to park and a van was on her tail, she had to go around, turning left onto a bridge over the Canal Royal and then left again on the opposite bank. She ducked into the only space available, and it being Florian's Fiat 500 she'd borrowed, took extra care not to prang it.

She completed the loop on foot, taking the next bridge down and walking back along the waterfront. A flotilla of small boats lined both sides of the canal, and the quayside was buzzing with life. Basking in the warm morning sunshine, Sète was living up to its reputation as the Venice of the Languedoc.

At Galerie Soleil, plate glass windows flanked a wide smoked door. Inside, it was all very hush-hush. A life-size sculpture of some mythical creature was the first thing to grab Margot's attention: a hideous nose-less woman with green scaly skin and long twisted fingernails.

"Striking, isn't it?"

Over to one side, a woman seated at a glass reception desk had clocked Margot's surprised reaction.

"What's it meant to be?"

"It's an interpretation of Qalupalik, from the Inuit legend. She was said to lure young children into the sea and then devour them whole."

"Hmm," Margot mused. "I think I once knew a teacher like that."

The receptionist snorted. "Sorry," she said, when a man looked over.

Margot wandered on. She passed through several interconnecting rooms, the black walls studded with artwork, many of them from the local area. Paintings and photographs in the main, punctuated with the occasional piece of abstract sculpture. A few of the artists' names were familiar to her from the art classes she'd been taking, and she recognised the locations of several of the landscapes. It would be nice to think that one day some of her own efforts would make it onto the walls of a place like this, though it was rather unlikely. Failing to find any mention of Sylvie B., Margot completed a circuit of the ground floor and then went back to the receptionist.

"I'd heard you were showing a collection of Sylvie B.'s work."

"That's right. It's on the first floor. Turn left at the top of the stairs and the exhibition space is right in front of you."

"Thank you."

Margot trod lightly up the steel and glass staircase, careful not to break the hush. The first floor was a higgledy-piggledy space, filled with an eclectic mix of contemporary art, though the exhibition area at the front was much larger and benefitted from the natural light flooding in through three tall windows. Sylvie B.'s work occupied the entire space, all of it photographs mounted in sleek glass frames. Her speciality was nature in art – plants and wildlife captured in the most remarkable ways. Highly detailed closeups, or shot from unexpected angles. Margot had looked her up on the internet before setting out.

Some of her pictures sold for thousands, and she had over a million followers on social media, though the artist herself seemed something of a recluse. Not a single image of her had come up in Margot's on-line searches. The 'B' was short for Babineaux; her father, Remi, owned Babineaux Construction, a sizeable outfit based in Sète but with offices all across the country. He was a self-made man, having worked as a stonemason for much of his life.

In real-life, Sylvie's work was even more impressive. This particular collection was a series of black and white prints taken in one of the nearby *étangs* – the saltwater lagoons that were a feature of this stretch of coast, running all the way from St. Cyprien in the south to the Camargue in the north. A land of pink flamingos and wild white horses, though it was refreshing to see that Sylvie had steered clear of cliché and concentrated instead on capturing the ethereal quality of the landscape. She'd employed several unusual methods of printing: some had been printed directly onto glass; in others, she'd used a method of processing which, according to the caption, involved soaking the film in a mixture of coffee and washing soda. The results were stunning. The second half of the collection focussed on the working life of the area: a canal barge passing through an industrial wasteland; an oyster fisherman knee-deep in water. The textural quality made some of them look more like paintings than prints, the combination of sand, sea and air so evocative that Margot was sure she could taste the salt on her tongue. Oh, to be so talented.

She became so engrossed that she lost track of time. Checking her watch, she was stunned to see that twenty minutes had gone by. She went back down to the receptionist.

"Find it?"

"It's a remarkable collection," Margot said. "I wish I'd been here for the opening."

"It was a good night, actually."

"You were here?"

"Oh yes. My partner curates the gallery. He's been trying to get Sylvie for a number of years."

"I'd loved to have met her."

"We were lucky. She doesn't often appear in public."

Margot hesitated. "Wasn't Jean-Paul Lefève here that night?"

"Yes, he was. He's good friends with Sylvie. Well, more with her father, I suppose."

Margot smiled. "Do you mind if I ask you a few questions?"

The receptionist's eyebrows went up. "Oh ... What kind of questions?"

Margot explained who she was, though not the precise reason she'd come.

"Can you remember what time Lefève arrived?"

"Well, the event started at eight. We had drinks and canapés while Sylvie was doing her introduction. I'm sure he was here for that."

"And he stayed until the end?"

"Oh yes."

"Which would have been ...?"

"Around eleven."

"Much after eleven?"

The receptionist shook her head. "I remember checking the clock when I was locking up. It was no more than two or three minutes past."

It was a two-hour drive from Sète to Argents, less at that time of night. Lefève would easily have had time to get back to Sandrine's for two a.m..

"Do you have any idea where Lefève went afterwards?"

Another shake of her head. "Sorry, no. I remember saying goodbye to them as they went through the door. Sylvie, her father and Lefève all left together. A couple of others were with them, I think. I got the impression they were all going on to a party, but I've no idea where."

Margot nodded her appreciation. "Is there any way I might get hold of Sylvie?"

"I could give you her official address – it's somewhere in Montpelier – though I doubt she'll be there. She said in her talk that she likes to spend time in an old fishing shack on the *étang*. Immerse herself in her subject."

"And where would that be?"

"It sounded quite isolated from the way she described it. Although—" Having seconds thoughts, the receptionist pulled open a drawer. "I could give you the name of a friend of hers. He might be able to help."

"That would be wonderful."

She took out an assortment of business cards, and finding the one she was after, handed it over.

"His name's Alain. Tell him I gave you his number and he should talk to you."

"Thanks." Margot tucked the card into her pocket. She made to leave, but then had another thought. "Doesn't Sylvie's father own a construction company in Sète?"

"Yes, he does – Babineaux Construction. They're building a big new apartment block on Route de Cayenne, in fact. Very chic, but a little bit too pricey for me."

They both smiled.

"Thanks again. You've been most helpful."

Margot stepped out onto the busy street. After waiting for a gap in the traffic, she crossed over and found sanctuary on the wide pavement that ran alongside the canal. A noisy motor cruiser was chugging by, searching for a space to moor up, so she moved to a bench where it was quieter and took out her phone. She called the number on the card. It rang for thirty seconds without reply. Margot hung up, checked she'd entered the number correctly, and then tried again. This time someone picked up right away.

"Hello." A chilled male voice.

"Alain?"

"Who's this?"

"My name's Margot. The receptionist at Galerie Soleil gave me your number. She said you could put me in touch with Sylvie B."

"What do you want with Sylvie?"

"It's about the murder of a woman in Argents."

"Sandrine?"

"You knew her?"

A pause. "So, what are you ... a reporter or something?"

Margot explained, bringing on another pause. She fully expected him to hang up, but the line stayed open.

"Are you still there?"

"I'm still here."

"Is there any chance I could meet Sylvie? I heard she has a shack on the *étang*."

"You know Café Olivier?"

"No, but I'm sure I'll find it."

"Meet me outside at three, if you like."

"Thanks. I'll be there."

Margot looked it up on her phone. The café was only a few streets away, but it was still only eleven. With one finger, she scrolled across the map in search of Route de Cayenne. She tapped on the nearest point-of-interest and then selected Directions. Her phone calculated a fifteen-minute walk.

The construction site was hard to miss: two huge tower cranes turning slowly over a large building wrapped in scaffolding.

Every viewable piece of hoarding carried the logo of Babineaux Construction, and a huge billboard by the gates spelled it out again just in case a passer-by might miss it. There was an artist's impression of the finished project, and a legend: '75 Luxury Apartments. Coming Soon!'

Margot worked her way along the perimeter fence, the restricted footpath forcing her to step down onto the road in places. It sounded like dozens of people were at work up on the scaffolding, hidden behind the hoarding, hammers clanging metal, power tools buzzing away, but when she got to the gates no one was there to stop her from going in. She was halfway to the building's entrance before someone called out:

"Hey!"

Margot turned to find a high-viz man approaching with purpose.

"You can't come in here. It's restricted. Site office first."

He put a hand to her elbow to steer her out, though Margot politely removed it. When they got to the gates, she gave him a smile.

"I'm looking for Remi Babineaux."

"Ask at the office." He pointed to a stack of Portakabins on the nearside boundary. He turned to head back but then promptly changed his mind. "Actually, he's over there." Now he pointed to a group of smartly-dressed men standing by some parked cars. "Remi's the one in the light blue suit."

"Thanks."

Remi was standing in the middle of the group, doing most of the talking. His audience appeared to consist of Far Eastern businessmen and his body language suggested he was putting on a sales spiel, keen to impress. Margot halted at a discrete distance and waited. If his state of attire was anything to go by – flowery silk tie, stylish Italian loafers – his stone-laying days were far behind him. Her continued presence seemed to be putting him off, and after glancing her way a few times, curiosity finally got the better of him and he cocked his chin.

"You looking for someone?"

Margot stepped closer. "Sorry to interrupt. Are you Remi Babineaux?"

"Who's asking?"

"I'm from the *Palais de Justice* in Argents. Would you mind answering a few questions?"

He gave her a searching look. His face was leathery and tanned, the hardness offset by a pair of piercing blue eyes. After giving it a little consideration, he finished up with the businessmen and waited while they dispersed. As soon as they were alone, he drew Margot to one side.

"What's this about?"

"Your daughter's exhibition last week. I understand you were there with Jean-Paul Lefève."

"That's right. He's a friend of mine. So what?"

"Do you mind if I ask where you went afterwards?"

He frowned. "We went to a party. Why? What's this got to do with anything?"

"I'm interested in Lefève's movements that night. Specifically what he got up to after the exhibition."

Babineaux glanced at something over Margot's shoulder and then back again. "What's with all the questions?"

"It's in connection with a murder in Argents."

"You mean that prostitute who was killed?"

It was telling that he didn't describe her as his friend's mistress, Margot thought. She answered with a nod.

Babineaux continued to look perplexed. He glanced around again as if hoping for a distraction.

"I see ... What did you say your name was again?"

Margot had carefully avoided revealing it but this time she told him.

"Would you mind waiting here one second?"

She watched him walk off in the direction of the site office. Two metres before he reached the steps, however, he turned sharply to his left and approached a row of three cars, parked in the shade. Without even glancing her way, he casually opened the door of a silver Mercedes, got into the driver's seat, and started the engine. Margot watched in amazement as he calmly drove off, a small cloud of dust rising in his wake. She angrily slapped the dust away from her face. It seemed both he and the mayor had perfected the art of the disappearing act.

She didn't bother waiting; he wasn't coming back. After standing there looking foolish for a full half-minute, Margot left the construction site.

She walked back into town and followed the directions to Café Olivier, finding it tucked away in a side street. With over an hour to kill before Alain showed up, Margot chose a table on the sunny pavement, and when a waiter came out, ordered a coffee.

She lit a cigarette, and quickly relaxed. With the sun shining brightly it was easy to while away the time watching the world go by. The tourists were often the most interesting; you could spot them a mile off. Pasty-white Englishmen ill-suited to their shorts; women fanning faces, complaining about the heat. Then there were the snap-happy photographers, and the young people who seemed to feel the need to point their phones at everything that moved (and quite a lot that did not). Margot flinched as a man pushing a bicycle went by, an annoying squeak coming from his wheels. A flamboyantly-dressed man who smiled at strangers. Margot shifted uncomfortably, stirred by an unpleasant memory.

She looked at her watch, and sighed. Ten-past-three. Still no sign of Alain. A man came in and took a seat two tables down, but he promptly immersed himself in a book and did nothing to indicate he'd come to meet anyone.

Margot ground out her cigarette. Two smokes down; only two more left for the rest of the day. When it got to twenty past, she went to the café door. The only one in there was the waiter who attentively looked up, wondering if she wanted anything. Margot shook her head and went back out.

She took out her phone, tempted to call him. He hadn't sounded like someone who was a stickler for punctuality but surely he would have called if he were going to be this late. She gave him until three-forty-five and then tapped his number. Two rings and it cut to voicemail. She didn't leave a message.

Run out of patience, Margot dropped the phone into her bag. She took one final look around and then set off back to the car. If no one was willing to help she would find this shack on her own.

The road out of Sète was as straight as an arrow and seemed to have no end. When a mini-roundabout came up, the only option was to drive straight on and she found herself travelling along an identical stretch of tarmac. The map on the satnav showed a narrow strip of land situated between two great bodies of water – the *étang* on one side, the Mediterranean on the other – but a sandbank fringed with dune grasses blocked her view of the sea, while on the other side of the road a mix of low scrub gave only glimpses of the lagoon. It looked like she'd found the road to oblivion.

With nowhere to pull in, she had to continue to the next mini-roundabout. At least this one gave her the option to turn right, though the road was blocked by a barrier and it turned out to be the entrance to a caravan site. A parking space came up, but it was occupied by a white pickup. And then, just as she was beginning to despair about ever finding a place to stop, a pull-in appeared. She braked hard, and turned in sharply, wheels dropping off the edge of the road and into soft sand.

Margot turned off the ignition. A deathly quiet encompassed her. She got out of the car, and stepped into the road. The tarmac disappeared into heat haze in both directions, and not a single vehicle was in sight. A chestnut picket fence was meant to stop people climbing up onto the dunes, but at the point where she'd pulled in the fence had been trampled and evidently used as a cut-through.

Margot scrambled up the sandbank. Emerging at the top was like arriving in another world. A huge sandy beach stretched for miles down the coast while the sea shimmered in the late afternoon sun. Straining her eyes, she could just about see a dozen tiny sailboats moving around like aquatic ants, racing along in the wind. Closer to the beach, a small group of multicoloured kite-surfers were out riding the waves.

The wind was strong so Margot turned her back to the sea. On the other side of the road, the lagoon was still hidden from view, despite the fact she'd gained several metres in height. She retraced her route down the sandbank, checked the road was still clear, and then crossed. The vegetation that bordered the *étang* was sparse and low, but the shrubs were gnarled and prickly. With no easy way through, she carried on walking down the road. A white van drove by, slowing as it passed, a curious driver looking out of his window to see what she was up to. Margot watched until he'd gone on his way, and then continued.

After a kilometre or so she found a break in the bushes. It led to a rough damp path, puddled in places, and after a few twists and turns she came to a clearing. But Margot promptly halted, dismayed by the sight of a small pile of white goods dumped on the far side. It seemed she'd found a fridge graveyard.

But she could sense she was close to the water now. She followed another gap in the shrubs and emerged on the edge of the *étang*. Away from the shelter of the dunes, the water was catching the worst of the wind and the surface was choppy. A few low houses could be seen far away on the opposite shore, but otherwise there was nothing other than water and scrub and a few small flocks of birds. Certainly nothing that resembled an old fishing shack.

Margot took out her phone and looked at Maps. There were several *étangs* along this stretch of coast, and judging by her location she'd barely explored a fraction of this one. She had no idea where she was meant to be looking or even what the shack might look like. This was starting to feel like the very definition of a wild goose chase. And time was getting on. It would be dark soon and Florian would want his car back.

18

It would have been a pauper's funeral – a direct cremation, no fuss, no frills – had it not been for a rather unusual request. Several days earlier, Gy Berger's mother had paid yet another visit to the Gendarmerie, this time brandishing a handbag full of cash. Learning that Sandrine's body had been released for disposal, Gy had insisted upon paying for a proper send-off and had instructed his mother to empty his savings account. The request had prompted some discussion at the Gendarmerie: the captain's theory was atonement; Margot had taken it at face value; Lieutenant Martel had sat on the fence, though had also gone out of his way to help organise things with the funeral director.

The service had been scheduled for eight-thirty a.m., probably the only time they could do at such short notice, and when the taxi dropped her at the crematorium Margot was the only one there. Standing in the shade of the portico, she scanned the car park, hoping to see Colbert's blue Tesla. Surely he would bring Lya to her own mother's funeral. He had been notified – Martell had called him at work, and later emailed him the details – yet there was no sign of the car.

An unmarked black van pulled in and took the loop through the car park that would bring it into the portico. Margot stepped forward, making her presence known, but the van pulled up short and a single, heavy-set man got out. After going round to the back of the van, he reappeared a few moments later with Gy Berger by his side. They moved out of the way and Berger caught Margot's eye, though nothing passed between them. He was a skeleton in a black suit, sleeves barely long enough to cover his shiny metal bracelets. Despite his mother's pleas he hadn't given up his hunger strike.

Margot scanned again for Colbert's car, still without success. At eight-thirty, another black van came in. This one drove right into the portico, and when it drew to a halt four men got out. They unloaded the coffin in silence, and then lead the small procession inside, moving rather more swiftly than normal, Margot suspected. They had the coffin laid out on the platform in under two minutes. Not that she blamed them. For them it was little more than a production line, repeated at forty-five-minute intervals, and then again the following day.

Margot took a seat in the front row; Berger and the prison guard sat down at the back. A few seconds after the music had ended, the celebrant came in and took her place at the lectern. She gazed out as if about to address a crowd of a hundred rather than a gathering of three, and to her credit made the effort and delivered a touching eulogy. Most of it could have come straight from the police report, though in many ways it was Sandrine's father who was the star of the show. Prior to moving to France, he'd been a professor at the American University in Beirut, and along with his string of academic papers, he'd written an article in *Time* magazine describing his experience of living through the Lebanese civil war. Margot had read it last night. The violence he'd witnessed had been appalling: mass killings, kidnappings, people being slaughtered on the streets on an almost daily basis. When a car bomb destroyed his home, killing his parents and grandparents, he'd decided enough was enough. He'd fled to France in 1977.

Sandrine's life was comparatively sparse on detail. That gap in her history after quitting university remained a blank page, and the only item of a personal nature was her graduation photo which someone had thoughtfully put into a frame and placed on the table next to the flowers. They could only hope her childhood had been happier than the years that were to come.

The service was over in eleven and a half minutes. They rose to their feet to the sound of Eva Cassidy's *Somewhere over the Rainbow* – it being one of the most-played songs in Sandrine's music library, as Lieutenant Martell had discovered. As the curtains closed on the coffin, Margot thought of all the remarkable people whose lives had gone unrecognised, forgotten by history, as their bodies went off to the oven. Trite to think it, but death really was the final curtain.

Since they'd taken seats at the back, Gy Berger and the prison guard waited for Margot to leave. As she headed towards the door, Margot glanced his way. Despite having paid for it all, Berger's face was a blank canvas, empty of emotion, hard to imagine why he'd gone to the trouble. It may have been her funeral, but there were no tears for Sandrine that day.

Célia had told her to take the whole morning off so as soon as she got home Margot changed her clothes and went for a walk around the shops. At noon, she called in at the Gendarmerie. It was Lieutenant Martell's day off, and the young gendarme who was manning the front desk was a little too keen, insisting on checking her ID before letting her in.

The captain wasn't in his office. Margot found her way to the glazed arcade and looked out across the parade ground. A light was on in the first-floor apartment, and when she eased open the fire escape door she could hear a radio playing. This time she didn't back out.

She crossed the parade ground and climbed the stairs. On the first-floor landing, she approached with caution, tapping on the window as she passed.

"Captain?"

The radio went off. A few moments later, Captain Bouchard appeared in the open doorway, shirt sleeves rolled up, a pewter jug in one hand and a polishing cloth in the other. He gave her an inquisitive look.

"Madame. Is there a problem?"

Margot smiled solemnly. "No, there's no problem. And I know it's lunchtime. Feel free to tick me off."

But he didn't tick her off. Instead, he continued to regard her with a wary look on his face, no doubt wondering why she'd come. Not in the mood for smalltalk, Margot looked silently back at him. She wasn't sure how but as the seconds passed some kind of understanding was reached between them and he stepped aside, inviting her in.

There wasn't a great deal to see. The salon was a rectangular box, open to the kitchen at the far end with only a breakfast bar to separate them. The front window looked down on the parade ground while an identical one at the rear had a view of some wasteland. The furniture was basic and old-fashioned; the dining table covered in a plastic cloth. Two plain doors were located in the wall to her left: the closed one presumably the bathroom; the open one a simply furnished bedroom. A double bed with the blankets neatly tucked in; a baby's cot reflected in a free-standing mirror. Breaking up the military starkness were a few feminine touches: a flowery lampshade, some nice cushions on the sofa, a sheepskin rug to the side of the bed. Naturally, everything was spotlessly clean. When Margot had finished looking round she turned to find the captain watching her.

"It's a shame no one uses these anymore," she said. "They look solidly built."

"Oh, they are," Captain Bouchard said, proudly laying a hand on one of the walls. "The French army doesn't do things by halves."

It must have made economic sense to someone, Margot supposed. Too expensive to maintain, or perhaps it was a matter of practicality. It can't have been easy raising a family in a place like this.

"I've just been to Sandrine's funeral."

"How did it go?"

"Apart from Gy Berger, no one turned up."

The captain sighed. "That's sad. In our job we're not supposed to get personally involved, but sometimes it's easier said than done."

Margot nodded. She studied him for a few moments, wondering if this were perhaps a good time. In the end, she came right out with it.

"Lieutenant Martel told me about your wife. I'm sorry I made fun of you."

Captain Bouchard stiffened. After a few moments, he gave a considered nod of his head and then turned away. He strolled towards the kitchen, straightening a chair along the way.

"These four walls hold a lot of happy memories. Probably the best years of my life."

"How long did you live here?"

"Fifteen years. We were married in Argents. We spent our wedding night in that bed over there. Our son was born and raised here."

"And you still come in and clean?"

The captain nodded. "My wife was very house-proud. Her family didn't have much. A place like this was luxury to her."

"That's very touching."

"She always kept it spick and span. It didn't seem right to let it deteriorate." He snatched a breath, and distracted himself by looking at a picture on the wall. "I do what I can. But it never looks as good as when she did it."

"I'm sure she would be proud of you."

Margot moved next to him and set her eyes on the same picture: a photograph of a younger version of Captain Bouchard, a baby in his arms, wife by his side. Another happy family.

"It's hard missing someone, isn't it?" she said.

"It is. I think the worse part is that moment when you realise you're never going to see them again. The finality of it all."

"It would be nice to think they were still around us, wouldn't it? Hiding in the air somewhere."

They both looked around as if longing for that to be true. Margot smiled fondly.

"You know, just after Hugo died, I often still saw him. Sometimes in the kitchen when I was drinking my coffee. Sometimes on the stairs when he would come down in that tatty old dressing gown of his. He would kiss me on the cheek, and we would talk for hours about what we were going to cook for dinner that night." Margot lowered her eyes, still smarting from the pain of those memories. "I know I must have been hallucinating, but I so wanted him to be real."

"It's been nearly three years since my wife passed away and I wish I could tell you it gets easier, but it doesn't. I suppose I'm lucky – I still have my son. I can't imagine how I would have coped without him."

A wave of raw emotion welled up inside before Margot put a lid on it.

"I would hide if I were you."

Margot froze, fixing Florian with a curious frown. "Why?"

"Cousineau's on the warpath."

Footsteps sounded in the corridor. The door to the office was still open and through it Margot could see a shadow come into the vestibule. She considered taking Florian's advice – there was a space next to the fridge in the alcove where she could hide – but in the next instant the bat appeared, filling the doorway like Count Dracula on the day he'd invited himself to tea.

"Madame Renard, could I see you in my office, please?"

"Actually, I was just about to—"

"*Now*, if you don't mind."

He turned and walked on, fully expecting her to follow. The contentious side of Margot's nature was tempted to stay right where she was, just to see what he would do. She'd never kowtowed to the Cousineaus of this world before and she wasn't about to start now. But Florian was giving her an expectant look, and deciding a little contrition was probably her best policy, Margot went after him.

She followed him across the internal bridge that linked the *Palais* to the courtroom and then took the first left to duck into his lair. It was probably just her imagination, but the senior *procureur's* office always felt a good five degrees cooler than the rest of the building. Cousineau was settling in at his desk, picking a piece of fluff from his starched white shirt-cuffs, mentally sharpening the words with which he was about to attack her.

"Close the door behind you."

Margot paused. Close it or slam it? It was tempting. As it was, she deliberately over-did it, closing it with a delicacy that would have shamed an angel.

"Sit down."

Margot faced him, hands behind her back. "I'd prefer to stand, if you don't mind."

"As you wish."

Cousineau leaned back in his seat, arching his fingers in true supervillain style.

"Did I or did I not advise you to tread carefully in your enquiries pertaining to the mayor?"

"Umm ... I believe you did say something to that effect, yes."

"Don't get cocky with me, Madame Renard."

"I wouldn't dream of it, Monsieur *le procureur*."

They stared each other out. Hard man vs. obstinate woman. Margot would not be budging one inch.

"You had no business going to Sète and harassing the mayor's friends."

"With respect, I didn't harass anyone. I was simply checking his alibi."

"And did it check out?"

Margot lowered her eyes. "That remains to be seen."

"Hunting down one of the mayor's business associates is not what I would call treading carefully. The mayor is not a person of interest in this enquiry. Is that understood?"

"I disagree."

Cousineau flinched. "I don't *care* whether you disagree or not. That is our position."

"Even though he was one of Sandrine's clients?"

"You have no evidence he's committed a crime."

"We're hardly likely to find any if we don't investigate."

"Besides which it's no reason to suspect him of any involvement in her murder. I'm sure this woman had hundreds of clients over the years."

"*This woman*," Margot said sternly, "was a unique and gifted individual and her name was Sandrine Bordes."

"I'm fully aware of her name."

Then use it, Margot was tempted to say.

Cousineau remained unmoved. Margot paused. After giving her head a few moments to cool, she went on:

"I'm guessing it was Remi Babineaux who told you?"

"Madame Renard—"

"Did I embarrass him in front of his business friends?"

Cousineau sighed. "Madame Renard, can we please forgo the theatrics? I've made our position perfectly clear. I'll be speaking with Captain Bouchard later today and when I do I'll be asking him to dispense with your assistance. You were employed at the *Palais* to review cold cases, and I respectfully suggest you confine yourself to doing just that. Do I make myself clear?"

"Perfectly."

"Thank you."

He picked up his pen and turned to his papers. When Margot failed to move, however, he looked up over the top of his glasses. "You may show yourself out."

Smouldering, Margot went to the door.

"Oh, and Madame Renard."

She spun. "Yes?"

Cousineau treated her to his smuggest of looks. "I will add that it was solely at the request of Judge Deveraux that you were asked to work here in the first place. In my view, your presence here is wholly unnecessary and I've yet to be persuaded you serve any useful purpose at all." He shot her a pinched smile. "Good-day."

Margot sensed Florian's eyes tracking her as she walked into the office and dropped into her chair, but she was too pumped up to acknowledge him. She snatched a stray sheet of paper from her desk, screwed it into a ball, and tossed it at the wastepaper bin. It missed. Typical.

"I'm guessing it didn't go well."

"Didn't you hear the screams from here?"

Florian pulled a strained face. "That bad?"

Elbows on the desk Margot sunk her chin into her hands. "Apparently, I serve no useful purpose at all."

He flinched. "Cousineau said that?"

She nodded.

"That man's unbelievable."

"I can think of a few other names I'd like to call him."

Florian got out of his seat. "Well, he's wrong. No one else in the *Palais* shares that opinion. We all think very highly of you."

Margot rallied. "Thank you, Florian. That's very kind." Though one small part of her couldn't help suspecting Cousineau had a point.

Her phone pinged. A text from Raymond:

Chef said I could cook one of the dishes from the tapas menu tonight. Would you like to be my guinea pig?

Margot replied immediately:

Your guinea pig will be there at seven. Fill me a bucket with wine, and have a straw at the ready.

19

The now customary visit to the pet shop on her way home: 2 packets of duck meat, gizzard and liver; 3 packets of salmon terrine; 1 bag of a new type of cheese treats they'd just had in. The feline wonder was stationed outside her kitchen door, looking none too pleased. If cats had wristwatches this one would be tapping its dial with a paw.

What time do you call this? Don't you know I have a stomach to fill? Here I am, literally STARVING to death, waiting for you to come home and feed me.

He followed her into the kitchen, and then wormed his way between her ankles while she opened the packet of duck meat, suddenly her very best friend in the whole wide world. Feeling rebellious, Margot took the saucer to the door of her salon and set it down on the threshold. Unmoved, the cat regarded her as if she'd taken leave of her senses.

"Come on," she said. "What's so different about eating in here, hmm?"

All the difference in the world, apparently. The feline wonder stubbornly rooted his backside to the spot.

Hands on hips, Margot gave him a look of consternation. “Aren’t I allowed just *one* small victory?”

Lacking the energy for another tug-of-war, however, she put the saucer back in its usual spot and stomped off upstairs.

After a shower, she changed into an oversized blue shirt, a pair of white shorts, and a tailored grey blazer. She wasn’t one for makeup but she applied a little rouge, a smear of lip gloss. She was in the mood to paint the town red.

Raymond, bless him, had a large glass of wine ready on the table. She kissed him on the forehead – “You’re an absolute star” – and settled into her seat. “So, what are you cooking for me tonight?”

“Cod cheek goujons with lemon aioli,” Raymond said proudly.

“Sounds delicious.”

“I tried it earlier and chef seemed to like it.”

“Have you filled in that application form yet?”

“I sent it off yesterday.”

“Well, fingers crossed.” Margot held them tightly crossed.

The moment he’d finished setting the table he hurried off to the kitchen. A minute later, Margot’s phone buzzed. A text from Stéphane:

I’m leaving for Strasbourg tomorrow. Can I see you before I go?

Margot put the phone down on the table while she lit a cigarette, though didn’t take her eyes off the screen. When it dimmed, she picked it up and read the message again. How did one go about trying to keep him interested while at the same time making it clear that all she was interested in was friendship? It had been such a long time since she’d last had to think these kinds of thoughts. Cigarette clamped between her lips, Margot thumbed a reply:

I’m eating at La Lune Bleue. Come and join me if you like.

She pinged him the location, then waited expectantly; excited when a reply came straight back:

I'll be there in ten minutes.

Smiling, Margot dropped the phone into her bag, still not entirely sure what she'd communicated.

The goujons were exceedingly tasty, the batter light and crispy, the cod cheeks perfectly moist. Stéphane turned up just as she was finishing, casting an uncertain look at the sea before pulling out a chair. A large wave had just come in, showering the flagstones just a few metres from where she was sitting.

"Are we safe here?"

"Don't worry, Toto. If we get washed away I'll save you."

He sat down on the leeway side of the table, and accepted the menu that Raymond brought over. Margot ordered another bottle of wine.

"This place is not easy to find," Stéphane said. "You'd think they would put up some signs."

"The owner dislikes tourists."

"Really? Isn't that rather like shooting yourself in the foot in a town like this?"

"A few of us discerning locals do rather appreciate it. What are you having?"

He ordered Moules Catalane. Margot asked for a plate of sea snails, shrimp and aioli to share. She emptied her wine glass, opened the second bottle, and gave herself a generous refill, prompting a raised eyebrow from Stéphane.

"Bad day?"

"You could say that."

She told him about her wild goose chase in Sète, the funeral, and then her dressing-down by Cousineau.

"He can't fire you. Speak to my mother. She'll put him in his place."

"I know," Margot said glumly. "It's just that, after being at

Sandrine's funeral this morning he caught me at a low ebb. Would you believe only three people turned up?"

"Why did you go?"

She shrugged forlornly. "I suppose I felt a connection with her. And then I began to wonder how many people would be at my funeral."

"Hundreds, surely."

Margot gave him a deliberate look, letting him do the maths: 0 children + 0 grandchildren + 0 nephews/nieces = 0 attendees to one's funeral. He seemed to get it.

Raymond came over with a small dish of olives stuffed with pimentos to snack on. Stéphane immediately got stuck in, happily spearing them with a cocktail stick.

"Anyway," he said. "Why would you want lots of people standing around, gawping? I certainly don't. Scatter my ashes over the nearest piece of turf, that'll do me."

"Don't you want your family to celebrate your life?"

"I'd much rather they did that while I was alive: a fanfare when I come home; a round of applause after I tell one of my jokes." He cocked his head, looking thoughtful. "Yes, I think I would like that. Or maybe, instead of a funeral, I could get blasted into space." He grinned excitedly. "Have my body drifting through the cosmos for the rest of eternity."

"Bumping into planets left, right and centre; your DNA spawning life on uninhabited rocks. Imagine that – a whole planet full of human rights lawyers." Margot shuddered. "It doesn't bear thinking about."

Stéphane grinned again, and had a big gulp of wine. "All right. So what did young Margot imagine she would be doing when she got to this stage of her life?"

Margot raised her glass. "Sipping cocktails on a yacht in the sunny Caribbean Sea."

He laughed. "What kind of job, I meant."

"When I was eight I wanted to be a ballerina. When I was eleven I wanted to be an Olympic diver. When I was thirteen I wanted to be a judge."

"So why aren't you any of those things?"

Margot looked into the bottom of the glass, watching the wine swirl. "Life has other ideas for us, I suppose."

Stéphane paused mid-chew, thinking about it. He tore off a piece of bread and used it to mop up the juices from the *moules*.

"I know what you mean. I'd been happily married for twenty years, I thought it would last forever. And then suddenly – *poof* – everything changed. My wife, who I thought adored me, had apparently met someone else. I wasn't what she wanted anymore, despite all the sweet things she'd said to me over the years. Inexplicable, I know, but true."

"Perhaps it was your ginormous head she'd taken exception to."

He thought about it. "Possibly, but highly unlikely."

Margot had to laugh.

"How have the kids been taking it?"

"Fine, on the surface. They've both got their heads screwed on. Manon will be going to *lycée* next year; Léo wants to join the naval academy."

He'd shown her photos last time he'd come down. Léo was his eldest at fourteen, Manon was ten. They'd seemed like nice kids.

"Will they stay with their mother?"

"We've not decided yet. They won't leave Strasbourg. Neither of us wants them uprooting. And if I do move I won't move far."

He offered her the last shrimp, and when she declined, used it to clean out the dish of aioli before popping it into his mouth.

"But my point is, even though my world got turned upside down and I have no idea what the future will hold, I'm excited. I can't wait to see what lies around the next corner."

He pushed away his plate of empty shells and gazed into her eyes. Shadowy in the candlelight, his face had a certain charm to it. More of the thoughts she hadn't had to think in a while crept into Margot's head. He reached for the wine bottle to top them both up, only realising it was empty when he tried to pour. Margot stubbed out her cigarette.

"Shall we go on somewhere?"

Stéphane twitched an eyebrow. "Where did you have in mind?"

"There's a nice bar up on Rue Militaire."

He nodded slowly. "Okay. But you have to promise not to throw anything at me."

Margot looked at him most seriously. "It will be hard, but I'll do my best."

They crossed the footbridge back to the harbourside and from there circled round to the promenade. Margot took him on a detour through the laneways so she could show him the new art installation – in the streets leading up to Rue Militaire, dozens of red and yellow umbrellas had been suspended on overhead wires. With the lights on and a breeze blowing, they looked like they were dancing on thin air.

At the top of the street, a set of old stone steps led down to a basement. One of the few things Margot missed about Paris was the night-life, but Bar La Liberté was one of the livelier spots in town, always full of chatter, and with live music on a Saturday night. They took stools at the bar, and after ordering a bottle of champagne Margot was tempted by the countertop menu.

"I feel a dessert coming on, don't you?" Chocolate and cherry tarte. Three different types of cheesecake. Apricot tarte tatin ... decisions, decisions.

Stéphane snatched up a menu. "Oh very well. If you insist."

Margot ordered the tarte tatin, he chose the chocolate cheesecake. The waiter brought the champagne in a bucket of ice and popped the cork, but Margot took the bottle from him and filled their glasses. She raised hers for a toast.

"To health and happiness, and no more funerals."

"*Santé.*"

Smiling, they clinked glasses.

"So tell me, Mister Human Rights Lawyer, what did you want to be when you were growing up?"

Stéphane had a quick slurp. "Well, not a human rights lawyer, if that's what you're thinking. Actually, I always wanted to be a magician."

"Really?"

He nodded.

"So why didn't you?"

He set down his glass. "My tricks kept going wrong. Every time I tried sawing a woman in half it didn't end well."

Margot laughed. "Would your parents have supported you if you had?"

"*Maman* certainly would have. She never pushed me to go into law."

"So why didn't you pursue it?"

He shrugged. "I suppose I just went with the flow. I was very academic at school. My teachers seemed to have a career path already mapped out for me."

"That's a shame. I can see it now, your name up in lights: The Great Stéphano and his troupe of one-legged assistants."

"You have a vivid imagination."

"Did you ever learn any tricks?"

"Oh yes. Quite a few. I can show you one now, if you like."

Margot had another sip of champagne. "Go on, then. As long

as it doesn't involve saws, knives, or any other sharp implements."

Stéphane summoned the bartender. "Could you pass me two straws, please?"

The bartender reached under the counter and handed him two black drinking straws. Stéphane made a show of unbuttoning his shirt cuffs, rolling his sleeves to his elbows, flexing his fingers like a bunch of wriggly worms. "Are you ready?"

"The suspense is killing me."

He started by holding the two straws together in an X shape, then began folding them at the centre, one over the other, in a seemingly random combination. After ten or so folds, he was left with a very tight knot with four stubby ends protruding. He held the lumpy piece of plastic up to her face.

"Am I meant to be impressed?" Margot asked flatly.

"I'm not finished yet. Blow."

She obliged.

He selected two of the stubby ends and pulled. Margot suspected they were meant to magically pull apart, but the look on Stéphane's face suggested something had gone wrong. The plastic lump remained firmly knotted.

"Oh."

"Maybe you should have pulled the other two ends."

"No. I'm sure I did it right."

His face was a picture of concentration as he began picking at the knot with a fingernail. Margot propped her cheek on her fist.

"Would you like a glamorous assistant?"

"No, thank you. I just need to undo this last bit here and then …"

"Is this going to take long?"

"Almost there."

"Only, I have a dental appointment at the end of next week."

"That's all very interesting, Margot, but you're really not helping."

"It's a good thing you're not chained up at the bottom of the ocean. I wouldn't think much of your chances, Houdini."

"Ha-ha, nearly there. If I can just re-fold this last bit like this, and then ..." His face brightened. "Ah – here we go."

He took hold of the two stubby ends and tried again. And got exactly the same result. Shoulders slumped, he glared at the straws in disbelief, and then threw it down on the bar-top in disgust. Margot laughed.

"You're not planning on giving up the day job, are you?"

He grumpily ignored her.

"Actually, I know a magic trick."

It took him a moment to get over his disappointment. He reached for his glass, and had a slurp.

"All right, smarty pants. Your turn."

"Are you ready for this?"

"I couldn't be more ready if I tried."

Margot licked her lips. She picked up her glass and held it in the space between them.

"Now. Watch me make this glass of champagne disappear."

She took a deep breath, raised the glass to her lips, and poured.

Margot ordered two Marc de Banyuls digestifs go to with their desserts, but when the food came she began to have second thoughts – Stéphane was already pie-eyed. The base of his cheesecake was a little overbaked and he spent a fruitless few seconds chasing it around his plate before finally managing to cut it with his spoon, shooting a piece over the edge in the process.

"Oops." He spluttered with laughter.

Margot picked it up off the floor.

"About that funeral of yours," he went on, slurring his words.

"What about it?"

He brandished his spoon. "I promise you, Margot, when the time comes I'll be there at your graveside, celebrating your life."

"Ah, you say the sweetest things."

"I mean it!"

"I'm sure you do." Margot downed the digestif. "Anyway. I suppose we'd better call it a night. You've got a train to catch in the morning and I have a lodger to pander to."

She paid the bill, but when she got up to leave, Stéphane remained on his stool, grinning. Margot gave him a curious look.

"What?"

"Nothing. It's just, this is how I always pictured you spending your evenings: a cigarette in one hand, a bottle of champagne in the other. Caro Emerald singing in the background."

Margot smiled sweetly. "Thank you. I do rather like Caro Emerald." Plus, she had enjoyed a liquid lunch or two.

Outside, the cool night air took them by surprise. Stéphane came to a halt at the top of the steps and swayed on his feet, looking a little green around the gills.

"I think I should probably sit down."

"I think you better had."

Margot steered him to a bench. She kept a close eye on him while she lit a cigarette, hoping he wasn't going to throw up. Sometimes she forgot other people lacked her ability to metabolise alcohol. She gazed down fondly at the town. She'd forgotten what a good view there was to be had from up here. There was something special about a seaside town at night that had always excited her. The water was there; you could hear it and smell it, but you just couldn't see it. Like some giant beast had taken a big bite out of the world. Stéphane was slowly tilting in her direction.

"When the time does come, Margot, what do you imagine you'll die of?"

"Hmm ... A bullet in the back from a jealous wife."

He laughed. "Somehow I really don't think so."

She was being flippant. The idea of cheating was anathema to her. She flicked the ash from her cigarette, and blew the smoke out of her lungs.

"I knew this man once," she said reflectively. "A proper old gent he was. He must have been well into his eighties when I met him. His fiancé had died during the war, but he never considered marrying anyone else. He said she'd been the love of his life so he spent the rest of his days living alone."

"Your point being?"

"My point being ... some people are like swans, they stay loyal for life. Yet others are like sparrows, they go with whatever's there."

He spluttered. "That's a little unfair on sparrows, isn't it?"

"It's not," Margot scoffed. "The sex lives of sparrows, look it up. They're the Don Juans of the bird world."

"Are they really? I never knew that."

"So, which are you, Stéphane – a swan or a sparrow?"

He gave it his fullest consideration. "A swan or a sparrow ... Isn't there a happy medium?"

"What – like a *swarrow*, you mean?"

He looked her in the eye, perfectly still for a moment, but then burst into laughter. He laughed so much his whole body shook.

"A *swarrow*!" he gasped.

Margot rolled her eyes. "It wasn't that funny."

But he just couldn't stop. Tears streamed down his cheeks; he clutched his chest like his rib cage were about to implode.

"Someone's going to have a thick head in the morning."

When he started to slide off the bench, Margot had to grab hold of his arm.

"I think we'd better get you back to your mother's."

"Yes. I think that would probably be a good idea."

Margot walked him up to the main road, put him in a taxi, and then headed home.

20

Célia was back from the hospital by eleven the next morning. Despite three days of treatment, she was bearing up well. Sitting up at her desk, she watched with amusement as Margot walked in.

"I gather you had quite a night."

"Ah."

Margot halted two metres from the desk, briefly lost for words. Célia went on:

"Not that I was able to get anything intelligible out of Stéphane last night. He could hardly string two words together."

"He got home all right, then?"

"Oh yes, he got home all right, although I don't think I've ever seen him so intoxicated in his life."

Margot covered the final two metres to the desk. "Sorry," she smiled, and Célia smiled back.

"There's no need to apologise, Margot. He could do with letting his hair down once in a while. Anyway, he sends his regards – he was vaguely awake when we dropped him off at the station." She came out from behind her desk and indicated the easy chairs in the corner. "I wanted to speak to you about Cousineau. I gather the two of you had words."

They sat. Margot told her side of the story. "I probably should have waited for the captain. Perhaps then Monsieur Babineaux wouldn't have run off on me."

"I have encountered Remi Babineaux before, actually."

"Oh – when was that?"

"It was some time ago. One of his employees was involved in a sexual assault on a sixteen-year-old. Babineaux vouched for him, but I remember at the time feeling he wasn't being entirely honest."

"Did you know he's a friend of Lefève?"

"Lefève wasn't mayor back then. It was only when I heard his name mentioned that it came back to me. But what I wanted to say was, this is my case now and far from warning you off I want you to pursue it. Be discrete, of course, but as far as I'm concerned Lefève is very much an active line of enquiry."

"And Cousineau?"

Célia patted her hand reassuringly. "Leave Cousineau to me."

Buoyed by the vote of confidence, Margot went back to Florian's office. She checked to make sure no one was lurking in the corridor and then eased the door to behind her.

"Florian," she said quietly. "Do you think you could do a little research for me?"

Florian pushed his spectacles up the bridge of his nose, intrigued. "Of course. What do you want to know?"

"I want you to find out everything you can about the mayor: his past and present business dealings; anything in his personal life that seems out of the ordinary."

"Okay."

"And in particular, I want to know what he was up to fourteen years ago. If he has any connection with Ginette Clément, anything at all, I want to know about it."

Florian seemed surprised. "You don't think he was involved in that case, do you?"

"He's hiding something. Her name struck a nerve when I mentioned it to him."

Florian seemed excited by the challenge. "I'll get onto it as soon as I can."

"Thank you. But Florian—" she pressed a finger to her lips "—keep it hush-hush for now. We don't want you-know-who finding out."

Her phone rang. Margot stepped back to her desk to take it.

"Hello."

"Are you the lady who called me the other day, asking about Sylvie B.?"

Margot recognised the voice. "Alain?"

"Yeah. Hey – I'm sorry I didn't show up at the café. I wanted to check with Sylvie first, see if she was okay with it."

"And was she?"

"If you're trying to find out who murdered Sandrine then she's happy to talk. I think you'll be interested in what she has to say."

Now Margot was intrigued. She sat down at her desk. "Okay. So how do I find her?"

"Are you free today?"

"I can be."

"Can you meet me at the same café? Two o'clock."

Margot checked the time. 10:07.

"All right. I'll need to get hold of a car, but I should be able to make it."

He rang off.

Margot didn't even need to ask: Florian, having evidently

picked up on what had been said, reached into his pocket and offered up his car keys.

The only solitary man seated outside Café Olivier was fortyish, had short grey hair, and was wearing a ring in his nose. Margot went straight to him.

"Alain?"

He put down the magazine he'd been reading and flashed her an up-and-down look. Half rising, he shook her hand, bangles and bands hanging loose on his wrist. Margot pulled out a chair, and signalled to the waiter for a coffee.

"Thanks for agreeing to see me. You said Sylvie had something to tell me."

"Is this an official visit?"

Margot looked him in the eye. "Does that make a difference?"

Alain half smiled. "Sylvie would prefer it to be off the record."

"It depends on what she has to say, but I'll see what I can do. How do I contact her?"

Alain hesitated, appearing to weigh her up. Margot waited, and after a few moments he gave in.

"I'll show you how to get to her shack."

He took a small sketchpad out of his bag and began drawing a map. From the way he was describing it, Sylvie's *étang* was not the one she'd visited last time but another further up the coast. He drew an X to mark the location of the fishing shack.

"The easiest way of getting to it is across the water. She keeps a rowboat tied up around here." A smaller x marked the spot. "But you can also walk." He drew a dashed line along the shore to indicate a footpath. "Just stay clear of the reeds."

"Is she there now?"

"I'll call her to let her know you're coming, but Sylvie's a free spirit. She'll probably want to check you out first. If she likes what she sees she'll come to you."

"And if she doesn't?"

Alain shrugged with his mouth.

Margot fixed him with a sceptical look. It all seemed a bit unnecessary, a little too cloak and dagger. "Can't you just give me her number?"

He firmly shook his head. "No can do. Sylvie doesn't like people bothering her. But you've got my number. Call me if you get lost."

He tore the page out of his sketchpad and handed it over. Margot hesitated, thinking if there was anything else she needed to ask. Despite his offer, she had the feeling that once he'd gone her only chance of speaking to Sylvie would go with him. Unable to come up with anything, she thanked him again and then returned to the car.

The road he'd told her to follow headed north, into a watery landscape that was becoming very familiar to her. A few kilometres out of town the road opened up, and the little Fiat got buffeted by a keen wind coming in off the sea. Margot was meant to look out for the entrance to a dirt track, and although a couple of likely candidates suggested themselves, both were blocked by barriers just a few metres in. After a few twists and turns, she entered an area where the vegetation was thicker, and spotting an opening at the very last second, slammed on her brakes. Luckily, no one was following.

She reversed. The track was wide enough to drive down, but a few metres in the vegetation started to encroach. Alain had told her to drive for half a kilometre, but with spindly branches beginning to scrape the side of Florian's car, Margot was forced to pull up.

She turned off the ignition, and got out. The track didn't appear to be well used. The ground was puddled and pot-holed, and her tyre marks were the only ones to be seen. Margot locked the car and continued on foot.

It was more sheltered on this side of the road and only an occasional flurry of wind made it through. She picked her way between prickly shrubs, and after fighting on for five or six minutes emerged on the edge of the *étang*. Miles of untroubled water spread out before her, while out in the centre a small flock of birds were taking flight. She could have been stepping into a scene from one of Sylvie's photographs.

The ground ahead was covered in reeds and tall grasses. Swarms of tiny flying insects began buzzed around her. Taking heed of Alain's warning, Margot came away from the reeds and moved in a wide arc, eventually finding a route to higher ground. A few minutes later she appeared to have arrived in the right place – protruding from the edge of the reeds was a small wooden rowboat.

The ground was too muddy to follow a direct route so she continued to take the long way round. An old wooden jetty came into view. The boat was moored at the far end, secured to an upright with a padlock and chain.

The planks looked rotten; Margot tested one with her foot before stepping out. She stayed close to one edge, using the handrail for support. Scanning the water, she looked for a shack. If she was interpreting the map correctly, the cross signified a point away to her right, and there was indeed a building over there, nestled on the inner shore of a small bay, almost hidden by trees. It looked very run down, and there were no signs of life, and since the rowboat was tied up here it was reasonable to assume Sylvie wasn't there.

Margot turned around, senses on the alert. *She'll probably check you out first,* Alain had said. Was she out there right now, hiding in those bushes, watching her every move?

She slapped a fly away from her face and took a fresh look at the map. The dashed line Alain had drawn showed the path skirting the shoreline, but there was no obvious sign of a way through, just more reeds and then scrub. Margot was tempted to swim across – it was the shortest route – but she hadn't brought her swimsuit, or a waterproof bag. And the light was beginning to fade. The reeds didn't look too thick on this side so she decided to risk it.

Her shoes moved on a slippery layer of mud. She wished she'd worn her boots, and something with long sleeves – sharp stems scratched horribly at her bare arms. To make matters worse, the swarm of flies appeared to be following her, and something began biting her ankles. And either she was sinking, or the reeds were getting taller. After a dozen or so metres Margot gave up. Angry and frustrated, she turned around and retraced her steps to the jetty.

A rustling in the bushes made her halt. Margot scanned around, eyes probing the vegetation.

"Hello," she called out.

A movement in her peripheral vision pulled her gaze to one side. But it was just a small bird, darting between the branches.

Margot exhaled. Enough was enough. It was starting to get dark, and there was no knowing when Sylvie might turn up, if at all. She checked her phone – no missed calls – and then went back to the car.

She decided to give it another ten minutes, and sat with her arms folded, listening to the quiet. When her eyelids started to grow heavy, she couldn't resist closing them. And it seemed she must have nodded off because the next thing she knew she was being woken by a gentle tapping on the window.

21

Darkness lay beyond the windows of Florian's Fiat 500 and Margot began to suspect she'd been hearing things. But then a torch came on and a bright light shone into her eyes.

Margot shielded her face. Behind the light, she had the impression a person was standing close to the car. After a few moments, the light swung aside and a grey shape advanced.

"Sorry. I didn't mean to startle you."

A female voice, muted by the glass. Margot lowered the window.

"Sylvie?"

"I'm guessing you're Margot."

Margot pushed open the door. With her retinas still green, she could only discern the outline of the figure wielding the torch. She appeared quite short, and solidly built. Suddenly alive to the possibility she'd been confronted by an axe-wielding murderer, Margot glanced at the woman's other hand, relieved to see she was unarmed. She got out of the car, and tried to relax.

"You're a hard woman to find."

"Suits me."

A vehicle drove by on the road, headlights cutting through the scrub. Viewed from a passing car they must have looked a suspicious pair. Margot offered a small smile.

"Did you just get here? I found your rowboat."

Wherever she might have been, Sylvie didn't own up. She flashed the light in Margot's eyes again, though this time it appeared accidental.

"We can talk in my shack, if you like. It'll be more comfortable there."

"Okay."

"Follow me, but stay close. There are a lot of potholes around here."

Sylvie moved swiftly across the marshy ground, clearly used to the lie of the land. In the space of a few minutes they were back at the jetty. She set the torch down on the planks while she kneeled to unfasten the padlock, and then clambered down into the boat, revealing a little more of herself in the process. Her black hair was tied into a ponytail, and she was wearing a green corduroy jacket with black, loose-fitting jeans. Safely seated, she retrieved the torch and aimed the light at the bench seat.

"Come aboard."

The boat rocked as Margot stepped in. Sylvie waited for her to get settled and then switched off the light. She pushed them away from the jetty, and once they were clear dug in an oar and pulled. With a gentle series of sploshes, they set off across the *étang*.

Sylvie handled the boat with ease and instantly found her rhythm. They glided across the water at a quick and even pace. Now that the wind had dropped, the lagoon was as still as a millpond, the quietness only disturbed by the wingbeats of late-arriving birds settling into their roosts. Surrounded by such serenity, it wasn't hard to see why Sylvie was so enamoured of the place.

After about five minutes they rounded the headland and entered the small bay. From over Sylvie's shoulder, Margot watched the shack slowly draw near. Another small jetty jutted out from the bank, and despite having her back to it Sylvie steered them in unerringly. As they drew up alongside she twisted her body, and in one fluid movement stowed the oars, reached for an upright, and then gently pulled them in.

Margot climbed out. Alone on the jetty for a moment, she cast a hesitant look around. She had visions of being hit over the head and dragged into the shack by a clique of fanatical artists, keen to incorporate her into their latest avant-garde installation. But after securing the boat, Sylvie merely flicked her a smile.

"This way," she said, and set off towards the shack.

It quickly became apparent the building wasn't as tumble-down as it had appeared from across the water. Tatty sheets of metal had been used on its walls, but they looked like they'd been installed for effect rather than utility. The two small windows were double-glazed, and although from a distance the roof had appeared rotten and carpeted with weeds, Margot could now see that it was a green roof, covered with sedums and other small plants. The gable end, which looked out over the water, was one large glazed frame.

The rear of the shack was raised on stilts meaning they had to ascend a short flight of steps. Sylvie unlocked the door with a key, reached inside, and flicked on the light.

Rather than a chamber of horrors, the interior was a tiny-house dream. The raised level contained a kitchenette and a bedroom that linked through to a bathroom, all three marvels of design. The roofline continued at the same level all the way through meaning that going down the steps to the lower level created the illusion of entering a much larger space. A daybed was built into one side, opposite that was a matching sofa, while bookcases filled in the spaces above. Old wide planks covered the floor, the remainder was strip pine.

"Nice place you have here."

"It beats working in an office. Make yourself comfortable." Sylvie gestured at the sofa. "Would you like a drink?"

She was holding up a bottle of whisky. Margot was tempted, but sensibly asked for a coffee instead. Despite being invited to sit, she turned to the big window and moved her face close to the glass. It was dark outside and all she could see was her own shadowy reflection.

"It's better in daytime," Sylvie said. "You can see right across the lagoon."

"I can imagine." Margot turned back to the kitchen. "I saw your work at Galerie Soleil. It was remarkable."

"Thank you. Two years I spent on that. Some people don't realise how long it takes to create art."

"Did you live out here the whole time?"

Sylvie came down with the drinks, handing the coffee to Margot, holding onto a glass of water for herself.

"Pretty much. I have a place in Montpelier but I prefer it here. You can't beat the smell of the water first thing in the morning." She sat on the daybed, right foot tucked under her left thigh. "Or maybe it's that I just don't like people."

She smiled. Properly revealed in the light, Sylvie came across as much more agreeable. Margot could only guess at her age. She had one of those faces that made it difficult to tell: she could have been thirty; she could have been fifty.

"Alain said you were asking about Sandrine."

"That's right." Margot took a seat on the sofa. "How long had you known her?"

"It must have been around a year. We used to meet up whenever she was in the area. I can't believe what happened to her, especially in her condition."

Margot frowned. “How do you mean?”

“Well, she was pregnant, wasn’t she. Didn’t you know?”

“We did, but we didn’t know if Sandrine knew.”

“Oh, she knew, all right, though it took her by surprise. I mean, she was on the pill. It must have been a lucky bullet.”

“Did she know who the father was?”

“I think she had an idea but didn’t want to say until she knew for sure.”

“Did she ever mention a Doctor Roche? Doctor Lucien Roche?”

Sylvie had a sip of water and then shook her head. “I’ve not heard that name before. I know she was worried about how she was going to feel about having another baby. I mean, given what happened with Lya. But I said to her, maybe this was her second chance. I think underneath she was excited. And she was already looking forward to getting Lya back.”

Margot regarded her in surprise. “What makes you think she was getting Lya back?”

“She told me so. She’d already done up her spare room; she showed me the pictures.”

“You do know the full history with Lya?”

“You mean how she abandoned her in the park?”

Margot nodded.

“That was all behind her. She was desperate to have Lya back; she talked about her all the time. She used to stand outside the school gates, watching her ex pick her up.” Sylvie bared her teeth. “He was such a bastard to her.”

“When did you last see her?”

“Two weeks ago. She’d decided to give up the sex work. She wanted to find a job that made use of her degree.”

“How did she seem at that time?”

“Happy. Happier than I’d seen her in ages.”

Margot looked for somewhere to put down her coffee cup.

The wood on the bookshelves was too nice to risk staining so she set it down on the floor instead.

"I wanted to ask you about the night she was killed. Jean-Paul Lefève told us he came to your exhibition."

"That's right."

"Did you invite him, or was it your father?"

"Well, it certainly wasn't me."

She held Margot's eye but didn't go on. After a few moments, she got up and went to the kitchen. Giving up on the water, she poured herself a small whisky and came back down the steps. Margot waited until she'd retaken her place on the daybed.

"You sound like you don't like him."

Sylvie had a sip of the whisky. "Lefève has no interest in art. He just likes to be seen at the right events."

"Did anything out of the ordinary happen that night?"

"Not that I recall. It was a good night, actually. Everyone was very appreciative. I sold quite a few prints. And Lefève was on his best behaviour."

"How do you mean?"

"Have you met him?"

"Just once."

"And once was enough, right?"

Margot couldn't resist a wry smile.

"He thinks he's a charmer, but he hasn't got the class. He likes to belittle people. Talk down to them. But he did seem quiet that night. Like he had something on his mind. He usually likes to be the centre of attention, the loudest voice in the room." She shrugged. "Maybe he was unwell."

"What time did you all leave?"

"We stayed until the end. Around eleven."

"And then ...?"

"My friend in Agde was having a party. We got there around eleven-thirty."

"Did Lefève go with you?"

"Yes ... Well, actually, no he didn't. I went with Alain in his van and Lefève got into a car with my father. But when we got to Agde it was just the three of us. Lefève had changed his mind."

"Why was that?"

"My father didn't say."

"So Lefève didn't go to the party at all?"

"No. My father stayed for an hour, and then went home. The rest of us slept over."

"And you didn't see Lefève again that night?"

"No."

Margot paused. So that was at least one lie he'd told them. Sylvie leaned towards her, an interested look on her face.

"Are you thinking Lefève had something to do with her death?"

Margot locked eyes with her. "Would it surprise you if I said yes?"

Sylvie gave it some thought, and then lightly shrugged her shoulders. Margot went on:

"In her diary, Sandrine suggested she knew Lefève had a secret. Do you know what she meant by that?"

Sylvie swallowed. "No."

"Are you sure? Alain seemed to think there was something you wanted to tell me."

Her eyes were saying yes but her body language said no. Sylvie got to her feet and went to face the glazed screen. She stared into the darkness for a little while, and when she turned, her face had changed, the friendliness gone.

"You need to look into his background. And if I were you I'd start by looking into the library project."

"You mean the library in Argents?"

Sylvie nodded.

Margot searched her memory. She vaguely recalled seeing a

flyer about a big redevelopment but couldn't remember any of the details.

"What's his involvement in that?"

"It's all there if you look for it. But I won't be giving a statement. If you try to involve me I'll deny everything I've just said to you."

Margot straightened, surprised by her sudden change of mood. She got to her feet.

"All right. I won't mention your name."

Sylvie looked obliged. "Good. If you're ready to go now I'll take you back."

22

Arriving at work at eight-thirty, Margot sat at her computer and typed: 'Argents-sur-Mer library' into a search engine. It came up with the same set of results she'd seen on her computer at home last night: articles from the local newspaper, some computer-generated images, even a scale model that someone had had mocked up. Despite having already been extended, the plans showed another large addition tacked onto the library's sea-facing elevation which, together with a complete re-modelling of the existing building, would create a 300-seat theatre, a gallery, a few small shops and a brand-new *Office du Tourisme*.

She typed in: 'Jean-Paul Lefève's involvement in Argents-sur-Mer library'. Internet search engines could be wonderful things yet they could also be annoyingly stupid. All it came back with were either results that had come up in the first search or items related to Lefève with no connection to the library whatsoever. The world was safe from AI for now.

Florian came in at nine. He shouldered off his bag and unloaded his files while Margot relieved him of the patisserie box. She took the box to the cubby hole and checked that all the cakes were present and correct, catching a little chocolate on her thumb in the process. She licked it off and then pushed the button to set the coffee machine in motion.

"Florian," she said, arms folded, shoulder against the door jamb. "What do you know about the library project?"

"The *library* project?"

Margot counted to ten. Given what time she'd returned his car to him yesterday, however, she forgave him that one.

"Not a lot. I know they've been talking about it for years. Didn't they want to start building it soon?"

"I've no idea. It was Sylvie who told me about it." The machine finished making his latte so she picked it up and carried it to his desk. "Is there anything controversial about it?"

"Not that I know of."

"Who would be the planning authority here – the Mairie or the prefecture?"

"Oh, the Mairie," Florian said without hesitation. "Nothing much goes on in Argents without Lefève's approval."

"So if I wanted to view the planning file presumably I would have to go there in person?"

"I would think so."

"Hmm." Margot pondered. She would have to choose her moment. Imagine bumping into Lefève while she was busy checking up on him.

She waited until ten. First, she called in at the Gendarmerie. Uncertain of the reception she was going to get, Margot approached the captain's office with caution. The door was open, but she knocked anyway. The captain looked up from his papers.

"Bonjour, Madame. I'm glad you called in."

"You are?" Margot remained on the threshold, giving him a puzzled look.

He returned an equally perplexed frown. "Is everything all right?"

"Has Cousineau spoken to you yet?"

The captain appeared to cotton on. He leaned back in his chair, trying to conceal a smile. "He came to see me yesterday afternoon."

"I'm guessing he wasn't very pleased."

"He was rather vexed."

"He told me he was going to ask you to dispense with my assistance."

"So he did, but that doesn't mean I have to comply."

Margot gave him a fond look. "That's very noble of you, Captain, but perhaps it's for the best. I wouldn't want you to get into any trouble."

"Trouble?" the captain said in surprise. He suddenly seemed keen to stand up. "There will be no trouble, Madame, I assure you. I am a captain in the *Gendarmerie nationale*. I answer to my commanding officer, not the *procureur*."

Margot could have hugged him.

A different receptionist was on duty at the Mairie. Margot asked for directions to the planning department and was pointed to a door beneath the first flight of stairs.

It opened into a short, covered passage that dog-legged into what must once have been the building's central courtyard. A modern single-storey building now occupied the space, its walls flimsy in comparison with the solid stone structures surrounding it.

Double swing doors opened onto a tiny reception area. Beyond the counter, a large open-plan office was crammed with all manner of shelves and filing cabinets, while the floorspace was dotted with small towers of books. Florian would have loved it in there. Despite there being at least six desks, only one was in use, and it was occupied by a rather grey-looking man who sat staring at a screen, looking like he hadn't abandoned his post for at least two decades. Margot's heart sank. Having experienced French bureaucracy before, she had visions of being trapped in a Kafkaesque nightmare and wondered if she should send out a message: *If I'm not back within three days someone come and rescue me.*

The clerk had seen her but he gave no indication of coming over. Margot made a point of staring at him while she pushed the little plastic buzzer on the countertop. A full thirty seconds passed before he stopped what he was doing, cranked some life into himself, and came to the counter.

"Yes, Madame."

She smiled politely. "I was wondering if I could view the planning file for the library extension."

"Did you make an appointment?"

"Sorry, no."

"Do you have the reference number?"

And here began the bureaucratic purgatory. Margot mentally rolled back her eyes, but managed to keep a cool head.

"Sorry, I have no idea what the reference number is. I'm not doing very well, am I?"

The clerk's face was a block of ice.

"It's for the big redevelopment," Margot went on hopefully. "You must have heard of it."

It looked like her words were falling on deaf ears, but the ice block slowly began to thaw. A glimmer of a smile even appeared on his face.

"All right. Wait here and I'll see what I can find."

After returning to his computer and making a note, he disappeared into the back. Margot feared he would be gone for an hour, but five minutes later the clerk returned with a bulging archive box in his arms. He groaned as he heaved it up onto the counter.

"There you go. Let me know when you've finished."

"Thank you so much."

Margot slid the box to the end of the counter, around the corner, and then let it drop onto the lower table at the side. It was full to the brim with paperwork. Not really knowing what she was looking for, she glanced at the various files and folders as she took them out. Public consultation documents, environmental impact studies, traffic flow reports ... the list seemed endless. Around halfway down was a folder of blueprints. The first one she unfolded was a set of elevations. Architecturally, it was a fine-looking proposal. An undulating roofline would mirror the adjacent hillside, big windows would look out over the sea. Timber, and other sustainably-sourced materials would be used in its construction, and much of the roof would be covered in solar panels.

Going back through some of the files she'd taken out, Margot found some notes from the council meeting at which the application had been discussed. None of the councillors had voiced an objection. Virtually all the comments she read were positive. A dozen full-time jobs would be created, and a big new car park would help ease the town's traffic problems. A dedicated cycleway would link the development to the cycle path that ran alongside the promenade. The only naysayer had been the owner of a local bar who'd feared the new building would spoil his view, but that seemed to have been discounted and the *Permis d'aménager* had been issued five months ago. She could find no details on how the project would be funded, but Margot was at a loss to see how any of it could reflect badly on Lefève.

She looked at her watch. Over an hour had gone by. Convinced she wasn't going to find anything of use, Margot began putting it all back. And it was as she was folding up the blueprint that a big red flag went up in her mind. Down in the title box in the bottom righthand corner she spotted a familiar logo: Babineaux Construction.

23

Margot failed to recognise him at first – the man in the wheelchair emerging from Célia's office – but as his two burly warders pushed him along the corridor she was stunned to realise it was Gy Berger. He raised his eyes as they passed, but his face remained blank. He barely moved a muscle as they wheeled him across to the elevator. They might as well have been pushing a corpse.

"Ah, Margot – there you are." Inside the office, Célia had spotted her through the open door. "Would you come in for a moment, please?"

Margot closed the door behind her and then approached the desk, still troubled by what she'd seen. "He looks terrible."

"I've spoken to his doctor. If he doesn't eat something today they'll start feeding him through a tube."

"Did you just interview him?"

"I did."

"What did you think?"

Célia put the top back on her pen. "He's clearly a troubled young man. I've asked for a psychiatric assessment. But as far as the evidence goes I'm afraid it doesn't look good for him."

Margot sighed. It would have been naïve to expect anything else but she still felt disappointed. "I just keep remembering the look in his eyes when he denied it. I'm sure in his own way he did love Sandrine."

"I don't disagree, but love can turn so easily to hate. We've seen it often enough. The DNA test confirmed he wasn't the father of Sandrine's baby. And neither was Patrice Fabron."

Thank god for that, Margot said to herself. The world didn't deserve any of his offspring.

"Any news on that mystery doctor?" Célia asked.

"I think Lieutenant Martell's still trying to track him down."

"And what about you, Margot? How have you been getting on?"

Margot filled her in on her visit to the *étang* and her lead on the library project.

"I still need to do some digging, but if Remi Babineaux is involved I'm not surprised something fishy is going on."

"Sylvie wouldn't give you any details?"

Margot shook her head. "I'm guessing she's conflicted. She wanted to implicate Lefève but not her father. I was going ask Florian to look into the financing of the project, assuming you've no objection?"

"None at all."

"And," Margot went on hesitantly, not sure of the response she would get after the way Cousineau had reacted, "I would like to arrange an interview with Remi Babineaux. It would be nice to question him without fear he might run off."

"Have you discussed it with Captain Bouchard?"

"I have. He's on board."

"Then go ahead. Confine your questions to Lefève's alibi for now. Let's wait and see what Florian comes up with before we quiz him on the library project."

Margot smiled. "Thank you."

Somewhere in the bowels of the building she imagined Cosuineau grumpily biting the head off a small rodent.

After being assured Babineaux would be at the construction site all day, they drove to Sète and arrived just after lunch. As they pulled into the dusty compound, Margot spotted the silver Mercedes parked in the same shady spot.

The receptionist in the Portakabin confirmed the boss was somewhere on site, but when they went back outside and asked around, no one seemed willing or able to pinpoint his actual whereabouts. A dump truck rumbled by, so close they had to step out of the way. Losing patience, Captain Bouchard strode back into the office and interrupted the woman who was now speaking on the phone.

"Madame, you can either contact Monsieur Babineaux and tell him we're here or I'll have the health and safety office, immigration, and every available member of the local tax department crawling over this site within the hour. Do I make myself clear?"

Surprised by the outburst, the woman cradled her phone. She switched to her mobile, and after mumbling a few words raised her eyes back to the captain.

"If you wait by the main gate someone will be right out."

"Thank you."

A workman was already there. Even so, it seemed Babineaux hadn't yet finished playing games with them.

"He's up on the scaffold. Top floor. If you want to speak to him you'll have to go up." He pointed skyward.

"No problem," Margot said.

"And you'll need to wear these." He handed out a couple of hard hats and a pair of *gilets jaunes*, grinning as he did so. "If you're afraid of heights I recommend you don't look down."

They followed him up six long ladders, Margot taking up the rear. The view down was indeed dizzying in places, but a combination of netting and hoarding screened them from the biggest of the drops. On the fifth level, the workman waited for them to catch up, still looking smug. When Margot stepped off the final rung, he pointed to the farthest corner.

"Remi's in the unit at the end. Tell him I said hi."

Without waiting for a response, he swung his body around the ladder and went back down.

Scaffold boards wobbled under their feet as they made their way to the end of the run. Around the corner, an opening in the wall gave access to one of the apartments, though it was a big step down. The captain went first, and then turned to give Margot a hand. Remi Babineaux, talking with two men, noticed them immediately. He dismissed the men and called them over to an inner room.

Building materials cluttered the space. After they'd negotiated their way around a stack of plasterboards, they joined him in the inner room. From the number of pipes and cables sticking out of the walls Margot guessed it would one day be the kitchen, though a good deal of imagination was required. On the other side of a partition, a noisy power tool was going full blast, sending clouds of dust billowing through a nearby doorway. Babineaux had to raise his voice over the racket:

"Sorry I couldn't come down," he said without a hint of apology. "You know what contractors are like: they'll stand around talking all day if someone's not here to crack the whip."

Yet he was the only one Margot had seen standing around talking.

"So what's the emergency?"

The captain cast an irritated look at the cloud of dust. "Could you ask them to be quiet for a moment?"

Babineaux didn't seem happy about it. He waited a full five

seconds before hanging his head around the corner and whistling a command. The noise of the power tool died down.

"Every second they're not working costs me money," he said as the dust began to settle. "I hope you realise that."

"This won't take long," Captain Bouchard said. "Assuming you cooperate."

"What do you want to know?"

"Two weeks ago," Margot said, "you went to your daughter's exhibition at Galerie Soleil."

"That's right."

"A number of witnesses saw you leave around eleven."

"So?"

"Would you mind telling us where you went?"

"Agde. One of my daughter's friends was having a party. I stayed for an hour and then went home. Next question."

"How did you get from Sète to Agde?"

"In a car."

"Was anyone in the car with you?"

He heaved a frustrated sigh. "Why do I get the feeling I should have a lawyer present?"

"There's no need for lawyers if you're telling the truth, Monsieur," the captain responded. "Lie to us, however, and there will be consequences."

Babineaux swallowed awkwardly, beginning to look a little out of his depth.

"All right. There was someone with me. John-Paul Lefève."

"Did he go to the party with you?"

"No. I dropped him off on the way."

"Where?"

"In town. Don't ask me the address. All I know is it's called Club Chinois."

"Why did he want to go there?"

"Beats me."

"He must have given a reason."

Babineaux shrugged. "Perhaps he wanted to meet someone. You'll have to ask him. I'm his friend, not his keeper."

"Did you see him go into the club?"

"Yes."

"What time was this?"

"I got to the party at midnight so it must have been around eleven-thirty."

"You didn't wait for him?"

"No."

"So, the last time you saw him that night was when he went into this club at eleven-thirty. Is that correct?"

"Bingo."

Depending on what he was doing at the club, that still gave him time to get back to Argents in time to kill Sandrine. It would be cutting it fine but it was still possible. And that was assuming Babineaux was telling them the truth, of course. Margot and the captain exchanged a glance. They were done.

"Thank you for your time, Monsieur," the captain said. "We'll be in touch."

"Fine." Babineaux sneered aggrievedly. "Mind your step on the way down."

The captain accelerated away from the toll booth and peeled off into the lane that looped round onto the autoroute. Beside him in the passenger seat, Margot slumped, overcome with drowsiness. Trying to stay awake, she flicked through the pages of the Babineaux Construction brochure that she'd picked up from the site office. It was a sizeable operation. Dozens of glossy photographs illustrated some of the projects they'd been involved in, ranging from office blocks to warehouses, landmark apartment buildings to state-of-the-art production facilities. On the scale they operated, the library in Argents would be small fry, hardly worth the risk for a man of Babineaux's means. If they had done a deal it was most likely favouring Lefève rather than the former stonemason.

Yet if this was the secret Sandrine had found out, she hadn't been blackmailing him. At least, not for money. There were other things she might have been leveraging from a man with the power and influence of Lefève.

But it was all just idle speculation at the moment. Margot turned to look through the window, watching the traffic speed by. Travelling on the autoroute always had a hypnotic effect upon her, and sometimes brought back unpleasant memories. She blinked deeply to try and stay alert, and went back to the brochure. The last few pages contained headshots of the board of directors, including a rather flattering one of Remi himself, and then, inside the back cover, was a list of the various organisations and sports teams the company sponsored. Nothing seemed in any way suspicious until one name jumped out at her. Margot flinched.

"That's interesting."

Captain Bouchard emerged from his thoughts. "What's interesting?"

Margot pointed, but since he was concentrating on the road she said it out loud:

"Babineaux Construction sponsor Argents rugby club."

24

"Lieutenant Martell – just the man I was hoping to see."

On the other side of the Perspex screen, Martell gasped theatrically. "Madame Renard, I thought this day would never come. How can I assist you this fine Saturday morning?"

If this guy ever decided to give up police work he had a future on the stage.

"Which rugby team do you play for?"

"Me? I play for SC Millas. And a very fine team they are, too."

"Do you know much about Argents SCR?"

He nodded his head appreciatively. "Argents are a good team. They're in the league above us so we've never actually played them. They had a very good season last year, narrowly missed out on promotion. Are you coming through?"

Margot nodded. The lieutenant moved round to the connecting door and let her in. "Why do you ask?"

"Lefève's friend, Remi Babineaux, is one of their sponsors."

Martell paused to think about that, though didn't seem to grasp the significance. "And you're thinking that ...?"

"It's a connection between Lefève and the murder of Ginette

Clément. Babineaux's only been in business for ten years so he wouldn't have been sponsoring them back then, but it's a link worth investigating, don't you think?"

The lieutenant nodded emphatically. "Oh yes. Absolutely."

"And there's another thing," Margot said as they migrated into the office. "How many players are there in a rugby team?"

"Fifteen for rugby union. Thirteen in rugby league."

"Argents SCR are rugby union, aren't they?"

Martell grinned cheekily. "You're learning."

"And if you included all the substitutes, the coaches, and the backroom staff, how many would you say?"

"For a team the size of Argents I'd say ... thirty or more."

"The night Ginette was murdered they were celebrating a big win. You would think they would have all been there that night. And along with the wives and the partners, the catering staff, various supporters ... I'm guessing there would have been closer to a hundred people at that dinner."

Martell nodded in agreement. "That seems a fair assumption."

"So why are there only sixteen statements in the dossier?"

"Is that all?"

"I counted them yesterday."

The lieutenant rubbed his chin. "That does seem odd. Could some of them have gone missing?"

"No. Only sixteen statements were taken; it was recorded on the case log. Standard procedure would have required them to take statements from everyone, wouldn't it?"

Lieutenant Martell nodded thoughtfully. "I doubt if any of the officers who worked on that case are still around. But I could try tracking some of them down, if you like."

Margot shook her head. "I'm not so worried about any shortcomings in the investigation. But I would like to go over there and see what they can tell me about Babineaux. Is the captain around?"

"He's not in today." The lieutenant's face brightened. "But I could drive you."

Margot gave him a dubious look but quickly gave in. "All right. Thank you."

"Give me just ten seconds to find someone to cover the desk," he said, and Margot had no doubt he would live up to his word.

It was a ten-minute drive to the rugby club. Signs directed them around the back of a newly-built Ibis where they found the staff car park, almost full. They parked in a corner and went to the main entrance, only to find the doors locked. The sound of shouting drew them around the side of the building but they could go no further – a steel palisade fence separated them from the pitch. On the other side, they could hear the men out on the field.

A knocking on a window made them look round – a man had spotted them and was pointing to a door to his left. They waited outside while he unfastened the locks.

"Hi there." A young man with a friendly face.

Margot made the introductions. "Is there a manager around?"

"He's out with the team right now. Can I help? I'm one of the assistants."

"This might sound an unusual request, but would you have a list of everyone who worked here fourteen years ago? Either played for the team or was employed in any capacity."

The young man raised his eyebrows. "Fourteen years? That's a bit before my time. But we do have an archive room. Come in. I'll see what I can find."

"Thank you."

He took them down a corridor that led towards the main building, passing several open doors along the way. The odour of embrocation and sweat was heavy in the air. Margot found it hard to associate the game with the south of France; to her mind, rugby was a game played on cold and muddy playing fields in the north of England. Martell, however, was in his element, and when they got to the foyer he gravitated to the trophy cabinet, his eyes like saucers as he took in all the silverware.

The assistant stepped behind the counter to retrieve a key from a rack. "Is this about that girl who was killed here? That was fourteen years ago, wasn't it?"

"You remember that?"

"I remember all the fuss on TV. People still talk about it now. In fact, you're the second one who's been round recently."

Margot gave him a puzzled look. "Really? Who else has been?"

"She must have said her name but I don't remember it. She said she was working with the police."

"When was this?"

"Must be ... four or five months ago."

"What did she want to know?"

"She was a bit vague. I think she just wanted to see where it happened. I left her to have a look around and when I came back she'd gone."

"Can you remember what she looked like?"

"Average height. Slim ... blonde ... in her forties, perhaps."

Margot tried to imagine who that might be.

"But about that staff list," the young man went on. "There are boxes and boxes of stuff in our archive room. It might take me a while. Would you like to wait in the café while I'm looking?"

He pointed to some lime green sofas in the corner – the café seemed to consist of a couple of vending machines and a microwave oven – but it was pleasant enough. He left her in front of a big TV that was screening a match with the sound turned down, though Margot's eyes were soon drawn to a sign above a nearby pair of doors: "Rose Room". She called Martell over from the trophy cabinet. Going in, she instantly realised where they were.

"This was where they had the dinner that night," she said, feeling the need to lower her voice.

Judging by the state of the décor not much had changed in the intervening fourteen years. A bar occupied one side with chairs and tables stacked neatly in a corner. The brown nylon carpet, sticky under her feet, was straight out of the 1970s, and the ceiling tiles looked no more recent. Ginette's mother had been doing the catering that night. When the dinner was over, Ginette had stayed behind to help clear up, and since there had been too much to carry in one load, Ginette's mother had driven the first load home alone. She'd returned half an hour later to find the function room empty and the last few stragglers out on the terrace, gathered on the spot where Ginette had last been seen. One of her shoes and her mobile phone lay at their feet. Apparently, she'd gone out there for a smoke.

Margot opened the double doors and stepped out onto the terrace. Out on the field, the coaches were putting the men through their drills. They were only a few metres from the edge of the pitch, though the scene back then would have looked different. The crime scene photos showed low-level bleachers surrounding the ground whereas now a multi-tiered stadium dominated the far boundary. As soon as the alarm had been raised, volunteers had poured in and a search got underway. If Margot's mental geography was correct, the woods where the body had subsequently been found lay on the far side of the new stand.

"I wonder what it would have been like for the team," Martell said, joining her on the edge of the grass. "Coming out to play their next match."

Her underwear had been pulled down, her tee-shirt ripped. According to her mother, Ginette hadn't had a regular boyfriend for months, though her friends had stated she'd hinted at a new man being in her life. One of them had got the impression he was an older man.

Margot gazed across the field, watching the men slam into one another. She pictured the stadium full of cheering fans, and had to acknowledge a tingle of excitement. Perhaps the attraction of the game wasn't so difficult to understand; all that raw power and energy, the heat and the passion.

The assistant manager came looking for them. He smiled happily as he held up a glossy brochure.

"I found this. It's a match-day programme from that year." He handed it to Margot. "It's a bit dog-eared, but all the pages are there."

Margot had a quick look through.

"If you want the full list of staff it'll take a bit longer. Our bookkeeper should have it on her system, but she's off sick this week."

"Could you email it to me as soon as you get it?"

"Of course."

Margot handed him a card. She leafed through to the team sheet at the back. All the people who'd played that day were listed, along with the substitutes, the manager and the coaches. From memory, only one of the men listed had been amongst the five players who had given statements that night, although ... Margot's pulse suddenly quickened. She looked up at the assistant.

"A Jean-Paul Lefève used to play for this team. Is that the same man who's now the mayor?"

Margot pointed it out, but the young man looked blank.

"Sorry, I have no idea. I didn't follow the team back them."

She turned to Martell who also seemed ignorant of the fact.

"Do you have any more information on him?" Margot asked. "Date of birth, home address ... anything like that?"

"Probably. There's a whole heap of stuff back there. You're welcome to take a look."

"If you don't mind."

They followed him back inside. The archive room was a small room piled high with boxes, and with the three of them in there it was rather cramped. As soon as the manager had located the relevant box, they took it out to the counter.

It was full to the brim with paperwork from the year Ginette had been murdered. They each took a handful. Margot came across several more match-day programmes, along with some newspaper clippings, dozens of loose photographs, and more in albums.

"He was on the team the previous year," Martell said. "His name's here in another programme."

"Here are some coaching notes," the assistant said. "He played number 4-lock. It says here the coach had been trying to get him to work on his tackling."

"Are number 4-lock's quite big?" Margot asked.

"Usually," Martell replied. "Some people call them enforcers. They like a bit of contact."

Margot pictured the silverback, head down, getting stuck into the scrum. It was a plausible image.

She pulled out an album of team photographs. According to the label, this one spanned two decades, and in each photo the team were lined up like schoolboys. Finding the one for the relevant year, Margot located Lefève's name in the caption at the bottom and then counted faces. A plump, pale-skinned young man looked back at her. Fourteen years ago Lefève would have been twenty-eight.

"This looks like him, doesn't it?" Margot said, showing the picture to lieutenant Martell.

After studying it for a few moments, the lieutenant agreed. "It certainly does."

The assistant handed her a clipping from the local newspaper: a two-page article, mainly concerned with Ginette's murder, but there was also a full match report. Not only had Lefève been playing that day, he'd also scored one of the tries.

What exactly all this meant, however, Margot wasn't sure.

As it was Saturday, Margot was reluctant to contact Célia, but when she did, she was surprised to discover that the judge was, in fact, at work. Not only that, when Margot arrived at the *Palais* Florian was there, too, his face brightening as she walked in.

"Ah, Margot. I'm glad you came in."

Margot pulled up a chair, eyebrows raised. "Two men pleased to see me in one day. Must be this new perfume I'm wearing."

Florian quickly sorted through some of his many papers. "The funding for the library project you asked me to look into."

"You've sussed it?"

"Pretty much. It's being funded by a PPP – a public private partnership. The developer will come up with the money for the building work and then lease the facilities to the town at an agreed rate. Free for the first six months and then rising in stages to the full market rate."

"And the developer then screws the taxpayer on the maintenance charges, I suppose," Margot added cynically.

"Perhaps. But I suspect you'll be more interested to hear who the developer is."

"Let me guess – Babineaux Construction?"

"Right first time."

Margot simmered. "So the mayor approves the planning application and gets his old friend a nice sweet deal on the side." She frowned. "But what's in it for Lefève?"

"Nothing I can see on paper. The contracts haven't been signed yet. The council are meeting in three weeks' time to make a final decision."

Margot's mood improved. "In that case, Florian, we'd better get a move on. Is Célia free?"

Florian checked his watch. "She's been working non-stop for two hours. I think she could do with a break."

Margot knocked, opened the door, and put her head through the gap. "Sorry to bother you. Could you spare a moment?"

"Of course, Margot. Come in."

Margot slowed as she approached Célia's desk. The judge wasn't looking so good: her face was drawn; her eyes grey. Margot gave her a concerned look.

"How are you feeling?"

"Just a little tired, that's all."

"Wouldn't you be better off at home, resting?"

Célia put down her pen and heaved a weary sigh. "That's very considerate of you, Margot, but please don't fuss. If I feel up to working I will; if I don't, I won't. It's as simple as that." She summoned a small smile. "I'll go stark raving mad if I have to lie in bed all day, I'm certain of that."

Margot admired her obstinacy – if she ever got cancer she liked to think she would be as equally determined to shake a fist at it – but she wondered how sustainable it was to keep bouncing back into work like this. Margot brought her up to speed on their discoveries at the rugby club.

"I've checked the dossier again. Lefève didn't give a statement that night, yet he would surely have been there, a party animal like him."

Célia had listened patiently throughout but appeared to grow more perturbed. "Are you suggesting he killed Ginette Clément, and Sandrine found out about it? And then he killed Sandrine to silence her?"

"It's a theory."

"An explosive one."

"He lied to us about his movements that night. And he was clearly lying about the state of his relationship with Sandrine. Surely that's enough to question him."

Célia mulled it over.

"You're close, Margot. Perhaps, very close, but I'll need a little more. Bring me some actual evidence of wrongdoing and then we'll speak to Lefève."

Margot felt quietly elated. All she had to do was keep picking at that knot. Like Stéphane and his straws. And there was one particular knot she was certain had more to give.

25

Margot was hoping to reach the *étang* before nightfall, but traffic slowed her progress, and when she finally arrived on the long straight road her headlights were tunnelling darkness. She missed the pull-in on the first pass and had to do a 360 at the next mini-roundabout. Slowing as she approached it from the opposite direction, she turned the wheel and pulled over, the underside of the car scraping tarmac as the wheels dropped off the edge. The ground was wet, and to add insult to injury it seemed she'd parked in a puddle.

Her foot disappeared into soft sand as she stepped out. Then the ground held onto her shoe as she leapt clear. What a wonderful start. With no chance of retrieving the shoe without wading back through the puddle, Margot took off the remaining one and tossed it back to the car with a curse. Barefoot, she set off through the bushes.

Without her guide, she blundered around for a full ten minutes. She finally managed to locate the jetty and used the torch on her phone to light up the silvery planks. The chain and padlock were wrapped tightly around the upright, but the boat was gone. Margot went to the edge of the water and looked out. A dim light was coming from Sylvie's shack.

How did one contact a person who didn't want to be contacted? Shout very loudly? Set off a flare? Use her torch to flash Morse code? After reviewing her options, Margot concluded the only solution was to walk.

Heeding Alain's advice this time, she steered clear of the reeds and took the long was round. Even so, the ground was swampy. Mud oozed between her toes as she entered a patch of low-lying ground. She made good progress until her right foot disappeared down a pothole and she sank halfway to her knee. Spinning her arms like Catherine wheels, Margot just about managed to remain upright. But she pushed on, the discomfort only serving to make her more determined.

The grass gave way to scrub, and as she emerged on higher ground Margot sighted the rear of the shack. Light was shining from the windows, and soft music could be heard coming from inside. She climbed the steps, but paused at the door. It was unlikely Sylvie was in the habit of receiving unexpected callers and Margot had visions of her coming to the door with a shotgun in hand. Tapping lightly on the woodwork, she softly called out:

"Sylvie. It's me – Margot."

Contrary to expectation, Sylvie didn't seem surprised to see her. Perhaps she had cameras hidden in the bushes and had been watching her comical progress with amusement. A smile wasn't far from her lips.

"You look wet."

"I don't suppose you'd be interested in a set of encyclopedias?"

Sylvie grinned.

They both looked down. Muddy footprints illustrated Margot's progress up the steps, and some type of stringy green weed was clinging to her feet. Her jeans were soaked up to her knees.

"You'd better take those off. Come in. I'll find you something dry."

Margot peeled the green weed from her feet and then took off her jeans. She waited for Sylvie to come back with a towel before drying her feet and stepping inside. Sylvie took the jeans from her and then produced a pair of green, wide-leg trousers.

"Try these on. They're the largest ones I have."

Margot pulled them on. They were a little on the short side but she wasn't complaining.

"Care for a drink?"

This time Margot accepted her offer of a small whisky. She went down the steps to the living area while Sylvie followed with the two tumblers. The old wooden floorboards felt warm under her feet. There was something inherently cosy about a house on a lake, worth the aggravation of getting here.

"It must be nice being so cut off. I think I'll try it myself one day."

"It does have its attractions." Sylvie handed her one of the tumblers and they both sat. "I didn't expect to see you back so soon."

Margot had a sip of whisky. "I think I'm going to need a little more help."

"That's a shame. I thought you'd have figured it out for yourself."

They shared a deep look. It seemed they'd reached a certain level of understanding but not quite enough for Sylvie to fully open up. But this time Margot was not leaving without some proper answers. She got up from the sofa and joined Sylvie on the daybed.

"I think I have figured out most of it. Lefève and your father made a deal. Lefève would swing the planning application and your father's company would win the contract to build it. In return, Lefève gets a payment on the side while Babineaux Construction profits from the maintenance costs – charging two hundred euros for changing a lightbulb, that kind of thing. Am I getting warm?"

Sylvie sipped her whisky, giving nothing away. Margot continued:

"You're reluctant to tell me the details because you're afraid it might cause trouble for your father. I understand that, but you don't have to worry – Lefève's the one I'm interested in. The problem is, we need reasonable grounds before we can question him, and unless I get something more in the way of evidence that's not going to happen. And that goes for Sandrine's murder, too."

"Do you have any evidence he was involved in her murder?"

"It's all circumstantial. But he had the opportunity, and the fact Sandrine knew his secret gave him a motive."

"Sandrine knew about the library project. She overheard Lefève and my father talking about it."

"Did Lefève know she knew?"

"I don't know. She wasn't sure what to do with the information. I think she thought of it as an insurance policy."

"Was she afraid of him?"

"Not physically, but Lefève's a powerful man. There were other ways he could have made life miserable for her."

"Was there anything else? Any other secrets she knew?"

"Like what?"

Margot had another sip of whisky and then put down her glass.

"Do you remember Ginette Clément?"

"The girl who was killed at the rugby club?"

Margot nodded. "Lefève used to play for Argents rugby club. He actually played in the match on the day Ginette was killed."

"Did he really?" Sylvie leaned forward, eyes full of surprise. "I never knew that."

"Ginette's friends thought she was involved with an older man. Back then, she was eighteen, Lefève was twenty-eight. When I mentioned her name to him the other day he got very touchy."

Sylvie fidgeted on the bed. "Now you're starting to scare me."

"Add to that his alibi doesn't stand up. Your father told us he went to a club in Sète rather than your friend's party, which is what he told us."

"Which club?"

"Club Chinois. Have you heard of it?"

Sylvie smiled wryly. "He was probably buying cocaine."

"Seriously?"

"A lot of dealers hang out there."

Margot shook her head in disbelief. "The hypocritical bastard. All that anti-drugs rhetoric he comes out with."

"How was Ginette murdered?"

"The same way as Sandrine – suffocated with a plastic bag. Why?"

Sylvie looked as if there was something she wanted to say though couldn't quite bring herself to speak. Margot shuffled closer.

"Is there something about Lefève you're not telling me?"

She continued to hold Margot's gaze but there was still no answer.

"Unless you help me, Sylvie, an innocent man might go to prison. I don't believe you want that to happen anymore than I do."

Sylvie nodded. "I can imagine him doing it. Holding a bag over her face, watching her die."

"You've known him a long time, haven't you?"

"He and my dad have been friends since school. My dad

always looked up to him, like he was the cool older brother or something, though I've never understood why. There's a lot he doesn't know."

"Such as?"

Sylvie picked up a cushion and hugged it to her chest. She looked away, an air of sadness coming over her.

"He used to come round to our house a lot. Saturday afternoons, the two of them would have a barbecue out in the yard. They would drink too much. Make all sorts of wild plans. Then this one time, I was alone in the kitchen when Lefève came in. He looked at me in that way. I was just about old enough to know what it meant."

"How old were you?"

"Seventeen. He didn't say anything. Just grabbed me from behind. He put one hand over my mouth, the other around my waist, then started rubbing up against me. It probably only lasted a few seconds but I was so surprised I couldn't move. When he'd finished, he went off, grinning, and put a finger up to his lips."

Margot swallowed. "So you didn't tell your father?"

Sylvie shook her head. "I was ashamed, I suppose. And it wasn't like he'd actually done anything. I mean, not really."

Margot squeezed her arm. "He assaulted you, Sylvie."

"I realise that now. But things were different back then."

"When did this happen?"

"Seventeen years ago."

"Did he ever try it again?"

Again, Sylvie shook her head. "The next time I saw him he acted like nothing had happened. I thought I might have imagined it, but I hadn't. And he's not changed. You can tell by the way he speaks about women, boasting about the things he's done."

Margot pulled the numbers together in her head. Ginette

was killed three years after he assaulted Sylvie. She would have been twenty. Margot asked if she could remember anything about him from that time.

"Nothing springs to mind," Sylvie said. "I was at art college when I was twenty. I didn't see them that often."

"You can't remember them falling out about anything? Or arguing?"

Sylvie thought about it, but then shook her head. After a pause, her eyes sought Margot's. "If you need me to, I'll speak up about the assault. It would only be my word against his but I'm willing to do it."

"I think you should."

"And as for the library project ... I'll tell you on one condition."

"Which is?"

"You keep my father out of it."

Margot admired her loyalty. "Unless he's broken the law that shouldn't be a problem."

"Okay. They set up an off-shore company to handle it all. They would make money letting out the space, split the profits fifty-fifty."

"So what's illegal about that?"

"Nothing, as far as I know. But it wouldn't do Lefève's public image any good if people found out he was profiting from a development he'd so vocally given his backing to. And it was never clear where his share of the capital came from. I'm guessing he wouldn't want anyone looking too closely into the Mairie's financial records. I can give you the details, if you like. Names and bank accounts. Will that be enough?"

Margot wasn't sure but she nodded. "Let's hope so."

They said goodbye on the jetty. It was after ten when Margot found her way back to the car. She rescued her shoes from the puddle, tossed them into the boot, and then climbed inelegantly into the driver's seat. Sitting in the dark, she typed a message to Célia:

Sylvie's willing to talk. Can I see you first thing in the morning?

Unsure she would receive a reply at this time of night, Margot started the car and reversed onto the road. Safely back on the tarmac, she pointed the car in the direction of Argents only to be interrupted by a ping from her phone. The road was deserted so she picked it straight up.

Come and see me at home now if you like. I'll wait up.

Ninety minutes later, Margot pulled into the car park underneath Célia's apartment block. She slotted the Fiat 500 into a space next to the candy red Bentley and then, still high on adrenaline, took the stairs to the top floor. The chauffeuse let her in. Célia was resting in the salon, the lights turned down.

"Now we can add sex pest and probable cocaine use to the list of reasons to interview him," Margot said after she'd given a recap of her trip to the *étang*. It only then occurred to her that she was still wearing Sylvie's green trousers and was glad of the soft light.

"Do you think we have enough?" she asked finally.

Célia left her in suspense for a few moments, but then smiled her approval.

"First thing Monday morning, I'll make the arrangements."

26

Cousineau was the first one in, marching into Célia's office with his habitual air of irritation. He blanked Margot, nodded to Célia in passing, and then took up his place in the leather armchair to the right of the judge's desk.

Next in was Lefève's *avocat*, a small man in an expensive suit, who walked with an assuredness that belied the importance of his role in the proceedings. Margot knew from experience that as far as most *magistrats* were concerned, defence *avocats* were a lower form of life.

Bringing up the rear was the mayor himself who entered confidently, haughtily surveying the scene before him as if baffled as to why he was dignifying it with his presence. Dressed in a light grey tailored suit, he unbuttoned his jacket and straightened his back. Any moment now, Margot imagined he would start beating his chest with his fists. He extended a hand across the desk for Célia to shake, but since he hadn't moved quite close enough for her to comfortably reach, Célia was forced to stretch. Formalities over, he sent a disapproving glance in Margot's direction where she stood in front of her chair on Célia's left flank.

"Is there any reason your assistant needs to be here?"

"Madame Renard is part of my investigation team. She's been instrumental in obtaining facts pertinent to the case which is why I've asked her to sit in."

The silverback flared his nostrils, making a sound that could have been mistaken for a grunt. He offered no comeback so Célia invited them to be seated.

They all complied, apart from Lefève who still seemed dissatisfied. He studied the arrangement of chairs, looking with displeasure at the one allocated to him – front and centre before Célia's desk. He nudged it aside with his foot before finally deigning to sit. Beside him, the *avocat* clicked open his briefcase and took out a sheaf of papers which he balanced on one knee.

"May I remind you, Madame *le juge*, that my client has agreed to this interview on the—"

"May I remind *you*, Monsieur," Célia cut in icily, "that we are here to listen to what the mayor has to say, not his *avocat*."

The little man looked a little put out but ventured nothing more. Célia turned back to Lefève.

"Firstly, Monsieur *le Maire*, I would like to thank you for agreeing to speak to me today."

Lefève inclined his head. "I'm more than happy to clear up any misunderstandings that may have arisen."

Célia took a page from her dossier. "As you know, we're here to investigate the murder of Sandrine Bordes. Your name came up during the course of the Gendarmerie's enquiry and there are certain matters I would like to formally resolve. Could we begin by clarifying the nature of your relationship with the victim."

"Of course. Sandrine was a friend of mine. I'd known her for three or four years. We'd been having an affair throughout that time."

"An affair?" Célia queried with a sceptical eyebrow.

"Yes. I am a married man."

"Were you aware she worked as a prostitute?"

"I was."

"And that didn't bother you?"

Lefève opened his hands. "What she got up to in her private life was of no concern to me."

"Even so, you must have had feelings for her, having known her for all that time. Wouldn't you have preferred her to be exclusively yours?"

He chuckled. "We clearly hail from very different worlds, Célia. My wife and I enjoy an open marriage. We've never been exclusive. Why should I expect anything more from my mistress?"

"People get jealous, whatever world they come from."

"Well, I can assure you, that didn't apply to me."

"Did you ever pay for her services?"

"Since I never viewed them as 'services' naturally I did not."

Célia spent a few moments looking at him, barely concealing her disbelief. Finally, she made a note and then turned the page.

"Could we now turn to the night of the murder? In your interview with Captain Bouchard and Madame Renard you stated that—"

"An interview which I understood to be off the record."

"My client has not been asked for a formal statement and neither has he provided one. If—"

"Monsieur, if you persist with these interruptions, this meeting is going to take up even more of your client's time. I'm sure you'd be happy for that to happen since you're no doubt charging by the hour, but I can assure you that my time and that of *magistrat* Cousineau is paid for from the public purse. Let's not waste it."

Despite her condition, Célia was putting on a good show.

Lefève mollified his man with a sideways glance. Célia paused only to take a sip of water.

"For the record, could you confirm your movements that night?"

"I'd be happy to, although I understood you were about to charge a man." He sent an enquiring glance to Cousineau, though it was Célia who replied:

"My dossier is still very much open and it would be remiss of me not to pursue all lines of enquiry."

"So I'm a line of enquiry now, am I?" Lefève seemed amused by the idea. He pursued his lips as he shifted his gaze between several different points in the room, nodding repetitively as he did so. Stalling for time, perhaps, or considering whether or not to continue cooperating. Margot wondered if he'd spoken to Remi Babineaux. She was intrigued to see how he would explain away his visit to Club Chinois.

"My movements that night ..." he repeated. "Well, I went to an exhibition in Sète around seven. After that I was invited to a party by some friends. The party went on for most of the night so I stayed over. Slept in a horribly uncomfortable bed, I recall. I returned to Argents the next morning and arrived in my office around ten. That was when my secretary told me about the murder. I was shocked, naturally."

"Where was the party?"

Lefève sent a glance in Margot's direction, creating a pause. He seemed to enjoy keeping them waiting.

"The party," he said, switching his attention back to the judge, "was in Sète. At a place called Club Chinois."

Margot shifted her chair, scraping a leg on the wooden floor-boards. Babineaux had clearly forewarned him. Célia went on:

"You told Captain Bouchard you went to a party in Agde."

"I told him I went to a party; I didn't say where." He smiled without humour. "You must understand, Célia, I'm a very popular person. I get invited to lots of parties. The people you're referring to may well have gone to Agde; the party I went to was in Sète."

"Would you care to give me the names of the friends you're talking about?"

"I'm not sure I could remember them. I had rather indulged myself."

"I heard that club's a notorious hang-out for drug dealers," Margot spoke up, prompting a series of sharp head-turns. Lefève regarded her with thinly-disguised contempt.

"If you have something to say, Madame, I suggest you come right out and say it."

"Very well. I was wondering if you would care to elaborate upon how you'd indulged. Alcohol, perhaps ... or was it something else? We all know that possession of cocaine, for example, carries a prison sentence, even for personal use."

The irony was not lost on any of them. The *Code pénal* was relatively lenient in what constituted a suitable amount for personal use, but local prosecutors were allowed to lower the limits as they saw fit. Lefève himself had put forward the proposal to lower the limit from 50g to 20g in the case of cannabis, and to exclude heroin and cocaine from the scheme all together.

"I'm not sure I should dignify that comment with a response."

Célia waited, giving him a chance to add more, but he wasn't taking the bait. His *avocat* looked as if he wanted to say something, but promptly thought better of it. As the silence persisted, Célia turned back to her dossier.

"When was the last time you saw Sandrine?"

Lefève re-composed. He cast his eyes up at the ceiling while he thought about it.

"Three or four weeks ago."

"And how were things between you?"

"Fine."

"No tensions, or disagreements?"

"None whatsoever."

"I believe you're aware Sandrine kept a diary."

"That's hardly unusual, is it?"

Célia unclipped a page from the dossier. "She refers to you in many of the entries. And if we go back a few weeks she talks about having discovered one of your secrets. I quote: 'I wonder if he'd be so smug if the whole town knew what I know. That would wipe the smile off his arrogant face'." Célia took off her glasses. "What do you suppose she meant by that?"

The mayor appeared wounded, clearly not expecting the insult. He cleared his throat. "I have no idea."

"She doesn't sound like the happy little mistress you would have us believe."

"Maybe she'd had a bad day. She could be quite unpredictable at times. There are any number of reasons why she might have written that."

"Did you know Sandrine was pregnant?" Margot piped up again, and this time received a look of mild rebuke from the judge.

But Lefève seemed amused. "You think I was responsible for getting her pregnant?"

"Were you?"

"No chance whatsoever. I always use protection."

"You do know they're not one hundred per cent effective," Célia said.

Lefève threw his hands into the air, growing impatient. "Fine. I'll submit to a paternity test if that's what you want. It will prove negative, I assure you. But I honestly can't see how any of this is relevant ..."

He turned to Cousineau again, hoping for support, perhaps.

The senior *procureur* looked as if he might have something to say but Célia quickly continued:

"Do you mind if I ask you some questions about the library development?"

Lefève looked mystified. "What on earth does the library development have to do with your case?"

"Your friend, Remi Babineaux, will be building it, I understand."

"That's correct. Babineaux Construction is a highly reputable firm. I've no doubt they will do a first-rate job."

"But you and Babineaux go way back, don't you? All the way to your school days."

"I'm not sure what you are trying to imply, but the council are fully on board with the choice of developer. All proper procedures were followed."

"Yet surely you can see the potential for a conflict of interest? In your role as mayor you gave your backing to the project; you've committed public funds to it. And if, for example, you were found to be benefiting from the deal in some way, you can see how a scandal might arise."

Lefève seemed to get it. "Speculation is one thing, evidence is another. You won't find any simply because there is none."

"I could order an enquiry."

"Yes, you could, and that would put back the start of construction for years. No one wants to see that happen."

"I quite agree."

Lefève gave her a closer look, trying to read her. "I'm sensing you have a proposition to put to me."

Célia paused. It suddenly seemed like they were the only two people in the room.

"There's a council meeting in three weeks' time."

"Correct."

"If you were to hold back on giving the project the green

light while you reconsidered your relationship with Babineaux, changed the agreement in favour of the town, for example, then I might decide that your activities at this nightclub are not worth investigating."

Margot mentally blinked. She couldn't believe Célia was offering to let him off the hook, even if it meant getting him to back down on the library project.

A thin smile played across Lefève's lips. "Are you offering me a deal?"

"Merely suggesting a practical arrangement. One that will suit all parties."

Silence fell. Lefève leaned to his side and had a quiet word with his *avocat*. When he straightened, he still seemed undecided.

"And if I agree will it put an end to this tedious charade?"

"Unless any other evidence comes to light."

He looked at Célia with what appeared newfound respect.

"Very well. I accept."

"Be in no doubt, however, that I will be keeping a close eye on the matter. Should I have any concerns of impropriety, any at all, I will order that enquiry."

"You can rest easy, Célia. I'm a man of my word."

"Thank you."

"Are we done now?"

They made a move to stand up, but Margot panicked. It seemed unreal that he was just going to get up and walk away.

"Not quite," Margot said, prompting them all to freeze. Put on the spot, she looked to Célia for support. "Might I be permitted to ask a question?"

This time Célia gave her a look of uncertainty. Cousineau had already risen from his seat and was poised to interject, but Célia quieted him with a raised hand.

"Is it pertinent to the case, Margot?"

"I believe so."

"Then go ahead."

Margot waited while they resumed their seats, ignoring Lefève's weary sigh. She cleared her throat.

"The other day, when I asked if you'd ever met Ginette Clément, you told me to get out of your office. Yet I subsequently discovered that you used to play at the rugby club where she was killed. You even played in the game on the day she was murdered, and presumably you went to the dinner that night. So would you care to explain why you were so reluctant to speak about her?"

This time Cousineau couldn't help himself. "You have absolutely no right to ask that question. We're investigating the murder of Sandrine Bordes, nothing more. Célia, I really must protest."

Before Célia had time to respond, however, Lefève spoke up:

"It's quite all right, Eugène. I don't mind answering the woman's question."

Cousineau didn't seem happy about it but he returned to his seat. Lefève spent a few moments adjusting his position, turning to face Margot square on, shoulders back, one hand planted firmly on top of his muscular thigh.

"The reason I asked you to leave, Madame, was because you upset me. That day holds many emotional memories for me. If you'd been there fourteen years ago then maybe you would have understood. Yes, I knew Ginette. I knew her very well indeed. She and her family were devotees of the club. Every Sunday, they would come down to the clubhouse to make coffee and sandwiches. When we had charity matches, they would bake cakes and sell them outside the ground. And on that night, when we heard Ginette had gone missing, the whole team turned out to look for her. I was in the group that found her, out in those woods. I saw her body, lying there in the undergrowth.

And believe me, if we'd found the man responsible we would have torn him limb from limb."

His eyes had glazed over but he didn't look away. He fluttered his eyelids while he gathered his emotions. No one spoke. He had the room.

"We held a two-minute silence before our next match. And wore black arm bands for the rest of the season. So yes, when you asked me about her the other day you did touch a nerve. But not in the way you thought. And if you seriously think I was involved in Ginette's murder, or had anything whatsoever to do with what happened to Sandrine, then, with the greatest respect, you're out of your tiny little mind."

Margot blushed, stunned to realise his emotion was genuine. Even so, she found herself hating him even more.

"Now, I think we're done here. If anyone has anything further to say you'll find me at the Mairie. Good-day to you."

With that the mayor got out of his chair and left, *avocat* trailing in his wake.

As the last of the three men to leave, Cousineau closed the door behind him. Feeling foolish, it was a few moments before Margot could find the courage to turn and face her boss.

"I'm sorry, Margot," Célia said. "I did my best. We'd have got nowhere trying to pursue him on a drugs' charge. No one at that nightclub would have talked to the police. Much better to use it as leverage to get him to back down on the library project."

Margot nodded. She knew Célia was right, but every nerve in her body still felt numb.

"And I don't think he was involved in either of the two murders," Célia went on. "You saw the emotion in his eyes. I really can't believe he's that good an actor.

Margot swallowed. She got to her feet and nodded again.

"Thank you, anyway. And I'm sorry for wasting your time."

Célia tutted. "You haven't wasted anyone's time. You had every right to pursue him. Thanks to you we've seen what kind of a man he really is. And if Sylvie's still willing to come forward it might prompt others to do the same."

She came out from behind her desk and placed a consoling hand on Margot's back. "He'll slip up one day. And when he does, we'll be waiting."

27

They were late finishing for lunch, and when Margot finally managed to escape to La Lune Bleue the time was after one. To spoil the day even further, the place was crowded and all the outside tables were taken. Relegated to a seat indoors, she had to wait five minutes for Raymond to get around to serving her.

"Sorry, Margot," he said, snapping through the pages of his notepad in search of a clean sheet. "It's been non-stop all day."

"You've been discovered?"

"It would seem so."

"Oh well. It was nice while it lasted."

"What can I get you?"

Craving salt, she ordered an anchovy salad with hard-boiled eggs and a large glass of white wine.

"I do have some good news, though," Raymond said when he came back from the kitchen. He kept her waiting while he set the table.

"Well, go on, then," Margot prompted. "Do tell."

"I've heard back from the *Lycée Hôtelier*."

"And?"

He grinned excitedly. "They've offered me a place."

"Oh, Raymond. That's wonderful news."

"Thank you."

She had to get up and hug him.

"When do you start?"

"January. Chef said I can carry on working here while I'm training."

"I'm so pleased for you. You're going to make a wonderful chef."

The salad was delicious, but less than halfway through Margot lost her appetite. Raymond was busy with other customers so she left the money on the table. In no hurry to go back to work, she walked home.

The courtyard was empty. For the second day running the food she'd put down had gone uneaten, and this morning she'd left him his favourite: duck meat, gizzard and liver. Margot picked up the untouched saucer and cast a forlorn look around her empty courtyard. Perhaps he'd found his way back to Rue des Arts, or had conned some other poor sap into looking after him. All that effort, and he'd just upped sticks and abandoned her. Notoriously fickle creatures, as Stéphane had said.

After scraping the food into the bin Margot went for a lie down. But she'd only just closed her eyes when her phone rang. Florian's name was showing on the screen.

"Florian – what is it?"

"What time do you think you'll be back?"

Margot pulled herself into a sitting position and rubbed some life into her face. "Why? What's happened?"

"I think I've found something. You might want to come and take a look."

"That was quick."

Checking her watch, Margot saw that she'd made it to the *Palais* in six minutes flat. She was rather hot from having hurried up the stairs and had to take a few moments to recover.

"What have you found?"

Florian called her round to his side of the desk. He pointed to number two in his line of three monitors.

"This is the calendar we use for the court bookings. I was just checking some dates when I found this."

He clicked back a few pages. A list of bookings came up, each one detailing the cases that had been allocated a hearing that day. Florian circled an entry with his pointer; Margot leaned over his shoulder to read the tiny text: a hearing in the Family Court for a custody case. The booking had been made in August, and the case was due to be heard in ten days' time.

"See who the appellant is?"

Florian clicked again, then leaned back to give Margot more space. She flinched.

"Sandrine Bordes."

"It looks like she was appealing the custody decision again. The booking was cancelled two days after her death."

Margot's mind raced. "Who was the *avocat*?"

"One second."

Florian reached for his mouse and did some more clicking.

"TNG Avocats. In Perpignan."

TNG Avocats were based in a smart new office block on the outskirts of Perpignan, rather more upmarket than the *avocat* Sandrine had used first time around. A sign in the lobby directed them to the fourth floor. On the way up in the elevator, Captain Bouchard stood quietly by her side, giving her sidelong looks. He'd seemed to want to say something ever since they'd left the Gendarmerie.

"For what it's worth, Madame," he finally ventured. "I think you did the right thing pursuing the mayor. Regardless of what happened."

Margot regarded him fondly. "Thank you, Captain. That means a lot."

"All we can do is follow the evidence."

That was true, but then the evidence had pointed to Gy Berger, and Margot still couldn't shake off her doubts about that.

The doors opened on the fourth floor. They emerged in a generic environment, the same as offices the world over: carpet tiles and beech veneer furniture straight out of an office supplies catalogue. A helpful young receptionist gave them a name and then pointed to a passage between two lines of glazed partitions. Halfway down, they came to a door marked: Alexandre Lalande. Inside, a young man in a smart white shirt noticed them through the glass and immediately came to the door.

"Captain; Madame – come right in."

"Thank you for agreeing to see us at such short notice," Margot said.

"Not at all." He indicated seats. "Tell me how I can help."

Margot explained. Alexandre nodded throughout, seemingly already up to speed on what she was saying. It looked like Sandrine's file was open on his desk.

"You're absolutely right. Sandrine came to us on the 3rd August this year. After hearing her story, I told her I was more than happy to take her case. I was looking forward to helping her get her daughter back and then, sadly, this. I was stunned when I heard the news."

"Did you think the appeal would be successful?"

"Yes, I did. She was in a much better place this time around, although I tried not to get her hopes up too much. She was asking for full sole custody, but in my view that was not realistic."

"What made her think she would get sole custody?"

"She told me the ex-husband was going to drop his objections. Apparently, he'd had a change of heart."

Margot frowned. "Really? That wasn't the impression he gave us."

The *avocat* shrugged. "I advised her it was unlikely, given that Lya was settled and happy living with her father. On the other hand, if the father had dropped his objections, I was sure we could have gained some more favourable access arrangements. Alternate weekends, something like that."

"Did she say why he'd dropped his objections?"

Alexandre shook his head. "I honestly have no idea."

Back at the Gendarmerie, Margot asked to be taken to the evidence room. The captain took her down to the basement, and after locating the box she'd asked to see, removed the lid and searched inside. After a few moments, he pulled out the shoe box of till receipts.

"What exactly are we looking for?" he asked as Margot began spreading the tiny pieces of papers across the nearby table.

"Here," Margot said, spotting one of the receipts from BUT. A child's bed, desk and chair. "She bought the bedroom furniture on the ... 5th of August. And these two—" Two more receipts from BUT "—on the 6th and the 9th." She put the receipts down and looked Captain Bouchard in the eye. "Why was she so confident Colbert was going to give up custody of Lya? She instructs the new lawyer on the 3rd, then a few days later starts doing up her spare bedroom."

The captain looked perplexed.

Was there some connection between Colbert and Lefève that she'd missed? Maybe Sandrine was putting pressure on Lefève to influence the Family Court and get the decision swung in her favour. But no ... Margot pinched shut her eyes. She was clutching at straws. It was hard to imagine a judge being influenced in that way.

Two hours later she was walking home when an email came through on her phone. The sunlight was too strong to read it in the street so she stepped into the shade of a shop doorway. The assistant manager from the rugby club had sent through the full list of staff who'd been working at the club fourteen years ago. She zoomed in on the text and swiped down the list. There must have been at least two dozen names. She quickly swiped back again, but halfway through one particular name jumped out at her:

Georges Colbert. Assistant groundskeeper.

Someone wanted to get by so Margot moved out of their way. She stared at the people passing by, suddenly gone numb. But her thoughts were starting to clear. It wasn't Lefève Sandrine had been blackmailing; it was her ex-husband.

28

Margot wasn't surprised to find him in a place like this: a gym with a blacked-out frontage in the middle of the sprawling commercial zone. Spotting the blue Tesla parked outside, Captain Bouchard swung into the car park and pulled up in front of the doors.

Martell had done some more digging. Colbert had worked part-time at the rugby club for over three years prior to Ginette's murder. He'd been a keen fly-half, and at the age of eighteen had won a place on the team, though had subsequently been dropped after failing to impress. Ginette would have been well-known to him, particularly as at the time they'd lived just two streets apart. Aged twenty-six, one failed career already behind him, was he the older man Ginette had been seeing?

"Sandrine found out he was involved in Ginette's murder and was blackmailing him," the captain mused while they were still seated in the car. "Is that what we're going with?"

"That's my take on it."

Was Sandrine the one who'd been asking questions at the rugby club? There had been a blonde wig in her wardrobe. After almost a minute spent thinking about it, Captain Bouchard decisively pushed open his door.

"Let's go and get him."

Beyond the blacked-out windows, the gym's lobby was softly lit. The desk was unmanned. They wandered through to the main exercise area where three or four people were straining away at the various machines. Colbert wasn't one of them.

Sensing a movement behind them, Margot looked round. A man with a sports bag over his shoulder had just emerged from a side door. He was heading casually for the exit when Margot called out:

"Georges Colbert."

He froze, head turning sharply. His eyes flashed with panic when he saw them and for an instant it looked like he might run. But the captain was soon by his side, a hand at his elbow.

"We need you to come to the Gendarmerie."

Colbert freed his arm. "Why?"

"Some further evidence has come to light. We would like to ask you some more questions."

He flicked his eyes nervously between them, seemingly unsure of his emotions but settling on indignation.

"This is ridiculous. I've already told you everything I know. I'm busy."

He turned to walk on, but this time the captain held onto his arm.

"Either come willingly, Monsieur, or I'll arrest you. It's your choice."

The receptionist, returning just at the moment, overhead. The spark went out of Colbert's eyes. Somewhere inside, he knew it was all over.

Colbert remained subdued on the ride back into town, relaxed even. Margot recalled the stories Hugo had told about people who'd lived with terrible secrets for years. When the truth finally came out they felt relieved, no matter how bad the crimes they'd committed. Colbert didn't even protest as they recorded his fingerprints and took a sample for DNA, thanking the gendarme who showed him into the interview room. A cup of water was brought and placed on the table in front of him, but all he did was stare into space.

This time Margot was allowed to sit in, albeit it on the condition that the captain asked the questions. She moved her chair a little way back from the table and sat with her arms folded, staring at Colbert with unflinching eyes. It seemed to make him uncomfortable.

"How long will this take?" he asked. "My daughter needs to be picked up from school."

"There's no need to worry about your daughter, Monsieur. She will be taken care of."

Captain Bouchard had brought in a file but he didn't open it. "I understand you used to work at Argents rugby club."

Colbert folded his arms. "That's right. It was little more than a Saturday job."

"According to their records, you were employed as an assistant groundskeeper for three years. Is that correct?"

He nodded.

"So you must have known Ginette Clément, given she was such a popular figure at the club."

Colbert shifted on his seat. "Maybe I did."

"She was an attractive woman of eighteen; you were twenty-six. Her friends thought she'd recently started seeing someone. An older man, one of them said."

A faraway look appeared his eyes. He was quiet for a long

time, a curious kind of wistfulness coming over him. He sat back in his chair, and unfolded his arms.

"She used to like watching me paint the lines. Sometimes she would stay over and we would sit on the grass. We would talk, about all sorts of things. She was very mature for her age."

"Were you romantically involved?"

"She didn't like boys her own age. She told me her last boyfriend hadn't a clue what to do with a woman."

"And you had?"

Colbert blinked, several times. For a moment it looked like he was defeated, ready to give in, but he rallied. The wistfulness disappeared and he refolded his arms.

"She wasn't my girlfriend."

"Did you want her to be?"

"That's neither here nor there."

"Were you at the dinner that night?"

"I was."

"Where were you when the body was found?"

"I don't remember ... with the others, I suppose." He reached for the water and had a sip. "It was a hectic night. People don't recall things correctly, do they? Not after all this time."

"We've taken a sample of your DNA, Monsieur Colbert. I've asked for it to be checked against the evidence found at the scene of Ginette's murder. If any of it matches, you do know what that will mean?"

He nodded.

"Is there anything you would like to say to me? If you tell us the truth now it may help your case."

He thought about it, for as long as ten seconds, but then shook his head.

"Did you kill Ginette?"

The question didn't faze him. He paused for longer this time, perhaps on the cusp of admitting his guilt. Captain Bouchard gave him more time, maybe as much as a minute, but Colbert still couldn't push himself over the line.

"What about Sandrine? We've been told she was confident you were going to drop your objections to her seeing Lya. Was she blackmailing you?"

Finally, something more like anger took hold of him. He leaned forward, a hand on the table.

"Do you seriously believe I was going to let my daughter go and live in the house of a whore?"

"Was that why you killed her?"

Margot couldn't help herself. "She was giving it up. Trying to make a new start. And not only that – she had a baby on the way. A baby which perished when you killed her."

Colbert flinched. "She was pregnant?"

"Yes."

Colbert swallowed hard, and then gathered his emotions.

"I'm not saying anything more until my lawyer gets here."

Outside the room, Margot stayed close to the captain, forcing her head to cool.

"I'm sorry. I pushed him too soon."

"Not at all," the captain replied. "I've never seen a man look more guilty. We'll bring his wife in next and see what she has to say."

"No need." Lieutenant Martell was advancing upon them at speed. "Victoria Colbert's just turned up at reception. She wants to make a statement."

The captain had her taken to a second interview room. When they entered a few minutes later they found her still on her feet, anxiously pacing behind the desk. She froze as they entered, startled like a rabbit.

"Have you charged him yet? Was it him? It was, wasn't it?"

"Please sit down, Madame," Captain Bouchard said calmly.

Perhaps fearing she'd shown her cards too soon, Victoria Colbert lowered her eyes. She pulled out the chair and quietly sat down.

"You've already provided a statement," the captain said. "Is there something you would like to add?"

It took her a while to speak. She seemed to need to consider her words before saying them like she had a confession to make.

"The other day, you asked me if my husband was at home the night Sandrine was killed." She tried to look him in the eye but didn't quite succeed. "I lied."

The captain nodded slowly. "Go on."

"He phoned me at around six o'clock to say he had to work late. He didn't want me to wait up, but I did, until around eleven. Then I went to bed and didn't hear him come in until around one. We've been sleeping in separate bedrooms so—"

"Why are you sleeping in separate bedrooms?"

Her eyes briefly met his. "I'd prefer it if you didn't interrupt. I'm not finding this easy and I'd like to say it in my own way."

It was the most assertive thing to have come out of her mouth. The captain stayed silent, and after gathering herself again Victoria Colbert went on:

"Around an hour later I heard him go downstairs. I waited a minute, and when he didn't come back up I went to see what he was up to. I found him in the kitchen, loading some clothes into the washing machine. He saw me, so I asked him what he was doing. He said he'd spilled some red wine down the front of his shirt, but I knew he was lying. He would never normally do his own washing. I asked him where he'd been but he was evasive.

"The next day, when I heard Sandrine had been killed ... that was when I began to suspect. I could tell he was on edge. He called me from work later that morning and said that if the police asked I was to tell them he'd been at home all night. When I asked him why, he said he'd been out gambling with a client and didn't want his boss to find out. But..." Her head tipped forwards, run out of steam.

"You didn't believe him?"

She shook her head. "I knew it was a lie."

"So why did you cover for him?"

She raised her eyes, looking first at the captain before turning to Margot.

"I was afraid of him. I thought that if he could do that to Sandrine who's to say I wouldn't be next?"

After a few moments, she reached into her bag and took out a bundle of small papers: pink envelopes tied up with ribbon.

"These are love letters. Sent from my husband to that girl from the rugby club."

"Ginette Clément?"

She nodded.

Both Margot and the captain leaned curiously towards the table, but left the letters untouched.

"It's all one-sided," Victoria went on. "Ginette never wrote back. I found them in our garage a few months ago – he'd got them hidden in an old filing cabinet. I already knew he used to work at the rugby club, but he told me he hadn't started until a year after Ginette was killed. He claimed he'd never met her. But then, a few weeks after I found the letters, we were having dinner with some of his friends. They got talking about the old days at the club, and when I left the room for a minute I couldn't help overhearing. One of them made a comment about how Georges had been infatuated with her ... with Ginette, I mean. I didn't quite catch what they'd said, but when I went back in, Georges looked very embarrassed. I asked him about it later and he got angry and refused to talk about it. So, I decided to do some digging."

"It was you who was asking questions at the rugby club?" Margot said.

Victoria nodded. "They told me he had been working there when Ginette was killed. I kept asking myself, why would he lie unless he was the one who'd killed her?"

"Did he know you suspected him?"

"He may have done. The more I thought about it the more certain I was. That was when we started sleeping in separate rooms. I told him it was because I hadn't been sleeping well; the truth was I couldn't bear him touching me."

"Why didn't you come and see us?"

"If he'd found out I'd gone to the police who knows what he would have done? But I had to tell someone, so I told Sandrine. I suppose it was like passing the buck. I thought that if I gave her the information she'd have the courage to do something with it."

"And she used it to blackmail your husband?"

"I knew she was desperate to have Lya back. Maybe part of me was thinking it was for the best. I'd always felt Georges had been harsh on her. I couldn't go on playing happy families knowing what he'd done."

"So he killed her to stop her going to the police?"

Victoria finally held their gaze. "He would never have given up Lya. Not in a million years. The thing is, these past few days ..." Emotion got the better of her and she struggled to finish. "I've blamed myself. If I'd had the courage to speak up then maybe Sandrine would still be alive today."

And wasn't that the truth.

"Well," Colbert said. "Is my lawyer here?"

Margot and Captain Bouchard said nothing as they returned to their seats. For a very long time they just sat and looked at him. Colbert remained perfectly calm. That inner voice telling him it was all over must surely have been getting louder.

"Your wife's just told us everything," Captain Bouchard said. "We have your love letters. You killed Ginette because she rejected your advances, and then you murdered Sandrine because you refused to be blackmailed. Is there anything you would like to say?"

Colbert considered. There was a long pause before he spoke, and when he did, he raised his head and fixed his gaze at a spot on the wall.

"I was a different man back then. Hot-headed. Full of unrequited ardour. I lost my temper. I really didn't mean to kill her."

"People don't change," Margot said. "You were a killer then and you're a killer now."

Colbert looked at her with what seemed like amusement, before his face hardened again. "Perhaps. The difference being, after what she did to Lya, Sandrine deserved it."

Margot flashed with hot anger. It took every grain of self-control not to retaliate.

29

"I've signed the discharge papers," Célia said cheerfully as she joined Margot at the window. "Gy Berger should be home by the end of the day."

"What about Victoria Colbert? Will she face any charges?"

"I'm not sure yet. If she'd told the truth at the beginning a great deal of time and anguish would have been saved. Think of what Gy Berger and his mother were put through."

"Quite," Margot said.

Perverting the course of justice carried a three-year sentence. What would happen to Lya if her stepmother did go to jail? Be farmed out with a relative, or taken into care? As if the poor child hadn't already suffered enough. Too young to understand it now, perhaps, but at some point in the future the reality would dawn on her – the fact that her father had killed her mother.

"I wonder if it was much of a dilemma," Margot said. "Sandrine was willing to let him go unpunished for murdering Ginette in exchange for getting her daughter back."

"A mother's bond is strong."

Victoria Colbert brings her this incendiary information. For

Sandrine it's a chance to escape. She starts turning her life around, plotting to get her daughter back, creating her perfect bedroom. Her future looks rosy until her plan horribly backfires.

"Did you ever find out about that mystery doctor?"

"Oh, yes," Margot said brightly. "The elusive Doctor Roche. It's a rather touching story, actually."

They came away from the window and retired to the easy chairs.

"Lieutenant Martell finally spoke to him last night. It was someone she'd known at university. It began with a chance encounter a few months back. They hit it off straightaway; spent a passionate week together, fell madly in love. But then his work took him away to Africa. He's only now been able to get into contact."

Célia sighed heavily. "What terribly bad luck."

"He knew about Lya. He'd been looking forward to meeting her. Even though they'd only been together a short time he said he and Sandrine had talked about marriage. My guess is he was the father of the new baby – that one-in-a-hundred chance. She was finally going to get her perfect family until fate decided otherwise."

They were quiet for some time. Alone with her thoughts, Margot imagined what a difficult call that must have been for the lieutenant to make. After telling him about the pregnancy, the good doctor had apparently choked up in tears.

Margot drew her breath. "Anyway. I should be getting back to work."

As she made a move to rise, however, Célia reached for her arm.

"Just a second, Margot. I've been meaning to ask ... have you ever thought about becoming a JI?"

"Me?"

"Sorry to bring this up right out of the blue, but, yes. You'd be perfect."

Margot was very nearly struck dumb. "I've never really considered it."

"Someone with your drive would make a fine addition to the *magistrature*."

Margot fidgeted, not sure if what she was feeling was excitement or fear.

"I'm not sure I could face all that studying. Not at my time of life."

"With your experience you'd only need to do the twelve-month course."

"But to go back to Paris?" She shook her head. "Too many bad memories."

"The magistrates' school is in Bordeaux."

"Oh yes, of course it is." For some reason Margot's brain had chosen not to remember that.

Célia smiled again. "Think about it. I'm not going to be around forever, you know. And when I do finally depart it would be nice to know I was leaving the job in a safe pair of hands."

Florian came in. Saved by the coffee. His usual practice was to leave the tray on the desk, but spotting them in the corner he came over and set it down on the low table instead.

"Is the coast clear?" Margot asked.

Florian cast a glance at the open door. "Why – are you expecting a visit from Cousineau?"

"I heard he'd made a voodoo doll of me."

Florian smiled. "Keep a clove of garlic in your pocket and you'll be fine."

"Or hide a sharpened stake under your desk," chipped in Célia.

A noise outside made them go quiet. They held their breaths

as a shadow entered the vestibule. Any moment now, the bat would swoop in and enact his revenge, put pay to Margot's present job never mind entertain any idea of her becoming a JI. But the silence lengthened, and whoever it was moved on.

The three of them shared a comradely smile.

The clock on the shelf lazily chimed midnight. Margot woke to find the TV still on, the sound turned down, her right arm numb from having been trapped between her torso and the sofa. She rubbed some life back into it, and stared with dismay at the detritus that had accumulated on her coffee table: empty wine bottle, open book, glass, plate full of crumbs. It looked like a racoon had been to visit.

Sleepy-eyed, she grabbed the remote and flicked through the channels: news; soap; movie; *Les Simpsons*; some reality TV nonsense. She laughed spontaneously; just imagine it – her as a JI – but just as abruptly grew serious. Was it really such a bad idea? She drained the last spot of wine from her glass.

On the TV, she flicked past a scene of some small children playing in a park. Curious, she flicked back again and turned up the sound. It turned out to be a documentary about foster parents. Various couples were talking about the process they'd gone through, and what a rewarding experience it had been despite the often troubled backgrounds of many of the children. Margot had a blinding idea. It came to her with the force of a punch: if Victoria Colbert did go to jail why didn't she look after Lya herself? She had plenty of room. It was the least Sandrine deserved. The ideas almost tripped over themselves as they tumbled out of her head:

She could re-do the room in the attic, just like Sandrine had.

She could get her a place in the local school; it was only a short detour from her route into work.

She could take her on holidays.

Teach her how to swim.

And dive.

And share her favourite books.

And they could go for long walks along the coastal path.

Margot grinned as she pictured that cheekily smiling face when she couldn't find her ballet pumps.

And they could have late-night chats about what a gifted person her mother had been and how she'd fought to get her back before events had conspired to bring her life to such a tragic end.

But no sooner had she hatched all of these wonderful plans than reality crept in. Like the idea that comes to you in the middle of the night made to look ridiculous in the cold light of day. The authorities would never allow her to look after a small child. She was far too old, her lifestyle unsuitable. What kind of role model would she be?

The documentary was annoying her now so Margot snapped it off. Balloon burst, she collapsed into the sofa, burying her face in a cushion.

"*Meow.*"

Margot's eyes sprang open. Staring into the darkness of the cushion, she thought she'd been hearing things. Maybe oxygen depletion was making her hallucinate.

The feathery filling was making her want to sneeze, but she suppressed it. Careful in her movements, she sat up, easing the cushion away from her face. It couldn't be true, could it? After all this time? Margot held her breath, heart racing, as she slowly turned her head. And her smile widened as she realised that no, she had not imagined it: Buster was finally venturing into her salon, giving her things a curious sniff.

THE END

PLEASE REVIEW THIS BOOK

Please don't underestimate how important reviews are to authors, particularly independent authors who don't have the backing of a huge marketing machine. If you enjoyed *NO TEARS FOR SANDRINE* please consider leaving a review on either Amazon or Goodreads, it will be very much appreciated.

FREE SHORT STORY

To receive a free short story featuring Margot Renard visit:
www.rachelgreenauthor.com

WHAT NEXT?

Look out for the next book in the series, coming soon to Amazon

For updates, sign up at: www.rachelgreenauthor.com

FOLLOW:

https://twitter.com/AuthorRachelG
https://www.instagram.com/authorrachelg/
https://www.facebook.com/AuthorRachelG
https://www.bookbub.com/authors/rachel-green?follow=true

Printed in Great Britain
by Amazon